ONE NIGHT IN THE LIFE
OF RV MULROONEY

ONE NIGHT IN THE LIFE OF RV MULROONEY

PJ CURTIS

POOLBEG

Published in 1995
by Poolbeg Press Ltd
123 Baldoyle Industrial Estate
Dublin 13, Ireland

The Publishers gratefully acknowledge the support of The Arts Council

A catalogue record for this book is available from the British Library.

ISBN 1 85371 540 9

Cover illustrations by Graeme Knuttel
Cover design by Poolbeg Group Services Ltd
Set by Poolbeg Group Services Ltd in New Baskerville
Printed by The Guernsey Press Ltd,
Vale, Guernsey, Channel Islands.

Acknowledgements

It's been a long road from first to final draft. Many thanks to those who gave so freely of their time and talent

Sincere thanks to Sandy Harsch, Carlo Gebler, Lelia Doolan, Cyril and Kit O'Ceirin and a special "thank you" to my editor, Gaye Shortland.

Thank you all for your constant support, encouragement and especially for your belief in RV and his pals.

This one is for you.

*To my fellow members of the Burren Action Group
and to a special mountain in County Clare*

Chapter One

In those few glorious no-thought moments before coming fully awake, before full consciousness blotted out the comforting mist of deep untroubled sleep, RV Mulrooney struggled to hold on for a few extra minutes. But as usual, as soon as he became conscious of trying to remain in that blissful state, the full weight of his waking world filled his mind like a freak wind whipping open the door of a warm room and filling it with the cold air of harsh reality. For RV Mulrooney was a man with duties and responsibilities. In his opinion, huge crushing responsibilities which he wore as a penitent monk would a hair-shirt. Responsibilities under which, as he often told his wife Hannah, a man with less character and moral fibre might have crumbled years ago.

Savouring what remained of that warm floating half-awake sensation, he raised his head from the pillow and, without any movement of the body, peered about the room. His eyes rested for a moment on objects now as familiar to him as his own face: the large turnip-shaped red alarm clock on his bedside table whose hands showed 4.32, the peeling ragged patch of flock wallpaper over the doorway which today took on the appearance of a fierce-looking Samurai warrior, and finally the large faded picture-print over the mantelpiece which held a number of china figurines and an assortment of cheap detective-story paperbacks – now barely visible in the room's half-light. His eyes lingered on the print and from the faded parchment Beethoven, the great Ludwig Von Beethoven – idol of his life – glared down at him with a look worn by a genius or a madman.

"Ludwig doesn't look so happy today," RV reflected, as a shaft of shimmering dappled light played on Beethoven's brow, giving him an even angrier look. Over the years, RV had come to regard it as true that when Ludwig looked happy, his own life, his duties and his world in general went well. When Ludwig wore that scowl, as he did today – well!, you could just not depend on events. RV sighed and transferred his gaze to the window. To glimpse anything outside from his position in bed, he had to raise his head several inches from the pillow, giving him a view of the sky to the south and the tall ash and sycamore trees at the bottom of his garden. This action usually brought his nostrils into contact with a number of agreeable cooking smells emanating from the kitchen. He sniffed the air. Nothing. Today the lack of any aromas, other than the permanent bedroom incense of mothballs and rising damp and the heavy musk of human bodies after sleep, brought him out of his lethargic musings and he came fully awake. He sat fully up and looked at the old stuffed armchair at the foot of the bed. On it was draped a dark blue uniform, clean-pressed and solemn. Garda Sergeant RV Mulrooney, chief constable and custodian of the peace for the seemingly uncaring residents of the village of Ballykeogh, was about to begin his day. Moving quickly, he swung his long legs over the side of the bed, while at the same time pulling his blue shirt over his head. He shivered as his skin came into contact with the cold crisp material, reached for his uniform pants and called aloud, "Hannah! Are you out there? Hannah!"

From the kitchen came the bustling sounds of kettles and cooking pans clinking on iron and ceramic. RV's wife Hannah hastily poured steaming hot water into a cream enamel wash-basin embossed with faded red roses. She then laid the basin, along with a bar of Sunlight soap, shaving brush, towel and cut-throat razor on a large tin tray. Picking up the tray she moved towards the bedroom to attend to her waking husband.

"Coming, Rudy, coming!" Hannah and the tin tray deftly negotiated doors and corners on their way to the bedroom.

"Ah, there you are," scowled RV from the edge of the brass bed that had been his parents' and on which he had been conceived and born. "I thought I was deserted. Are the rashers on? Time to be going. I fancy I've a hard night ahead of me."

"Hello dear, how're you feeling after your long sleep? Your breakfast will be on the plate waiting for you – I was out longer than I expected – bank-day today you know – I met Father O'Malley – he says we're for a spell of dry weather. He's all excited about the funeral in the morning – and that Mrs Flanagan in the shop above would hold up a hurricane with chat, so she would – will you be wanting your flask tonight? God, is that the time?"

Hannah laid the tray on a marble-top washstand and stood for a moment watching her husband shake the sleep from his thin frame. He glanced at her, still blinking away sleep. She was dressed in a thick knitted cardigan over her best floral dress and still wearing her low-heeled town shoes. It was obvious to RV she was excited about something or other. He was about to enquire but decided to let it pass. Whatever it was it could wait. Hannah

3

practically bubbled with vitality on bank-days. Today she looked and sounded flustered. She nervously patted her hair before moving quickly about the room, re-arranged a few figurines on the mantelpiece then quickly moved to the other side of the bedroom to flick at some imaginary cobweb behind the dressing-table. She avoided any direct eye-contact with her husband who was now busy muttering and fumbling while stuffing long spindly legs into his uniform pants.

"Father O'Malley and his dry spell indeed! Hummph!" RV stood bolt upright, snapped braces and ran a finger over the knife-edge crease in his trouser-leg. "Father O'Malley should know by now that it's more likely for Moses himself to come down off Sliabh Cullen over there with a brand new set of stone tablets than for a dry spell to come to this side of the hill! He's been praying for a dry spell since 1950 and as far as I can see not one of those prayers have yet been heard by the Man Above. And yes, I'll be needing my flask – not too much salt in the soup this time – Tom Duignan's mongrel got the most of it last night."

By the time RV was finished speaking, Hannah was back in her kitchen busy with her daily ritual of preparing her husband's breakfast which, since he started his night shifts some weeks ago, she served promptly at 4.45 p.m. each afternoon. Today, as usual, his breakfast consisted of porridge, several thick fresh juicy rashers from Doyle's butcher shop to be washed down with a glass of hot milk and stout. The latter RV frequently recommended as a panacea for all ailments, as did his father before him. "Iron and calcium – a powerful mixture. Good for blood and bones," he would declare. "Especially for those in a job like mine – out day and night in all weathers." Other than this daily administration of body and spirit-building elixir, RV

4

never let a drop of intoxicating liquor pass his lips. And he saw to it neither did Hannah; though he suspected she sometimes took a drop or two when he was out of the house or when she went on her occasional outings to Ballyglen. But he was happy enough to allow this and never mentioned it to her.

While breakfast was being prepared, RV busied himself stropping the cut-throat razor that had been passed down from his grandfather. He then lathered his gaunt sunken jaws, trying to catch a glimpse of his reflection between the chipped patches on the wash-stand mirror.

As the cut-throat slid carefully over jutted impossible jaw angles, RV felt as those Spanish bullfighters might before facing the crowds, the bull's rage, the glory – or the gore. As for himself and his civic duties, the only difference was for that him there was usually more bull and gore than glory. He sighed a long sigh and steadied the slight shake in his right hand.

The keen blade slid effortlessly over the last dour jaw-angle, leaving only his neatly clipped steel-grey moustache untouched. Shaving complete, he donned his uniform tunic and turned to inspect himself in the wardrobe mirror. He stood over six feet, his slightly hunched bony shoulders struggling to fill his ill-fitting uniform jacket. Someone in the village once described his thin bony frame as 'spidery'. The long high-cheekboned face which stared back at RV was that of a man who held and carried considerable authority and responsibility. Beneath his neatly-trimmed moustache, a slightly turned-down mouth gave the impression of a man who rarely smiled. With his penetrating intelligent eyes, close-cropped hair greying at the temples, receding hairline and resolute jaw-set, he could be taken for an army officer, doctor, barrister or bank manager. Puffing out his chest to the girth of a man befitting his rank, he looked up and down at the figure facing him in the mirror: first full on, then sideways, then back view.

Satisfied enough with the image, he drew a wet comb across his remaining strands of hair while wistfully regarding Beethoven's tousled mop. "Why is it," he mused, "that great men often have more hair than they seem to need. Look at old Ludwig there – a healthy mop. And Einstein – a fine thick mane. Albert Schweitzer even! All of them! Thatches of healthy wiry hair enough for two ordinary mortals! But then they don't have to live in this part of the world. What with the weather, the worry and some of the clients I have to deal with they'd soon be rid of most of it."

He marched out of the bedroom into the kitchen. The kitchen looked invitingly cozy and warm in the late afternoon light and smelt of the usual aromas of basil, thyme, coriander, mixed spice and garlic – scents that always had a calming effect on RV. His mother used exotic spices and he was glad Hannah, unlike the rest of the local women who smothered most of their meat-dishes with an excess of pepper and salt, made frequent use of a variety of deliciously pungent spices in the foods she prepared.

Though a little later than usual preparing his "breakfast" Hannah, still somewhat flustered, laid a gurgling bowl of Flannaman's Oatlets alongside a folded newspaper on the table by the range. Inside the black No. 9 Stanley range a coal fire hissed and sizzled, warming the room in the fast-approaching twilight of the day. Glancing underneath the range he saw the protruding ends of a highly polished pair of leather boots. He nodded with some satisfaction.

"A policeman's lot *can* be a happy one," he thought, "if he possesses a good woman, a good home and – a decent

6

pair of strong handmade leather boots." RV's mood began to lift. "Maybe Ludwig's wrong today," he muttered through his first spoonful of porridge.

"What's that, dear?"

"I think I'm in for a long day," RV said aloud.

"Surely you mean night, dear." Hannah poured hot milk from a saucepan over a half-glass of Guinness.

"And I feel I'm about to make a break-through on the case I'm working on." RV ignored his wife's correction.

"What case is that, dear?" Hannah inquired, pouring herself a cup of strong tea.

"Don't you ever pay attention? The big case – the only case – the brazen trafficking of illegal liquor – here in our very town!" he retorted sharply. Lowering his voice to a whisper, he continued, "If you hear anything – whispers – loose tittle-tattle – idle gossip – chance remarks – anything relating to poteen – rumours about the village, that sort of thing – you will let me know, won't you?"

"Of course I will, dear," Hannah replied. "But I sometimes feel people are extra careful when talking to me. They always keep their distance. They never make too free with me – they see me as – as – well, different! I suppose I can't blame them. I am the Sergeant's wife, after all!"

RV could see her point. Of course he understood how things were and was quickly coming to appreciate just how little assistance the townspeople of Ballykeogh actually offered him in his quest to bring the local law-breakers to book.

"Well, you never know what you might overhear – in the shops, the butchers, in the bank – wherever – women often gossip about things men will never mention – unless they're under the influence, that is! So keep your ear open to every little tit-bit. It may seem insignificant to you but it

7

may prove to be the most vital of clues, as far as I'm concerned."

For the moment however, this quiet untroubled time was his and he banished all thoughts of duty from his mind. Settling himself closer to the range he smacked his lips and smirked at the front page of the newspaper. It carried a photo of a well-known local politician, now sporting a grey blob of porridge for a face. "Goes well with his politics," he thought to himself before turning to the comic section and the daily adventures of the ageless Rip Kirby.

A slow quiet peace descended on the room, broken only by RV's eating sounds. He began to feel more alive and by the time the rashers and his glass of milk and stout were placed on the table in front of him, things seemed to be in far better order. Sergeant RV Mulrooney liked things to be in order, both at work and at home. While things outside the world of his charge were often not to his liking, here in the village of Ballykeogh, in all matters concerning law and order, and more especially here in his own home, RV insisted on things being just so.

In this respect RV took after his father, James, who also held the rank of Sergeant in the old RIC and who had served long and loyally during those dark and dangerous days of the "Troubles". In fact, RV took after his father in almost every respect, except for one: his great passion for music, which he undoubtedly took from his mother — though that passion extended only to the entire works of the Master, Ludwig Von Beethoven, whose picture dominated his bedroom wall and whose bust took pride of place on the sitting-room sideboard. He possessed a large collection of old 12 inch 78 RPM recordings of most of Beethoven's symphonies; these he treasured above all else.

If the house was to go up in flames, RV had stoutly resolved, he would not hesitate a moment to risk life and limb to save those precious shellac platters.

RV's late mother, before she married his father James, had led a carefree life in Dublin city. She was then, by all accounts, the very life and soul of the high social circles she moved in, where her piano and singing recitals were the toast of every drawing-room soirée and social gathering south of the River Liffey. Cecilia Spiers, as she was before she became the wife of James J Mulrooney, was a member of a well-to-do old Dublin Protestant family who had made their fortunes in the wine-importing business. But though a well-respected family, it was a colourful family of some notoriety. Cecilia revelled in recounting to RV when he was a boy the adventurous escapades of some of her errant forebears. Her Uncle Joshua had departed in the 1880s to explore the Amazon, and after a period mining for silver in the hills around Tombstone, Arizona had ended up working the Mississippi Riverboats between Natchez and New Orleans as a professional gambler and met an untimely end in a gambling-hall duel over a beautiful Creole belle. Her great-uncle Daniel had accompanied the legendary explorer-missionary, Dr Livingston, wandering the wastes of darkest Africa. Like Joshua, Daniel was a lover of high adventure, of women, of good food and fine wines. More than all else he was a lover of danger and sought it out in that most savage of continents, in the late 19th century. Cecilia swore she possessed a letter from great-uncle Daniel, postmarked Mombasa 1880, complaining bitterly of the poor native cuisine throughout his entire journeys in the African interior and of his passionate resolve to "do something about it." Ironic then, Cecilia remarked, that poor Daniel, a gourmet to the end, was to end his days as the main item on the menu for a cannibal tribal feast somewhere west of Lake Victoria. She laughed heartily as she conjured up pictures of poor Uncle Daniel berating the natives from within the roasting-pot for their lack of attention in using the appropriate seasoning of herbs and spices with their meal-to-be.

There was however, one ancestor that Cecilia spoke of more than all the rest. He was, she confided to RV and his brother RN, the most notorious of them all: the most feared man during the terrible years of the French Revolution – Robespierre himself. As usual, the boys listened with amazement. "His true identity," she would whisper breathlessly, as if telling some ancient dreadful secret, "was never really divulged. But we knew – and they knew – the whole world knew – that he was none other than one Robert Spiers." Cecilia's face glowed radiantly whenever she spoke his name. "Robert Spiers! A first cousin to my great-great-grandfather, William, and," her eyes blazed with excitement, "it is said that he was as dashing, handsome and brilliant a lad as ever entered Trinity College."

Robert, it seems, because of his extremist radical views and actions, not to mention a paternity suit being pressed by the daughter of a powerful Dublin merchant, was eventually forced to flee Dublin for the relative safety of Paris. There, at the close of the 18th century, the radical Robert became 'Robertspiere'; now known to history as 'Robespierre', a central figure and guiding hand in the events which led to the French Revolution.

"Our Robert was the cause of many an aristocrat tyrant losing his head," Cecilia would relate to the spellbound RV. "But though he strove to keep his head when all about him were losing theirs, in the end the poor brave boy lost it." She always touched her throat whenever she told this part of the tale, her voice low and trembling. "Oh, the French would never admit it of course. They still claim him for one of their own. History in the writing always suits itself. But I'll tell you one thing! They've always held more than a sneaking regard for young Irish Trinity students from that day to this." Cecilia always wore a knowing smile when she related this fantastic tale. Wasn't it at Trinity College she met her future husband, James Mulrooney? James, already in the police force and detached to Dublin on a training course, had managed to get into a Trinity Ball with a detective from Dublin Castle. There, according to Cecilia, they met, fell in love and before the evening was out were practically engaged to be married. The truth was it took three long years before Cecilia finally convinced the reluctant young Guard to even consider an engagement and a further three before they were wed.

Cecilia changed little on marrying RV's father. Within months of arriving with James to take up his new post in Ballyglen, the small west of Ireland town was throbbing with all kinds of social activities, the like of which it had never experienced before. Cecilia's tea parties, bridge parties, piano recitals, concert performances, poetry readings and amateur dramatics became the talk of the town. When the silent movies arrived in Ballyglen, it was Cecilia who organised the very first to be screened in the town. To the townspeople of Ballyglen it seemed that the twentieth century had well and truly arrived with all its glamour and excitement with the coming of Sergeant James J Mulrooney and his vivacious and energetic wife Cecilia.

The silent films were to become her passion. Cecilia adored them all: the Chaplin and Keaton comedies, the tear-wrenching dramas, the DW Griffith epics – all accompanied of course by Cecilia herself on an out-of-tune

11

piano with less than two working octaves. Griffith's "Birth of A Nation" was screened so many times it deteriorated to resemble nothing more than shapeless grey shadows lost in a raging snowstorm.

But it was due to her unswerving devotion to two of the silent screen's biggest romantic heroes that she insisted on christening her only two sons in honour of them. Thus it was that James and Cecilia Mulrooney's two baby boys – the first-born, Rudolph Valentino Mulrooney, born in 1918 and Ramon Navarro Mulrooney born two years later – got saddled with names neither one ever quite learned to live with.

"In heaven's name, Cecilia," James pleaded with his strong-willed young wife. "Rudolph Valentino! Ramon Navarro! You cannot be serious! I never heard of such names on child or man. They're not Catholic names are they? They're maybe not even proper Christian names! What will the people say? How will the poor fellows live with such names? Will you not have them Patrick and John – or maybe even James?" He looked hurt.

"No such thing, James," Cecilia was adamant. "I do not intend to follow the rest of the sheep in naming my offspring. Isn't the entire country overflowing with Patricks, Johns and Jameses – not that there's anything wrong with your name, my dear – it's a fine strong name – like you are, James dear, but only the common and uneducated won't have heard of the great 16th century Spanish Saints, St Rudolph and St Ramon. Both of them as Christian as Peter or Paul, from civilised families in civilised Christian countries. So don't be such an old-fashioned bore, James – a great name signifies a great life and our boys will have great lives. Don't you want our – your boys to have great futures, James?"

This seemed to pacify James for the time being, though

it continued to nag and bother him. Sons, bearing the names Rudolph and Ramon! Well, he would have to learn, as they would, to accept them and live with them. Cecilia, he knew, was just not going to give way on this one.

"And not only will they be as handsome as their Hollywood namesakes, they will be famous singers, or musicians or actors as well!" Cecilia repeatedly remarked to her taciturn husband who by then was well out of his depth when dealing with his wilful young wife and was now resigned to accept her judgment absolutely in these and other, if indeed not all, domestic matters. He rarely argued with her ever again on any subject, even accepting her insistence that both Rudolph and Ramon be brought up in her religion, which was Methodist.

"Whatever you wish, dear. Anything to make you happy," James would meekly agree. "The running of the household affairs are yours and yours alone." Outside the home, things were different. Especially down at the police barracks, where the men in his charge often had cause to both fear and respect the fierce and silent power of this formidable law-enforcer.

Time passed, and as Rudolph and Ramon grew to adolescence, endless and in the long run fruitless piano lessons from old Miss Rosenstein had proved one fact. Whatever about either one of them becoming as handsome or as famous as their film-star namesakes, the possibility of either Rudolph or Ramon becoming concert pianists was absolutely out of the question. While Rudolph displayed some natural, though lazy, musical talent, his skittish younger brother Ramon seemed more interested in Miss Rosenstein's pretty 15-year-old niece Rachel, who appeared out of nowhere one April day and stayed with her aunt for two years. Ramon's piano lessons were to end abruptly on a Summer evening in 1934, when Miss

Rosenstein caught Ramon and her niece together in a somewhat compromising position in the wood-shed at the bottom of her garden. Next morning, Rudolph overheard an extremely angry Miss Rosenstein in heated and loud conversation with his mother in the sitting room. Voices were raised and a red-faced Miss Rosenstein hurriedly departed, her long tweed skirts swishing angrily about her. Ramon was quickly summoned for a long private conversation with an angry and cold-eyed Cecilia. Though he asked many questions of his mother, and later of a smirking Ramon, Rudolph never did learn what exactly transpired between his brother and Miss Rosenstein's niece in the wood-shed that summer evening. Cecilia never informed James of the incident and despite this and many other indiscretions, Ramon had become his mother's favourite. Indeed, Ramon continued to scheme and carry out the most outrageous escapades with what often seemed, to both Rudolph and James, full support from Cecilia.

"He's his mother's son, all right. Don't know what to make of him," James once commented to Rudolph, who by now had grown more and more attached to his father. So much so indeed, that he was now fully intent on following his father's footsteps in deciding to join the police force as soon as he came of age; much to his mother's growing chagrin and dismay.

"The life of a policeman, James!" Cecilia argued. "That's no life! That's a sentence – especially for your – our – son!"

"The life of a policeman – there's no life like it, RV." James never called his son Rudolph Valentino – somehow the name stuck in his craw as did Ramon Navarro, who had become RN. "Can there be greater satisfaction at the end of a working-man's day than to know he has

14

contributed in no small way to maintaining law and order? 'Keep ye the law – be swift in all obedience, clear the land of evil, drive the road and bridge the ford.' Kipling – wonderful words, my boy, never forget them – they should be carved in the heart of every policeman. Of course, in this case it should read 'cycle' and not 'drive the road'. No matter – there's great satisfaction in knowing you're on the side of Good and pitting your wits against the Forces of Evil. And make no mistake my boy, there's evil and badness everywhere you turn these days. It stalks the land winning converts in every town and village, in every dark secret corner." James laid a heavy hand on his son's slender shoulder and continued solemnly, "A man can do no better while making his way in this world than do battle with evil wherever or whenever he exposes its cancerous growth. Be a policeman, my boy. Be a good, honest policeman. There's no better calling."

This speech always had a great effect on RV who more and more now saw himself in the role of "Champion of the Good and Right" and less and less the concert pianist his mother had hoped he would surely one day be. And so it was that, one day in early 1938, RV, to the delight of his father James and the utter dismay of his mother Cecilia, packed his case to follow in his father's footsteps and became a Garda cadet.

Now, all those fleeting years later, RV held the rank his father once held – that of Sergeant. He carried the rank well enough, although in the lonely moments of self-doubt and self-pity he often wished he possessed his father's qualities, especially those of firmness, leadership and natural authority.

Now stationed here in Ballykeogh, Sergeant RV Mulrooney needed those in abundance. And, he knew, all the inner strength and resilience he could muster if he was to confront and conquer the gnawing worm of evil his father had convinced him existed all about him and now existed right here in his very own patrol patch.

When RV remarked to Hannah that he was in for a long day, he could never have imagined just how long it was going to be. It was, of course, not a "day" that lay ahead of him but another long, most probably wet, damp and marrowbone-chilling night watching and waiting on a bleak hillside some distance from the town. Sergeant Mulrooney had been on night-duty for over three weeks now; it began at six o'clock p.m. precisely each evening when he relieved Guard Behan. The night shift ended next morning at eight a.m., when Guard Behan reported back for day-duty. RV's duties rarely saw him in the station, unless there was important paper-work to be completed. This tedious chore was completed between six and eight p.m. or so. Then it was time to set about his outdoor duties which kept him occupied until the wee small hours of the morning, when he returned to the station cell to catch a few restless hours of sleep. Unless, of course, there happened to be an occupant already confined within – which was often the case, particularly at Christmas, Easter, horse and cattle fair-days or at election time. More than once the cell held a suspect or two he himself had taken into custody until they were charged, suitable alibis were forthcoming or the occupant had sobered sufficiently to be released. Though RV had to admit he relished the relative comforts of the station-house, for the bulk of his time on duty he was engaged in what for him had become an obsessional task. A task, he also had to admit to himself, that filled his duty-hours to the exclusion of all else and which drove him with the intensity of an explorer about to stumble on a lost city of gold.

The task which drove him on was simple: to seek out and rid the community once and for all of possibly the greatest threat to beset the land since the coming of Cromwell – the making, distribution and consumption of that most vile and heathenish of man-made brews – poteen! This Devil's own concoction was, he was fully convinced, being distilled and distributed by a person or persons unknown within the boundaries of this very parish of Ballykeogh. With his late father's words – and Kipling's – ringing in his ears, he had committed himself utterly to unearthing the illegal still, or stills, and bringing the persons responsible to a quick and overdue judgment.

"I'm on the verge of a major break-through on this case – any day now," RV would declare to Guard Behan and to Hannah, more to bolster his own flagging resolve than anything else. "And let me tell you that a superior intellect and mind trained in detection is more than a match for any one of the low criminal classes to be found around these parts. Yes indeed! Vigilance, intelligence, perseverance, a fair smattering of footwork coupled with native cunning, creative flair and intuition – a strong hunch, as you might have it – will win the day every time. The clues to the whereabouts of these poteen-making vermin are all about us to be seen by the trained eye. Make no mistake, the net is closing, the complex net that is the law is closing. It's only a matter of time before we- er- I have them where I want them."

"You're right, Sergeant, absolutely right! Only a matter of time, as you say, only a matter of time – you'll nail 'em surely!" Guard Behan would mutter, continuing to fill in his *Sunday Press* crossword, barely hidden atop the station desk under an assortment of official documents. The truth was, Guard Behan knew, Sergeant Mulrooney's investigations were bringing him no nearer to unearthing the whereabouts of the illicit still.

In fact it was RV's considered opinion that the persons engaged in the manufacture of the illicit liquor were part of a highly trained and organised gang of international bootleggers. Otherwise their detection and capture would not have eluded him for so long.

"You know, it's possible," he confided to Guard Behan. "It's just possible that the men we're after aren't from around here at all. It's possible that what we're dealing with here is not a local boyo giving us the run-around but an international criminal organisation – possibly organised directly from London or New York or Chicago – or," his voice trembled with excitement, "maybe even Moscow."

"Moscow? Oh, I don't know Sergeant, the Rooskies only drink Vodka and as for Chicago – I'd rule that out entirely," Guard Behan replied without looking up from his unfinished crossword. "Sure isn't my own uncle Francis well up in the Chicago police force. Higher than Sergeant too he is. No, no! He would never allow that kind of skullduggery to go undetected under his nose. Anyway, since they put Capone and his gang away – with the help of my uncle Francis I might add – so he wrote my father – they've had no trouble with poteen-makers in Chicago for several years now. So I doubt if it's the Chicago boys. I think it's those tinkers who come around from Kerry every year, just after the Puck Fair."

"Don't you believe it, Guard! Don't you believe it for an instant. Those are professional imbibers, not makers. No, it's obvious we're up against serious professional brains here, as sure as rashers are rashers!" Sergeant Mulrooney thundered. "I mean we must set our wits against the best of theirs and flush out their operative agent in this area. It's that simple!"

Guard Behan had to admit his Sergeant was indeed determined to get to the bottom of this troublesome case and had to agree with him that it was indeed time to close this file once and for all.

The large clock with the smoke-stained face which hung by the kitchen door ticked up 5.15 p.m. as RV sipped the last of his glass of milk and stout. Smacking his lips, he patted his porridge and rasher-filled belly before turning to engage himself in what he believed to be his only real pleasure. From under the sofa he drew an old wind-up HMV gramophone and placed it carefully on the kitchen table. With equal care he placed a large shellac disc, which he had taken from a suitcase behind his chair, on the turntable. Having wound up the machine he released the brake-gear then dropped the bulky needle-arm on the revolving platter. Soon the scratchy but stirring cacophony of chords that introduced Beethoven's Fifth Symphony filled the tiny room with sound. A smile of great satisfaction spread over RV's face as he lowered himself into the well of glorious sound and the swell and flow of the Master's most patriotic of works, with only the odd rhythmic intrusion from the clock's pendulum and the rattling of windows facing the west.

"My mother might have been right," RV mused and considered his long tapering fingers. "These hands were made for activities a little more artistic than police work. Fingers designed for music, surely. I should have gone on with my piano lessons. Who knows where I'd be today." One of his fingers wagged gently in time with the symphony's slow pulse. Eyes closed, conducting the revolving shellac symphony, RV was transported to a higher plane, where time and space were one and nothing mattered but the merging of body and soul with the

19

majestic spirit and grandeur of Beethoven's Fifth. Ballykeogh locals who passed at these times were used to overhearing that "posh" orchestral music coming from the Sergeant's cottage. But to the uninformed traveller coming up from Ballyglen, the sound of the wind moaning its accompaniment to various passages of Beethoven's works emanating from a place somewhere in the heart of the mist that hung over Ballykeogh was nothing short of awe-inspiring.

Hannah was by now engrossed in one of her chief occupations – that of rug-making. This pastime she resorted to often to pass the time when RV was on night-duty and in times like this, when her husband and Beethoven communicated in some other realm. She started to say something to RV, stopped and turned her eyes to her work. Ever since trying out a pattern she got from a *Reader's Digest* Christmas issue ten or so years ago, Hannah had produced a fantastic array of rugs, carpets and wall-hangings. These emerged in all kinds of different shapes, sizes and designs – from the complexities of ivy-leaf patterns to fierce-looking Bengali tigers or African ivory tuskers to the high art of Leonardo Da Vinci's *Last Supper*.

Apart from decorating every square inch of their small cottage with her imaginative creations, Hannah managed to sell several rugs and carpets to some of the more adventurous local women and some to a soft-furnishing shop in Ballyglen. This gave her a modest personal income, which she banked regularly. More importantly, her pastime provided her with a time-consuming hobby on long winter nights while RV was away from the house. At least, that's what RV liked to believe.

"Well!" RV said at last. "It's fifteen before six – duty calls, I'm afraid. Time and crime waits for no man." He always said this. "Guard Behan will be wanting to be away home after his day-duty – though the odd extra hour on duty wouldn't do him much harm either."

The silence following the final strains of Beethoven's Fifth seemed louder than the symphony itself. Hannah put aside her unfinished rug and before speaking, glanced for a moment at the work already completed on a huge Indian bull elephant – yet without a rear end.

"I'll fill your flask," she said, moving towards the Stanley No. 9. "It's pea soup. Good strong thick pea-soup to keep you going up there on that hill tonight." RV winced. Pea-soup, his least favourite, and definitely no friend to bolster one on a cold dark night vigil. He glanced sideways at Hannah, busy at the range, and it crossed his mind for the second time that evening that she was not her usual self. He couldn't quite put his finger on it. He considered saying something but changed his mind. He had, after all, problems enough of his own pressing down on him. He stood, stretched himself and walked stiffly to the hall.

From a peg on the wall he took down a well-worn dark blue cape – the same one his father James had worn – and swung it around his shoulders. This style of cape was long out of use in the force, but Sergeant Mulrooney insisted on wearing it, believing it gave him an added air of authority, not to mention dignity. He also refused to wear anything other than the old-style tunic that buttoned all the way to the neck. "The man looks like a relic from 1924, not 1964!" the Inspector below in Ballyglen often joked to his men. "But he'll have to conform to the force rules and regulations, just like the rest of us." The Inspector, however, took no action to change Sergeant Mulrooney's old-fashioned ways.

"I just do not go along with change for the sake of change," RV had complained to Hannah. "These newfangled uniforms are for postmen or train porters, not for members of the Garda Siochana. A policeman should not only act like a policeman, he should dress to look like a policeman." It was going to take a lot more than a misspelt memo from Ballyglen or Dublin to change Sergeant Mulrooney's ways and convince him to hang up his father's RIC tunic and cape.

Placing his cap on his head, RV opened the cottage door and stepped outside into the misty twilight. His head automatically sank into his shoulders. This he did to brace himself against the sharp biting edge of the Atlantic wind which he knew would strike him with full force when he rounded the corner of the house to fetch his bicycle from the back shed.

"Father O'Malley and his dry spell indeed. Hummph!" RV grumbled to his bicycle-clips before rolling his sturdy Armstrong up the path to where Hannah stood waiting with his food-box.

"Try not to stand around too long in the rain, dear," she said, handing him his night's rations. "You know what it does to your arthritis."

"I know, I know, but I can't let the elements get in the way of my work," RV grumbled. "The weather doesn't stop the lawbreakers from their criminal doings, so there's no reason in the world it should deter the lawkeepers from keeping the law. Anyway, my old bones are used to the wettings by now – keeps them lubricated. Lord knows, I've had my share of 'em in my time."

The sky to the west still glowed amber, gold and blue through the grey mist. For a brief moment it seemed as if someone had ripped a huge tear in the clouds heaped up against the horizon, just wide enough to squeeze out a spray of purple, blue and sea-green spikes of October light. Away to the east sharp spikes of light fell softly on wet stones on the side of Sliabh Cullen, making them look like

22

huge silver doubloons scattered among the purple heather. A single curlew shrieked a long, lonesome call.

"See you in the morning then, old girl. Make sure you lock and bolt before turning in," RV called as he turned his bicycle in the direction of the Garda station in the village, a little over a half a mile away and all uphill.

"I'll be fine, Rudy. Have a good night-duty." From the cottage door, Hannah waved to her husband's back.

All around, the dead leaves of summer, with the consistency of soggy copper-coloured cornflakes, lay as a carpet underfoot on the wet tar road. It was not going to be an easy or pleasant cycle to the station. The sky darkened. Somebody up there had zipped up the cloud bank to the west and the thin film of mist had turned to a light rain. It was practically night.

Chapter Two

As the final strains of Beethoven's Fifth died away in Sergeant Mulrooney's cottage, Ramon Navarro Mulrooney, his brother – better known in Ballykeogh as RN – was crossing the street between Mrs Flanagan's grocery shop and the church. In the tiny cluttered shop he had purchased his next day's supply of forty Gold Flake cigarettes, a half-pound of extra lozenges and a pair of leather bootlaces. While there he had also caught up with the latest news and items of gossip from Mrs Flanagan, one of his chief sources of information in the village. Ahead of him the old church sat firm against a slate-grey sky; squat and solid with the permanence of a sleeping sphinx, its spire a wizard's pointed cap. In the failing light the spire glowed like some strange, lost beacon, its dull beam probing the fine evening drizzle. In spite of the weather, RN's mood was one of buoyant ebullience. He ignored the brittle, salt-tanged wind whipping up the mountainside from the restless Atlantic. This razor-edged wind raked the village streets daily, bending trees, plants, shrubs and the back of man and woman to its will. The wind, coupled with the hardening drizzle, did not impinge on RN's feeling of general well-being as he swished his way through the dead-leaf slush on the gravel pathway leading to the church door. In fact, the world had never looked rosier to RN, who quietly hummed a version of "Autumn Leaves" – appropriately seasonal, he thought – as he walked along the path. It was a partially remembered version of a song he had learned from Mrs Rosenstein all those years ago, though such was his interpretation now that even the composer would have great difficulty in recognising it. Squinting towards the church, he spotted the plump figure of Father O'Malley silhouetted against the open church door and peering out into the fading light. RN attempted a rapid change of direction. "Ah, RN!" Father O'Malley called out. "There you are! The very man I wanted to see. You're a hard man to track, RN – I've been looking out for you all day."

"Oh, Christ," groaned RN. "Just what I needed. What's he doing poking around this time of day?" He raised his voice. "Oh, hello there Father – I was on my way over to see you. Just getting the few smokes before Mrs Flanagan closed for the night. Another damp evening again, Father!"

"It is that, RN – fine days are rare these days – "

"As rare as hens' teeth, a straight-talkin' Kerryman or an honest politician, Father."

"But there's a dry spell on the way – I can feel it in my bones."

"Mmnn, when it comes to weather-forecasting the bones are more reliable than the weathermen in Dublin! We can but hope and we can but pray. God is good." RN brushed raindrops off his jacket and stepped into the church-porch light. A fine spell indeed! Some bloody chance, he thought, considering this side of the hill had not seen a dry day in well over four years.

"Yes indeed. God is good, RN! God is good!" Father O'Malley said. Then putting on his Sunday-sermon face he

25

added in a solemn voice, "We have a little Church business to attend to in the morning, RN."

"We have, Father? What business is that?" RN scraped dead leaves from his muddied boots.

"You must have heard the news, RN – Mr Dwyer! Mr Daniel Dwyer, Black Jack's – er – that is – I mean Jack Dywer's uncle, has passed away in the Bronx. God rest his poor soul! His remains are expected off the Galway train down in Ballyglen in the morning. From the railway station there he will make his final journey home to the church here before being laid to rest among his dear departed relatives, God rest their sleeping souls." Father O'Malley crossed himself – his hand made a high-speed flicking across his face as if warding off a swarm of stinging bees.

"By God!" a wide-eyed RN exclaimed, sounding surprised – though he was already in possession of all the details from Mrs Flanagan. "I hadn't heard a word about it. I can hardly believe it! Daniel Dwyer! Well, well – the great Daniel Dwyer – dead! You don't say!"

"I do indeed say, RN! Mr Dwyer's allotted span in the vale of tears has run its course. The Avenging Angel comes to touch us all eventually, RN. Kings and paupers alike. He knocks at the door of both cottage and castle and when he knocks we must all answer. Poor Daniel Dwyer is no different. He's answered the Angel's final call. It was his dying wish, though, to be carried back here to Ballyglen to be laid to rest with his own on the side of Sliabh Cullen. I only pray he was prepared to meet his Maker."

"Ah – yes, but is Dwyer's Maker prepared to meet him?" RN smirked.

"We'll leave that to God and Mr Dwyer, RN. Judge not, lest ye be judged! Anyhow, there it is. Dan Dwyer is returning to his home-sod and what more could a person ask from life than to be laid in Catholic soil to face eternity with his own departed kith and kin." Father O'Malley joined his hands.

"Oh, indeed, Father, indeed." RN thought anything would be better than having to spend eternity on the side of this particular mountain, especially if it was in the everlasting company of the Dwyer clan.

"Now, about the funeral itself – " Father O'Malley placed an arm around RN's shoulders and spoke in hushed confidential tones. "I'm quite sure that the – er – financial arrangements will prove to be more generous if we ensure Mr Dwyer a good and proper burial. From what I hear, he was not without considerable personal wealth and I've no doubt but that he has set an ample sum aside to ensure he be given a send-off befitting a gentleman of his rank and stature. And who knows! He may have remembered Mother Church in his Last Will and Testament."

Father O'Malley rubbed his hands with satisfaction.

RN stared ahead, nodding slowly.

"What I'm saying, RN, is that this is no ordinary funeral service. This must be absolutely top-shelf service. I'm sure you know what I mean. So, I want you to take care of all the details – church open and ready – vestments aired – heating on – oh, and the digging of the grave, of course."

"Don't worry about a thing, Father. Leave everything to me. We'll give old Dan a send-off a Bishop – er – I mean a statesman – would be proud of. Leave it all to me,"

"Fine, RN, fine, I knew I could depend on you."

"That's what I'm here for, Father."

His mind racing, RN experienced a tingling sensation inside and recognised it for what it was. He already had the smell of American dollars itching in his nostrils. This little caper might mean a nice little windfall and one which could do everyone a bit of good – unless, RN figured, the

Yank's rake of a nephew, Black Jack, gets his greedy paws on the lolly first. Still, he smiled to himself, there would be a lot of thirsty customers lining up tomorrow for a drop of the Pure. It would be the first bit of real good Daniel Dwyer ever did for anyone around Ballykeogh.

"Oh, and by the way," Father O'Malley continued, "The man that brought the word from Ballyglen says it was Mr Dwyer's dying wish that a lament be played at his grave-side as they lower his body to his final resting-place. Not that he ever had a note of music in him to my knowledge, but it seems that he wants his last earthly affair to be one of high style and ritual. Any ideas on that one, RN?"

RN scratched a three-day-old stubble. "Mmnn . . . there's only one man I can think of who would fit the bill, Father, and that man is Jamie O'Connell. He's your man for the music – a great man for the laments, is Jamie. He'd bring tears from a lump of Italian marble. I've no doubt but that you'll find him in his usual haunt up at The Gloves with his drinking cronies anytime after nine or so."

Jasus! thought RN, if only I'd learned the bloody tin whistle instead of the piano, there would an extra dollar or two in that cushy job.

Father O'Malley stepped out of the doorway, looked at the sky – now no more than six feet above his head – peered at his watch and then in the direction of McGarrigan's Bar. On most evenings at this time, he was comfortably settled in the snug, his hands cupping a heart-warming glass of hot whiskey. He placed his palms together as if in prayer and raised them to his lips. "Ah yes – young O'Connell – the man who won't darken the church door Christmas or Easter – a lost sheep – an errant son and brother – ah well – no matter. He'll do, I've no doubt. I'll drop around to The Gloves after nine to see if he'll agree to play over the grave in the morning. Let's see what else – mustn't forget anything. Mr O'Flaherty is gone to collect the coffin. I'd better not forget while I'm up at The Gloves to recruit a couple of strong lads to help you dig the grave. Yes, yes! It will be a great send-off for a great man. Oh, before I forget, RN," he lowered his voice to a whisper and furtively looked right and then left. "Could you possible organise – em – a few more bottles of – emm – 'holy water' from your usual source? You know what I'm talking about . . . They'll be sorely needed before this is over, I'm thinking."

"You can count on me, Father," RN said quietly and smiled a knowing smile. "No problem there at all! I'll have several bottles of the best ready and waiting in the morning."

"Good man, good man! Right, I'm on my way. I'll try and drop by later to check on things." Father O'Malley pulled his pork-pie hat down over his ears and moved off down the gravel path leaving RN smiling to himself and rummaging for the sacristy keys.

"He's bloody enjoying this," RN muttered to himself. "He hasn't caught a fish this big for bloody years! We'll all get mileage from this little caper! This will make the others look like paupers' funerals." It was possible the Bishop himself would put in an appearance, not to mention every other priest within thirty miles of the village. There was nothing quite like the pound or dollar to get the clergy excited and out in force at funerals or weddings. RN found his keys and whistling loudly he set off towards the sacristy.

Father O'Malley's excitement had certainly been rising since hearing of Daniel Dwyer's demise earlier the same day. Life for him in the hillside village had fallen into a predictable and mostly boring routine. Apart from the annual Novenas, the odd vigil, his daily eight a.m. morning

Mass – attended only by Mrs Flanagan and Mrs O'Reilly – and the occasional impoverished local's funeral, what else was there here to occupy his time? There had not been, he regularly complained to RN, a single marriage in over fifteen years. He had once harboured hopes that RN and Clara O'Dowd, the spinster village postmistress, might be enticed into taking step towards the altar but it came to naught. Everybody else left in the village and neighbourhood were either married, widowed or confirmed spinsters and bachelors. Not one marriage, or christening for that matter, in fifteen long years. Not since a younger, fiercer, Father O'Malley had descended on the sleepy and unprepared village like the wrath of Jehovah on Sodom and Gomorrah. His early Sunday sermons were both electrifying and memorable, promising unimaginable and unending torments in the "raging fires of Satan's Domain" – he never referred to it as Hell – for the innumerable and inveterate fornicators, gamblers, lovers of strong drink and other sinners he knew to reside in Ballykeogh. His weekly fire and brimstone pulpit tirades, directed at a stunned, and mainly aged, congregation finally took their toll. Within six weeks of his arrival in Ballykeogh, numbers at confession had dropped away to a handful and there was hardly a man or woman between the age of sixteen and forty – with the exception of Tom Duignan's six moon-faced daughters – left in the entire locality. Since his arrival in Ballykeogh, he had hoped to shepherd his flock down the paths to grace, innocence and temperance. Instead he witnessed them depart one by one to continue their sinning – or so he believed – in the flesh-pots of sin that were Piccadilly and Manhattan. It was a somewhat deflated priest who was left to hear the sins of children and soothe the fears of those parishioners facing the grave. His sermons these days concentrated on the central message of the need for all to contribute towards the upkeep of the church and its pastor. "Give generously and give often" was now his weekly pleas to his aged and apathetic flock.

"Tomorrow *will* be different. Tomorrow is no ordinary day and no ordinary funeral service. I'll have to prepare a special sermon to suit the occasion," he mused as he stepped briskly towards McGarrigan's Bar.

Mr Daniel Dwyer's impending funeral was like Christmas Day come two months early and Father O'Malley was determined to make the most of it.

RN continued his off-key improvisations of "Autumn Leaves" as he fumbled to find the correct key before unlocking the sacristy and stepping inside. The familiar acrid sting of damp camphor-balls and incense assailed his nose. He walked toward a large pine chest of drawers which contained Father O'Malley's Mass vestments. Tugging open the middle drawer, the smell of damp cloth and camphor pinched his nostrils. From beneath a yellowing alb he drew a bottle and, pulling the cork with his teeth, raised it to his lips and took a long draught. The pure white liquid cut a path of searing silver over his tongue and down his throat to his gut to shoot those familiar arrows of tingling pleasure to his extremities.

"Sheesh!" he grimaced and hiccoughed. "That's powerful stuff. It's holy water all right, no doubt about that. The best drop so far, even if I do say so myself." Moving to a tin bucket of water standing behind the oil-stove in the corner, he submerged the bottle in the water, allowing it to fill to overflowing before replacing it in the folds of Father O'Malley's alb.

"If I can keep up this standard with my next production batch, there will be no one in the country to touch me for quality." He chuckled loudly, launched into yet another almost tuneless interpretation of "Autumn Leaves" and set about his chores. There was the pair of brown coffin-stands which had to be placed at the rear of the church, next to the confession box, to receive Daniel Dwyer's remains. Next, there was the placing of four tall ornate brass candlesticks with four large wax candles, one for each corner of the coffin. As he busied himself at these tasks, his footfalls echoing eerily in the cavernous church, he smiled with some satisfaction and congratulated himself yet again on his extraordinary run of good fortune He smiled as he recalled some of the events which had led to his arrival in Ballykeogh and obtaining his present post of church sacristan and general church groundsman. And though Father O'Malley might not see it in the same light, RN had also become general financial advisor to the priest and indeed consultant in most of the day-to-day running of church affairs. The difference between the Protestant and Catholic pastor, he reasoned, was that a Protestant pastor would involve his wife in parish matters. Here, Father O'Malley was forced to rely solely on RN for the advice and direction he might have sought from a spouse. The truth was, since his arrival in Ballykeogh several years ago, Father O'Malley had grown to depend on him almost entirely, a fact which RN now exploited to the full. This dependence allowed him to be more or less a free agent, with full control over his daily actions. It especially gave him the freedom to develop his other talents and "interests" outside the running of the church and it now looked to RN as if, at last, his endeavours were about to pay dividends.

"Things are working out nicely," he congratulated himself. "Things are working out very nicely indeed."

It was indeed true that things were turning out nicely for RN here in Ballykeogh. But then, things had worked well for the quick-witted, resourceful RN ever since, at the age of sixteen, he had escaped the clutches of his doting mother, Cecilia and those intolerable piano lessons. Regardless of his own past, he could never deny the fact that it was most assuredly the talents which he had inherited from Cecilia's side of the family that had helped him to get ahead in his many and varied employments since running away from home. While his older brother RV took after their dour and silent father in almost every respect, RN not only resembled his mother in physical appearance, but also in many of her outgoing, if not eccentric, personality quirks and traits. Like Cecilia, he could be at once creative, imaginative, charming, plausible and likeable. He could, like Cecilia, also be stubborn, wilful, ruthless and cunning in his dealings with others. When set on a course of action he could turn his quick mind to overcoming any obstacle, however difficult. His chameleon-like ability to adapt to any given situation sometimes astounded even him and he possessed the uncanny knack of playing out whatever role any given situation called for. Just as he was playing out his role for Father O'Malley here in Ballykeogh. Down inside him, RN felt, there was a great actor trying to break out. Either that or a corrupt unscrupulous scoundrel – which he suspected was closer to the truth. He liked to believe that some of these traits might have come down to him through his mother's blood from his notorious supposed ancestor, Robespierre.

"Only I'm not going to lose the head," RN said when considering his illustrious lineage. "Ancestor Robert thought too bloody much about the plight of his fellow-man. Too considerate a soul he was entirely. And fine thanks the Frenchies gave him for all his high-principled efforts. Had the poor misfortunate sod looked after number one he might be alive today! Look after number one and let the world look out for itself, that's my motto!"

Since leaving home on that spring day in 1936, RN's life had been one he himself often marvelled at. He often wished he had kept a diary in the years in between. His life would read like one of those cheap adventure paperback novels he sometimes purchased on his visits to Ballyglen. While his introverted and dutiful brother RV prepared to follow his father's advice and join the police-force at age seventeen, RN secretly plotted an escape from any such regimented future. Soon he was to be catapulted into the outer world where he flitted from adventure to fantastic adventure with all the daring, dash and bravado of his silent-screen namesake. His mother Cecilia, to whom he wrote occasionally, would be proud of him, he knew. She would have expected no less of her favourite son.

On leaving home, the teenage RN had set out to reach Liverpool by way of Dublin city. Here, he reasoned, he would sign aboard a tall clipper ship and sail to some exotic shore where he would discover the buried treasure which, as he had read, lay waiting for those courageous enough to seek it. His sudden and unannounced exodus from home was aided by the proceeds gained from the sale of a couple of choice pieces of Cecilia's most valuable jewellery. She was later to forgive him even this, as she forgave him most things.

His travelling expenses secure, RN packed a small suitcase, scribbled a hurried note and climbed out his bedroom window one dark and moonless night, leaving behind a distraught mother and – though he strove not to show it to Cecilia – a somewhat relieved father. Not so, however, was Mrs Corrigan from the other side of the village, whose only daughter, Molly, was having difficulty disguising the visible fact that she was many pounds heavier than she had been eight months earlier. Soon after Mrs Corrigan extracted a full account from her daughter, old Murty Duggan from higher up the mountain complained in the town of the disappearance of several of his best sheep – supposedly stolen and later sold to a passing jobber. Though there was much talk and much speculation about both the missing sheep and young Molly Corrigan's condition in shops and dark pub snugs, RN's name was never mentioned in public – mainly out of respect for Sergeant James Mulrooney and his wife Cecilia.

There were no clipper-ships waiting for RN in Liverpool, only a hard depressed sprawling city and work on dirty coal-tugs plowing the far-from-exotic Mersey. The impending war, in the England of 1939, had forced RN to take several jobs under different guises in his efforts to both raise himself in the world and escape conscription into one of Her Majesty's Armed Services.

"You're not going to find me in uniform. It's their bloody fight, not mine!" RN told an Irish work-mate. "I've better things to be doing with my time than traipsing around France trying to not become cannon-fodder for one of Adolf's gunmen. Anyway, this little bru-ha-ha is unfinished business left over from the 1914–18 tiff. At the end of the day, it's a squabble between the Brit and Hun wealthy and powerful about wealth and power – oh, and land. Only why bring the working man in to do their bloody fighting – and especially their dying, for them! 'Give your all for King and Country,' they say. What a load of horse-shite! You don't see too many Royals or the moneyed classes slogging it out at the front – and you never will! If I'm going to give my all, I want to give it for RN and not HM."

RN continued to dodge call-up to one of the Armed Forces but, knowing the net would soon close, he packed his bags and headed north to the comparative safety of the Scottish Highlands and pastures new. While Hitler was preparing an all-out assault on southern England, RN Mulrooney was engaged in an all-out assault on the unsuspecting inhabitants of the Outer Hebrides. His plan, in RN's mind quite a brilliant plan, was supremely simple. His ultimate aim was to place, through his persuasive and proven sales techniques, a complete set of *Encyclopaedia Britannica* in every crofter's cottage on the islands.

To his utter chagrin and dismay, the initial campaign was to fail utterly. The Scots crofters, like their Irish cousins, had little love or thirst for literature that bore the word 'Britannica' on the cover. After a re-think, his follow-up campaign was, to his delight, an unqualified victory. Returning from Edinburgh, where he had exchanged his unsold Encyclopaedia for a consignment of Adolf Hitler's *Mein Kampf*, RN sold every single copy to the same people who had refused his initial sales advances. This he achieved by convincing the canny and careful crofters that by purchasing a copy of this book they would in the coming months increase their chances of survival by 100%. The Germans were days away from conquering the Sassanachs to the south, then they would push north to the islands and the Scots would not be spared either. Their only chance, he told the wide-eyed islanders, of surviving the inevitable German onslaught – which was literally days away – would be the possession of a copy of the Führer's famous work. "When the storm-troopers stick their helmets inside your half-doors," he warned, a note of danger and urgency in his voice, "show them your copy of Adolf's *Mein Kampf*! That's bound to convince them of your long and unswerving loyalty to Hitler and his struggle. It may be your only chance! There'll be precious little else to aid you in your hour of need!" The result astonished even RN; a copy of *Mein Kampf* found its way into the cabins of every single crofter he visited.

RN was preparing yet another business trip to Edinburgh to replenish his now-depleted book stocks when he got word that the local police were interested in interviewing the travelling book salesman on a number of matters. It was time to pack his bags again and move on.

A year or so later, a certain Dr Ranjit Singh, Ph.D (Calcutta), bone-setter specialist, herbalist and faith-healer of some international repute (or so he pronounced himself to be) disembarked from a Swansea mail-boat and checked through Customs at Cobh harbour. Soon afterwards the affable, if exotic, Dr Singh's practice grew and flourished, with a speed that alarmed the Doctor himself. His growing reputation was earned through his work at every horse and cattle fair, sport meeting, hurling and football match in Kerry, Cork and Limerick. In a short time, Dr Singh's horse-drawn and gaily coloured caravan became a well-known sight on the lanes, highways and byways of the three counties. There was no day but this travelling healer was besieged by the sick and ailing – some seriously so. To his utter astonishment, he claimed more than a few completely cured patients. The fame of the Indian doctor spread to such a degree that Dr Singh seriously considered opening a permanent office in Killarney Town or even Cork – a move, he felt, that would truly establish his medical practice and cement his growing reputation as a healer and physician of great power.

His medical career, however, came to an abrupt end one wet night at the Puck Fair at Killorglin, when a giant of a tinker-man refused to accept that Dr Singh's special course of treatment to ease the pain and tension in his young wife's back was within the bounds of strict medical etiquette. Dr Singh's career could never hope to command the same respect again once it became known that the incensed tinker-man had left the good doctor in such a condition that a *real* bone-setter had to be brought in from Co. Clare to re-set several damaged parts of Dr Singh's anatomy. Added to that was the fact that, according to the tinker's wife, from the neck down Dr Singh was as pale-skinned as any sun-starved Kerryman.

"A mighty funny Indian he was. A black face but his body as white as a swan on a pond!" the tinker was later heard to say in the local pubs. "But the leathering I gave the 'oul bastard sort of evened up the black all over him."

It was the end of a promising career for the Indian doctor who bore more than a passing resemblance to James and Cecilia Mulrooney's errant son. Though sore and sorry, RN was not going to be discouraged by such a trivial and temporary setback. It was while recuperating from his injuries in County Clare's Lisdoonvarna Spa that he hit on his next idea for self-employment. He now saw himself suited to the role of professional matchmaker to those lost loveless – and, as he saw them – hopelessly desperate souls who thronged to the Spa town each August to partake in the numerous Bacchanalian rituals performed there annually. To this age-old ritual RN returned each summer to set up his newly established practice in a small room off the lounge of a small hotel in the town's centre. He never ceased to be amazed at the complex hurdles and difficulties ordinary Irish men and women had created for themselves in doing something that even the most primitive and uncivilised of peoples on the planet found little trouble with – that of forming a natural healthy male-female bonding relationship. Where else on the planet did healthy single males over the age thirty need to wallow in up to twenty hours of heavy drinking, before they could pluck up the courage to simply ask a maid to dance a set or a waltz? From his tiny office, RN was now doing brisk business in getting grown men and women to do what what should have come naturally. If you were an ageing bachelor farmer looking for a young wife or a sad-faced spinster looking for a husband, 'The Matchmaker' Mulrooney was the man to see.

"It's a funny old world, no question," RN remarked to Mrs Duggan, his landlady in Lisdoonvarna. "Men and women have been thrown together on this planet since the beginning of time and yet the poor misfortunes in this godforsaken country still find ways of creating all kinds of barriers and problems when it come to getting together and doing what nature intended them to do."

"Well, nature often needs a helping hand," Mrs Duggan replied. "And wouldn't yourself be out of a job if nature did her job?"

"Oh! I'm not complaining, I'm not complaining, Mrs Duggan. It's a job that sorely needs to be done and there's a rare satisfaction from bringing lost lonely souls together to enjoy the – er – pleasures of wedded bliss."

"What about yourself, RN?" Mrs Duggan often inquired. "Are you ever going to take the plunge yourself?"

"Not a chance, Mrs Duggan! Not a chance. Marriage, as somebody once astutely remarked, is an institution and I'm not prepared to be committed to *that* particular institution just yet."

It was on one of these visits to the Spa town that RN struck up a drinking relationship with a silent dour giant of a man from outside the town. Their regular drinking bouts eventually led RN's companion to confide in him as to how he supplemented his meagre farming income. Eventually RN was introduced to the arcane secrets of the making of poteen – the Pure Drop – the clear white liquid that fired Irish blood and imagination for centuries and now played so large a role in Lisdoonvarna's yearly mating-ritual festivities. RN had to concede that the poteen brewed by his brother-in-booze was as good as ever he had tasted. His companion swore that but for frequent and copious libations of the drop of Mountain Dew half the country would have gone stark raving mad years ago.

"Mind you," RN observed, "half of those who do imbibe *have* gone raving mad."

"Not on the product of my still, they haven't. The really pure stuff never harmed anybody – and my brew is the best, and the purest. The making of good poteen is an art form and there are few artists of note in my business. You want to learn how to make liquid gold? The *real* Uisce Bheatha – the Water of Life? Stick with me, son, I can show you how to concoct the purest of the pure – after that it's up to you."

Time passed and having learned how to distil the liquor to the satisfaction of his mentor, a new plan began to take seed in RN's mind. His work as a matchmaker in the Spa town, though challenging and often rewarding, was too sporadic to engage his restless spirit. Perhaps it was time, he mused, to go home to Ballykeogh where he would ply his new-found trade and practise his art. The village, as he learned from a man from that part of the country, was under the watchful eyes of his own brother RV who had been promoted to Garda Sergeant and Father Finnius O'Malley whom he had yet to meet.

The church was in order and ready to receive the mortal remains of Mr Daniel Dwyer. From here he would make the short journey to join his forebears in the Dwyer family grave-plot situated in the north-east corner of the graveyard adjoining the church building.

RN glanced quickly around the gloomy church for a final check to ensure everything was in order before returning to the sacristy. There he drew from his inside coat-pocket a brown paper bag and began to fill it with fistfulls of church incense from an old biscuit-tin standing in the corner next to the oil stove. "That'll do nicely." he said, savouring for a moment the aromatic incense. "We don't want any tell-tale smells of poteen in the making coming from a certain place during tomorrow's little affair and this lot here will do the job nicely, so it will." He stood for a moment in deep thought. "Maybe I should slip down to the vault to see how things are progressing." He considered this action, then shrugged and shook his head. "Naah – I'll go down and check later when things are quiet around here. Plenty of time then to do what needs to be done." He checked his watch, nodded and resumed his off-key, tuneless whistling. It was 6.35, close to suppertime and RN was hungry. Curious, he thought, how being in a church for any length of time always gave him a terrific appetite. Force of habit, possibly? He recalled when he was a boy, rushing home from church, kneecaps bruised and numb from the rough pew kneeling-blocks, to tuck with great relish into a large fry-up of free-range egg, sausage, home-made black pudding and fried potato. All to be polished off with steaming mugs of hot sweet tea and slices of fresh-baked soda-bread smothered with bitter-sweet gooseberry jam which his mother Cecilia made every summer without fail. RN remembered, slowly shook his head and sighed a long sigh.

With visions now in his head of the succulent leg of local lamb or best braised local beef with mint followed by hot sweet apple crumble being prepared by Mrs Scully, the priest's housekeeper, his mood improved. He quickly extinguished lights, locked the sacristy door and strode through the church grounds in the direction of the priest's house, a few hundred yards or so behind the church, where he himself had his living quarters.

Leaving RN to his sacristan duties, Father O'Malley decided on a brief visit to McGarrigan's Bar, his usual haunt. There, he felt, he could relax and, as much as was possible and allowable for a man in his position, relate on a man-to-man basis with the few of his flock who frequented the establishment. These included a few well-to-do local shopkeepers, wealthy farmers, the local schoolteacher who harboured political ambitions and a sitting County Councillor.

Seeing Mrs Flanagan with her sharp nose flattened against her shop window-pane, as usual, he decided to drop in. He needed cigarettes in any case and who knows, he thought, he might gather a fresh tit-bit of local news. Whenever she had a mind to, Mrs Flanagan kept him up-to-date and well informed on whatever local gossip he might not hear down at McGarrigan's Bar.

"Good evenin' to you, Father. Damp evenin' we're havin' – wasn't it terrible about poor Yank Dwyer – and him a man still in his prime. What can I get you this evenin'?" Mrs Flanagan gushed and headed to the cigarette shelf without being asked.

"Ah yes – poor Mr Dwyer. He will be sadly missed, Mrs Flanagan. But such is God's will. When Death comes knocking we all have to answer. I barely knew him of course. He left for the Bronx shortly after I came to Ballykeogh. Strange he never returned but from what I hear of him, he was an upstanding Christian God-fearing man and a leading figure in the community in his younger days."

"Oh the Yank was a rare character to be sure, Father, a

42

rare character and no mistake!" Mrs Flanagan added with a glint in her eye and laid twenty Players Please cigarettes on the counter.

"It's the good that go the soonest, Mrs Flanagan. Let's hope he lived a decent Christian life for which he will gain his just reward when he meets his Maker in Heaven above."

"The Man Above coming face to face with the bauld Yank Dwyer – that's a moment I would dearly like to witness, Father – that is, if I didn't first have to answer the knock, as you put it, Father." Mrs Flanagan grinned the crookedest of toothless grins as Father O'Malley rummaged in his pocket for loose change. "That'll be two and four pence for the twenty Players, Father."

"The good God will examine his earthly deeds, both good and bad – as He will each one of us – and judge and reward him accordingly. Tell me, Mrs Flanagan, did you hear at all if Mr Dwyer was a wealthy man? Or if there was a will? I'm wondering if Jack, his nephew, stands to gain from his uncle's estate?"

Mrs Flanagan grinned another toothy grin. "Sure all them Yanks are wealthy, Father. They pick money off the trees out there along with the oranges and lemons. Oh the Yank Dwyer had money but sure he knew full well he couldn't take it with him – none of us can. There are no pockets in coffins, are there, Father – but to answer your question, there is talk around of Black Jack coming in for a hatful of Yankee cash – but sure that's the same as the Yank Dwyer leaving it directly to McGarrigan in the pub below. That's where it will end up in the long run. He's a martyr for the drink, Father."

"Hmnnn – ah yes, Jack's love of the sound of glass on bar-marble – I see what you mean, Mrs Flanagan, I do see what you mean. Dear me, is that the time! Well, I must be off – see you at the funeral Mass in the morning. Good night to you, Mrs Flanagan." Father O'Malley stepped into the street and headed off in the direction of Big Tom McGarrigan's Select Bar and Lounge, a regular haunt of the deceased's nephew, Jack. A thought nibbled and tugged at the edges of his mind. He could not help noticing that Mrs Flanagan's tone indicated she knew more of Daniel Dwyer than he and far more than she was prepared to tell him. "What of it?" he muttered to the thickening fog, "We must not speak ill of the dead."

As he walked, he fell deep in concentration in an effort to focus his mind on composing a suitable church and graveside eulogy for the late Daniel Dwyer. This was not to be the usual run-of-the mill eulogy. Certainly not of the standard of his usual Sunday sermons, cobbled together last thing on a Saturday night on returning from McGarrigan's Bar. After all, it wasn't every day a man as important, or indeed as wealthy, as Mr Dwyer came back, from America no less, to be buried among his own in his home soil. There was something noble about that, something proud, even epic and great. A slain Chieftain returning to rest in his native earth with the other departed warriors of his Clan. His homily in the morning, he knew, would have to match the nobility and grandeur of the occasion. This might be – no, it *must* be – his finest, his most important moment. After all, the Bishop himself was to attend the service. Get the words right, impress the Bishop, he thought, and promotion must be on the cards. He had to concentrate. Just as he was getting to grips with a grand-slam opening line, a tall gaunt familiar figure on a bicycle loomed out of the mist. It was Sergeant Mulrooney on his way to the Station.

"Good evening to you, Sergeant."

"And to yourself, Father."

"Moist evening."

"Seasonal, Father, seasonal."

"We're in for a dry spell, I think, Sergeant."

"Possibly, Father O'Malley. Very possibly."

Father O'Malley was prepared to linger awhile and engage the Sergeant in general conversation. Conversation, he reasoned, leads to conversion. Their conversations on meeting, however, never seemed to progress beyond banal weather-related observations of the patently obvious. The Sergeant was not to be lured into deeper discourse with the priest on this occasion and continued to cycle in the direction of the station without a glance either left or right.

"Ah well," Father O'Malley sighed and stared at the disappearing policeman. "Some other time, perhaps."

The Sergeant was a rare fish, he thought, stiff and dour and not at all like his most affable brother, RN. Strange how two brothers could differ so much from one another – both physically and in personality. A good four inches shorter than his dour brother, the devil-may-care RN was outgoing, sociable and well-liked while the Sergeant remained aloof, distant and even feared by many of the locals. Perhaps, Father O'Malley reasoned, the fact that RV was a Methodist accounted for his difficult, somewhat autocratic and often tetchy nature.

For several years now, Father O'Malley had made every conceivable approach to the Sergeant with the singular aim of wooing him over to the Catholic fold. So far none of his efforts in that direction had borne fruit. But Rome, as he well knew, wasn't built in a day. The harder the fight, the sweeter the victory would be when – and he prayed for it daily – he finally won the Sergeant over. He still prickled with pride at how he had saved the Sergeant's brother RN from the wilderness of non-belief. It had crossed his mind, however, that perhaps Sergeant Mulrooney felt that his brother's desertion from the Methodist flock was some sort of family disgrace.

In no less than six months after arriving in Ballykeogh, RN, having had several soul-searching discussions with Father O'Malley, had finally embraced the Roman Catholic faith. Despite RN's conversion, he had made no headway with RV, who remained aloof and distant, impervious to even Father O'Malley's more subtle approaches. Still, time can wear down even the most solid of objects and miracles do happen; he truly believed that still. And when all was said and done, he *did* have RN's conversion to his credit, his first and only one since he entered the order over thirty years ago. But even one soul saved is a whole world saved and he felt a great satisfaction in having at least one victory to his credit to help balance the Heavenly Scales on the Last Day of Judgement.

"When the Great Book of Accounts is finally opened," he told himself while picturing in his mind's eye a sort of celestial *Book of Kells*, "that one deed – that lost soul saved – will be etched in gold alongside my name." He could claim his brief span on earth had had some meaning.

The arrival of RN in Ballykeogh had been a God-send. From that day, Father O'Malley's worries regarding the day-to-day running of the church and parish affairs came to an end. He had to admit RN had worked wonders financially to balance the parish books. Was he not, after all, a fully-qualified chartered accountant, or so he had informed Father O'Malley. In a short time, things begin to change, the most important being the church finances. From being several hundred pounds in the red, there might soon be enough in the account to perhaps begin thinking about the building of that church Father O'Malley had dreamed about for so long, at the other end of the town. In the meantime, essential and long-overdue repairs to the existing church were carried out. All of this, he freely admitted, was due to RN who organised lotteries and whist-drives, weekly *céilí* and modern dances, sports days and even point-to-point races to get the church books back in the black. The dances were held down in Ballyglen, as there were few now left in Ballykeogh old enough to attend or young enough to want to. And didn't a large portion of good grazing-land higher up on Sliabh Cullen now belong to the church estates? Again he had to admit this was entirely due to RN's financial wizardry. He marvelled at RN's uncanny ability to gain access to the homes of several aged and fast-ailing, well-to-do bachelor farmers within a radius of ten miles of the village and befriend them. It was no less than a miracle how he always managed to be on hand a day or two before their final moments, to persuade them of the fabulous rewards to be gained in the hereafter if only they would sign over their lands and money to the church. The last one to respond to such advice was old Pakie Galvin, who donated to the church a four-figure sum of money and thirty-five acres of good winterage shortly before dying suddenly from what the Doctor described as 'an inordinate intake of alcohol – probably poteen.' He also noted other such cases, further commenting that there were far too many old farmers around Ballykeogh who had succumbed to the same fate in recent times. "Mighty strange business," the Doctor puzzled. "Old Pakie Galvin was never known to have touched a drop of intoxicating liquor in his life."

RN proclaimed himself to be as baffled as everyone else in Ballykeogh at Pakie Galvin's sudden conversion to the pleasures of the "Pure Drop". He commented to Father O'Malley, as they examined the deeds to Galvin's farm, "The poor man was well past it. Well into his eighties he was! He was happy to leave the world as he came to it, and even happier to leave his earthly goods to Mother Church. And as for the drink, if you're going to go, can you think of a better way? Well and truly pickled and at peace with yourself and the world! It's how I'd like to go myself. In fact I'm counting on it!"

Lately, RN was speaking to Father O'Malley of yet another sure-fire money-raising "scheme" he had in mind. A "big one", so he said, one that would get that new church built with money to spare; enough even to get a new car for Father O'Malley and perhaps a sturdy truck or van for himself. Father O'Malley had promised to discuss this "grand scheme" with RN in the coming days.

The inviting sign on McGarrigan's pub window which read *Select Bar & Lounge* cheered his spirits and dispelled from Father O'Malley's mind all thoughts of graveside orations, RV's refusal to see the "True Light" and RN's proposed mysterious scheme. He squared his shoulders, brightened his step and pushed open the door to the lounge bar, leaving the world and its troubles outside with the wet autumn night.

Chapter Three

Guard Barney Behan did not even have to look to see who it was scuffling up the pathway leading to the station door. Quickly putting his unfinished crossword out of sight under some documents on the woodworm-honeycombed desk, he glanced at the clock, stretched and sighed a satisfied sigh. "Aahh. Five fifty-nine precisely! He's punctual, as always. I'll have to give him that," he muttered as his mind still worked to solve 10 down, today's crossword stickler. "If it wasn't for the crossword and the radio to relieve the boredom," Guard Behan thought, "a man could wither like a flower in winter in this place."

He could hardly remember a single evening that Sergeant Mulrooney had not clocked in at exactly 5.59 p.m. to take over his night-shift duties which commenced at six p.m. Punctuality was one of Sergeant Mulrooney's strong points. He was punctual in all his duties and expected the same of other people. The station door creaked slowly open to receive the punctual Sergeant, his cape and cap glistening with silver droplets of mist, and his antique bicycle, into the shabby station duty-room.

"Good evenin' Sergeant, 'tis yourself that's in it," Guard Behan called.

"Of course it's myself." The Sergeant blinked in the weak light emanating from a single 40-watt light-bulb hanging in the centre of the room, snapped off his bicycle clips from around his ankles and placed them on the handlebars. "Who else were you expecting at this time of evening – the Minister of Defence perhaps?"

"Another moist evening, Sergeant." Guard Behan ignored the comment.

"Moist is putting it mildly, Guard Behan, putting it mildly indeed. There's no shortage of moist evenings in Ballykeogh." RV removed his cap, wiped the cap-peak with his elbow and then, with a matador-like flourish, swung off his rain-cape and shook it twice. A shower of raindrops sprayed on the documents lying on the desk and Guard Behan, who winced and pretended not to notice. A tinny-sounding radio blared in the background.

"What's that infernal noise, Guard?" inquired RV, sternly nodding in the direction of Guard Behan's cluttered desk.

"What noise, Sergeant? Oh, that noise, is it? The radio! That's no noise, Sergeant, that's The Beatles! They're the rage of the music world – more famous than Elvis or even Sinatra – more famous these days than the Royal Showband even."

"Hummph! You call that fame? Fame, my good fellow, is relative."

"It's true. And I heard tell that there are experts who say that their music is as important to modern culture as Mozart's was to his," Guard Behan declared, proudly showing off to the Sergeant his profound knowledge of the pop-music scene and the world beyond Ballykeogh.

"If that sound – that – din is a reflection of modern music and culture, then we are in far worse shape than we realise! Who are they again?"

"The Beatles, Sergeant, the Beatles – as important as Mozart, they are, or any of those other fellas who lived when classical music was all the rage."

"The Beagles? Braying beagles is how they sound to my ears. As important as Mozart? Or – or even Beethoven? What utter poppycock! Has the world gone crazy or what?" RV guffawed, his face having turned a deep red. "If the Master was alive today, he'd be turning over in his grave, so he would – to think that this infernal *din* would be classed as anything even remotely related to *real* music! Good grief!"

RV stepped briskly to Guard Behan's desk, foraged beneath the clutter of documents, found the blaring radio-set and switched it off. A great silence fell immediately on the room, broken only by the clock's ponderous ticking. Guard Behan's shift had ended.

RV moved toward the tiny fireplace which was choking the life out of a turf fire attempting to survive in the grate. Standing with his legs apart and his backside to the sullen sods, he rubbed his hands together and asked, "Well, Guard, anything to report after your duty?"

Taking a well-thumbed note-pad from his tunic breast-pocket, Guard Behan cleared his throat and replied, "A slow day, Sergeant." Then flicking over the pages of his note-pad, he continued, "One summons issued to Tommo Larkin for failing to display adequate lighting on his bicycle – remember, you nabbed him yourself on your way back from Tom Duignan's place last week – one summons to the Widow Mallin for failing to produce a current licence for her sheepdog – I got that one – " He paused for a moment, threw the Sergeant a long sideways look and said slowly and deliberately, "Oh yes! This one could be serious. One report from Tom Duignan's wife Dotty concerning the sighting of a peeping-tom – skulking in the general vicinity of the Duignan household – observed, she reports, by both herself and her husband Tom. She was extremely concerned for both the safety and the chastity of her daughters, and not to mention herself. She gave me a right good lecture on how disgusting and disgraceful it was for the law – meanin' us – to allow this sex-crazed pervert to roam scot-free over the countryside and to spy and prey on innocent God-fearing womenfolk. He had only one thing on his mind, according to Mrs Duignan, and that was to commit all manners of unspeakable crimes on their innocent young bodies. Quite excited she was, Sergeant."

Clearing his throat, RV scowled and stiffened at the mention of Tom Duignan's name. "What did you say to her, Guard?" he asked.

"I asked her to describe the peeping-tt – er – the suspect, which she did. Tall and thin she said he was – over six feet – dressed in dark clothing and sighted on several nights recently between the hours of midnight and two o'clock in the morning skulking and dodging between hedgerows and bushes on the mountainside overlooking their house. You've been patrolling up there, haven't you, Sergeant? Seen anything – em – suspicious in that vicinity, have you?"

RV cleared his throat, stared at the ground and rocked uncomfortably on his feet.

A smirk played about Guard Behan's mouth as he continued, "I said of course we would launch an immediate and thorough investigation and have this sex-maniac behind bars in no time at all and that herself, her husband and – ahem – her half-dozen attractive daughters could sleep without fear of prowlers, peepers or other local bogie-men. She went away giving off about all men being sex-maniacs and so forth, but she seemed satisfied that we would apprehend this unsavoury midnight rambler.

Otherwise, Sergeant, a quiet enough day, all things considered." Guard Behan folded his note-book with satisfaction and returned it to his pocket.

RV again cleared his throat, walked to his desk and sat slowly down.

"Thank you, Guard. I'm sure you allayed Mrs Duignan's fears and handled it all with tact and sensitivity. Naturally, we will investigate her report – though I must say it sounds a bit hysterical to my mind – and she always was a nervous, over-imaginative woman. A peeping-tom – out on the side of Sliabh Cullen? In this weather? I somehow think not. However, duty is duty and we will investigate. You can start inquiries tomorrow, Guard. Now," RV shuffled some documents before him on his desk. "Have you any other information to report? Any suspicious-looking farmers in town purchasing inordinately large amounts of brown sugar? Any unusually large sales of potatoes? Or barley? That kind of thing. Clever detection work is what's required here, Guard, clever and informed detection work – and attention to detail, however small or insignificant." RV was irked at Guard Behan's continual and dogged refusal to take any real interest in – to RV's mind at least – the most important of all their official duties here in Ballykeogh, namely, the detection and ultimate smashing, once and for all, of the poteen-making operation being run with daring impunity under their very noses.

Guard Behan did not, however, share in his Sergeant's unswerving commitment to that particular mission. He knew that should the Sergeant ultimately apprehend the man responsible for making the poteen, the backlash from the maker's clients in the locality would be more than the Sergeant was prepared for or could handle. He had served his time as second fiddle to Sergeant Mulrooney here in Ballykeogh for longer than he thought good for his career.

He knew his ticket out would be won with the right amount of well-placed summonses to his credit. Particularly summonses issued to trespassers of the law – though never to the local well-heeled local farmers or business-people of the village – which could be brought before the district justice and convictions won. Then he could expect to earn that longed-for early transfer. Away from Sergeant RV Mulrooney, away from his unattractive digs in Mrs Blaney's cold cheerless house and away from this miserable rain-sodden God-forsaken outpost at the back-of-beyond. When that day dawned, Guard Behan believed that the coveted three Sergeant's stripes which had eluded him for so long would soon be his.

"No, Sergeant, nothing to report on that front, I'm afraid," he said with resignation, "Just the usual comings and goings."

"Hmnn – I see. Well, not to worry. Keep your eyes peeled and your ear to the trail. Something will break – wait and see. In the meantime, pay heed to everything – no minute piece of information, no matter how trivial, or anything you see, no matter how innocent-looking, is as it seems to be. Everything that moves, everything that happens in this village, or indeed outside it for that matter, has significance and may be an important and crucial piece of the jigsaw to help us in solving this puzzle. Never forget that, Guard Behan. Also remember that in solving this business, we will earn the undying respect of our flock, not to mention our masters at HQ. Anything else before you go?"

"By God, I almost forgot to mention the Yank Dwyer – Daniel 'The Yank' Dwyer. The Yank, did you know, died suddenly last week in the Bronx – that's in New York, Sergeant – "

"I know where the Bronx is, Guard; do continue."

" – died in the Bronx, New York as I said and they're carting his body all the way back here to Ballykeogh to be buried. Did you ever hear the beat of that one! Died while on official duties they say – while working as an undercover agent for the FBI no less – or so the boys below in Ballyglen would have it. Tombs O'Flaherty is going to collect the remains off the eight-thirty train in the morning from Galway and then drive back here for the funeral Mass at eleven."

"Mr. Dwyer dead, eh? Well, well! I never knew he was in the FBI." RV registered surprise and asked, " Anyway, what's all that got to do with us here at the station?"

"Ah, well!" Guard Behan suddenly became animated with the importance of the news he was about to impart to his superior. "You see, it's going to be a pretty big affair, so it seems. The word from below in Ballyglen is that there's going to be a right royal turn-out to meet the train – brass band, contingents from the old IRA and Cumann na mBan. The lads below from the station in Ballyglen are laying on a full guard of honour and escort for the remains. It's going to be the Real McCoy, looks like to me, Sergeant."

"By the lord Harry! That's red carpet treatment, to be sure. I would hardly expect that sort of turn out if it was Al Capone's corpse – or the Bishop of the Bronx – that was arriving. All that for Daniel Dwyer?"

"Oh, yes. Death-notices and obituaries singing his praises in the *Ballyglen Bugle*, so I'm informed. Seems he was a big shot around here in the War of Independence – before he emigrated to the States, so he's in for the full treatment. That's all I know."

RV stroked a jutting chin and said after several moments of deep thought, "Well, we better prepare, in that case. If his old IRA comrades are going to be present, there'll be guns for sure – shots fired over his coffin at the graveside – that sort of thing. The presence of the law will definitely be required to keep a vigilant eye on proceedings." The full implications of the forthcoming funeral on the morrow were beginning to dawn on him. "I'd better speak with my opposite number down below," RV said, referring to Sergeant Kelly in Ballyglen. "Call Clara at the post office and ask her to get me Ballyglen 13."

Guard Behan cranked the side-handle of the single decrepit telephone on RV's desk and waited. Getting no response, he cranked the handle with ever-increasing force and waited. He shook his head and looked at RV. "No answer. Looks like Miss Clara is having one of her turns again."

"Give me that!" RV snapped, snatching the telephone mouthpiece from Guard Behan's hand and shouting into it, "Hello! hello! Miss Clara! Are you hearing me? Miss Clara! Oh! what's the use – the woman is impossible. I'll have to walk over to the post office and make the call to Sergeant Kelly from there. You wait on here till I return. I won't be a moment longer than I have to." RV reached for his cap and marched towards the door.

"Christ! It would be more efficient if we employed a bloody one-winged carrier pigeon to take our messages to Ballyglen than to depend on that daft Clara to answer our telephone calls," Guard Behan grumbled, angry with this delay in his signing-off duty. Waiting until RV was out of sight, he switched on the radio and continued with his unfinished crossword.

RV walked briskly down the village street towards the post office, spotting from the corner of his eye Mrs Flanagan's nose pressed to her shop window. "There's not much in this place that doesn't go unnoticed by that madam," he thought. "She probably knows more about what goes on in the locality than I do." As he approached the post office, he pondered the difficulties the station was experiencing in making the simplest phone call. "The phone situation is a pure disgrace – a fiasco! God forbid we should find ourselves with a real emergency on our hands. A direct line, yes, a direct line is the only answer to the problem." He drew near the tiny post office situated across the street from the Garda Station at the north end of the village. He resolved to make an official application for a direct phone-line link with the station in Ballyglen as soon as possible.

Clara O'Dowd, referred to only as "Miss" Clara, had been postmistress in the village PO since her mother died in the late forties. Clara had been considered a little 'odd' by the people in the locality and her behaviour in carrying out her official duties as postmistress was somewhat erratic, to say the least. Over the years however, the villagers and customers from the general locality had come to accept her for what she was and had come to regard Miss Clara and her foibles as perfectly normal, Accordingly, they had adjusted their letter-posting, pension-collecting and the making of phone-calls to suit her little "turns". Nobody but Sergeant Mulrooney seemed unduly troubled or irritated by Miss Clara's strange ways and moods, but then hardly anyone other than the Sergeant or Guard Behan made any phone calls out of the village, especially after six p.m. on winter evenings.

Before Clara O'Dowd took over the responsibilities of postmistress to the village, her mother Brigie, a none too bright, rather snobbish and haughty lady of unwarranted airs and graces, had operated the small post office from the first day it opened in 1913. The first telephone to be seen in the area was installed in her office with great pomp and circumstance almost thirty years later in 1942, while a war raged in Europe and the Emergency lay over Ireland like a heavy turgid mist. It was two years later, however, before any phone-calls could actually be made from the PO. Clara's mother, a deeply religious and superstitious woman, was utterly convinced this black box of gadgets and bells, winders and speaking hand-grips, was the work of the Devil himself. On the day it was connected, she had to be physically restrained by a PO Engineer and a County Councillor – present for the "Grand Opening" – from attacking the complex, highly suspicious-looking installation with her knobbly blackthorn walking-stick.

"Get this Satan's contraption out of this house!" she screamed, when on holding the black hand-grip to her ear, she distinctly heard a thin ghostly voice call her by name. Not until the priest, also present at the Grand Opening, promised to exorcise and – as Brigie demanded while brandishing her blackthorn – to "banish Beelzebub's brothers" from the simple black box, did she allow the post office engineer to fix the device on the wall of the sitting-room she had converted into the Ballykeogh post office. For two years after the installation, regardless of pleas and even threats from the post office head office in Galway, Brigid remained unconvinced that the black box fixed to the wall was anything other than an "unnatural, heathenish contraption". It was not until she was assured that an Italian, Signor Marconi, whose mother was an upstanding Catholic from Dublin, was the creator of this "hellish" invention, that she grudgingly accepted the device with all its hissings, crackling and unexpected bell-ringings.

While she lived however, she never felt entirely happy or comfortable having to answer the startling, jangling bell or speak to the strange, disembodied voices coming from the ear-piece. It was only with great reluctance she assisted customers with their calls to the outside world. The consequences of this resulted in very few phone-calls being made to, or from, Ballykeogh.

Shortly after she gave birth to her daughter Clara in 1910 her husband Francie died of TB and a liver complaint, brought about, the doctor said, by "an excess of conviviality" over many years. This left Brigie to bring her only child up on her own. As was the custom, the local matchmaker had made overtures to her to fix a marriage with several local farmers but she shunned each one in turn.

"Why should I marry again," she scornfully informed Duxy Dinann, the matchmaker, "when I have three pets at home which answer the same purpose of a husband. I've got a mangy cur of a dog that growls at me in the morning, a bad-tempered budgie which babbles away all afternoon and a tomcat that stays out all night! I'm well rid of the last one! Why would I want another husband?"

Brigie's desire to raise a daughter of quality, breeding and education inspired her to send Clara away to a finishing school in Paris at the tender age of fourteen. She was determined that her "one and lonely" daughter, as she called her, was going to grow up as refined a lady as was possible in this barbaric country, regardless of what cost. To finance this plan, she sold off Francie's small-holding outside the village and soon Clara found herself on her first, and last, journey to experience the world outside Ballykeogh. It was in Paris that Clara was to meet the dapper young English "gentleman" to whom she gave her heart, her body and eventually, most of her meagre living allowance sent regularly from home. Clara was sixteen, free of her mother's overbearing, smothering care, far away from the prying eyes of her neighbours at home in Ballykeogh and very much in love.

Now, thirty years on and residing once again in Ballykeogh, Clara still grieved for the loss of her youth, her frail beauty and most of all the loss of her English lover. One day in 1933, or so the story went, Clara's beau disappeared out of her life forever, to seek action, adventure and promotion in the Spanish Civil War. Clara never saw him again and later heard that he had been killed in action by a German fighter plane while defending Madrid. On receiving this news something in her snapped. Clara was never quite the same again. Heartbroken, her plans, hopes, desires and dreams – her entire world – shattered, she returned to Ballykeogh and her doting mother, Brigie. She was rarely seen outside the door again, except at Easter or at Christmas Midnight Mass and then she was dressed from head to toe in mourning black. When Brigie finally passed away, Clara took over as postmistress, but still remained aloof from what passed as normal village life. Other than her regular customers, no human ever visited Clara socially. She never left the house to visit the few family friends she still had, never went to local parties or dances or entertained men friends – despite a few futile attempts at courting her.

Now Miss Clara lived in a world where reality and fantasy regularly waltzed around her living room. It was a room now filled with bitter-sweet memories of glittering Paris nights, and empty never-to-be-fulfilled longings. The room, still wearing the faded Victorian decor favoured by her mother, was filled with Victorian furniture, bric-a-brac and piled high with hundreds of old newspapers dating back to her mother's time. These papers she read and re-read, for ever scouring the small ads and foreign news columns for some news of her dead lover. One day soon, she fancied, she would read the news of him having survived that German attack, and, even as she read the thrilling news, desperately seeking to make contact once again with his lost Irish sweetheart. On the days or nights when fantasy led the dance, her wandering mind assumed whatever date printed on the paper she happened to be reading at the time to be the actual date. Thus did the days, and youth, slip Miss Clara by.

That evening, as Sergeant Mulrooney crossed the street to attempt to get her to put his call through to Ballyglen, Clara was engrossed in reading a tattered and smoke-stained copy of *The Daily Mail*, dated September 3rd, 1939. The paper's bold headlines informed her that Poland was under attack from German Forces while Mr Winston Churchill, speaking from the War Room in London, warned the English-speaking nations of the evils of Nazism and the imminence of a full-scale German attack. Clara stared at the headlines and tried to evaluate the import of the news. This was indeed shocking, dreadful news, the evil of the Nazis which Mr Churchill warned could be upon her at any moment! At that precise moment, Sergeant Mulrooney rapped loudly on her front door. To the alarmed Clara, it seemed that the Germans were already in the village and at her very door attempting a forced entry.

"Miss Clara! Miss Clara! Are you inside? Can you hear me?" RV rapped again, impatiently.

"Saints protect me this night! They're here already! And they speak English! It's the end for us all!" A terrified Clara clutched her 1939 *Daily Mail* to her breast and sat as still and silent as she could, her heart fluttering in her rib-cage like a small frightened bird cupped within closed hands.

"Miss Clara!" RV called loudly, "I know you can hear

me! Will you please come and open this door! I wish to make a very important telephone call. It's extremely urgent, Miss Clara. A matter, you might say, of life or death! Can you hear me in there, Miss Clara!"

Recognising the booming voice outside her door, Clara sighed with relief, gasped and, in a small tremulous voice, called out to RV, "Sergeant Mulrooney! Thank heaven it's you! So you've read the terrible news too. They'll be here any hour now. We'll all be overrun! We have to do something!" she said, her small voice rising in panic and her mind filled with visions of brutish, jack-booted Hun storm-troopers about to inflict the most hideous of tortures on her trembling body.

"No, no, Miss Clara," a confused-sounding RV shouted at the still-closed door. "They are not expected here till morning. The train doesn't get in to the Ballyglen railway-station until eight or so. I don't expect they will get to Ballykeogh till just before ten o'clock or so. And anyway, Miss Clara, there's nothing to fear from a funeral!"

"A funeral? Heaven spare us all – if the Germans get here it could be all our funerals!" Clara's voice piped from the darkness of her room.

"Mr Dwyer's not German! And it's just one coffin for one grave – nothing to upset you, surely!" RV's jaw tightened. He was beginning to lose his patience. "Now look here, Miss Clara! I have to put an urgent call through to Sergeant Kelly in Ballyglen – it's to do with firearms. There'll be volleys fired over the coffin, you know – things have to be in order. I have to be fully prepared. I have to make that call – *now*!"

Clara breathed another sigh of relief. "Thank God!" she thought. "The brave Sergeant is making plans for the village's defence. He even knows what time they will get to Ballyglen!" After a long time, she pulled back the window curtain a few inches and peered out at Sergeant Mulrooney standing in the continuous rain. "Oh Sergeant! I just knew we could depend on you. The village has to be defended and saved, at all costs – but I can't – I *won't* let you in. I'm not opening this door to anybody! Even if St Peter himself was to knock this very minute. I'll let you make your call, but I'll push the phone out to you and you can make your call from there. In these troubled times, a body can't be too careful!"

RV shook his head in confusion. "What in heaven's name is she babbling on about? What harm can Dwyer's funeral do her? The poor creature gets worse by the day," he thought. "Still, I'd better humour her, otherwise I'll never make contact with Ballyglen." He waited silently while Clara shuffled about inside the darkened house.

At last, the side-window of the post office opened a fraction and a skinny arm emerged to place the receiver on the window ledge. "Now Sergeant," Clara whispered from within, "I'll crank the handle and you give the number you want in Ballyglen to Mrs O'Neill."

RV sighed, shook his head as he picked up the receiver and wondered what Sergeant Kelly in Ballyglen would think if he could see him now, standing in the falling rain outside the Ballykeogh PO window, attempting to make a simple official phone-call. He would be the laughing stock of the entire Ballyglen Garda Station.

When Mrs O'Neill came on the line, he asked for Ballyglen 13 and after what seemed like an age, RV heard the distant sound of Sergeant Kelly's voice from the spitting ear-piece. His opposite number in Ballyglen confirmed the facts of the funeral already imparted to him by Guard Behan and was also able to confirm that yes, there was indeed to be a volley of shots fired at the graveside by whoever of the Yank Dwyer's old IRA comrades were still alive. Sergeant Kelly also stressed the need for both RV and Guard Behan to attend the funeral as official representatives of law and order.

RV assured Sergeant Kelly that he could be entirely depended on to ensure that things ran smoothly and that all would be in order before, during and after the funeral. Wishing Kelly a good night, RV rapped loudly on the window-pane to indicate to the invisible Clara that he had terminated his telephone call to Ballyglen. "Thank you, Miss Clara. I've finished my call," he called and waited for a skinny arm to reach out and retrieve the handset. The receiver quickly vanished inside and the window was slammed down sharply. "Good grief! she's almost as bad as her mother!" RV shook his head, sighed and started back for the station-house.

"God help us all in these terrible times!" Clara called after the disappearing Sergeant. Sitting in her dark room of shapes and shadows, she was once again alone to watch the past and present spin, whirl and dance around her chair with ever-increasing frenzy

As RV walked the short distance back to the station-house, he began to formulate his plan to set in motion the drafting of an official request to HQ. Namely, that Ballykeogh be equipped, as soon as was possible, with that direct, and indeed vital, telephone link to Ballyglen to deal quickly and efficiently with emergencies – such as this one, for instance. Arriving back at the station he found Guard Behan standing by the open door, his civilian raincoat on over his uniform, ready and eager to hand over to the Sergeant and be off home. Without a word, RV snapped off the radio and glared at Guard Behan.

"That Miss Clara is becoming impossible to deal with! She's practically away with the fairies!"

"Residing with them full-time at this stage, I'd say!"
Guard Behan retorted.

"She should be removed from her position forthwith! I
can not abide people who fail, for whatever reason, to
execute their official duties and responsibilities in a wholly
professional manner!"

"She's a nuisance sure enough but – ah, sure, the poor
thing is daft as a March hare and totally harmless,
Sergeant."

"That may be, Guard, but duty is duty – and her actions
may one day lead to some disaster or other. The rigmarole
I had to go through just now to make one simple phone-
call – it was laughable! Why do we put up with her and her
carry-on? She should be retired – or replaced!"

"Well, you know how it is around here, Sergeant. They
wouldn't put up her for a week if she was efficient.
Without people like Miss Clara to gossip about, people's
lives would be empty, boring and dull. That's why they
tolerate her ways. And, as I said, there's not a jot of harm
in her. Well, I'll be off then, Sergeant." Guard Behan
headed for the door, not wishing to get involved any
further.

"Don't forget! We have extra duties to perform in the
morning, Guard. I want to see you here in the morning
spick and span – and on time! Good night to you."

With Guard Behan departed he was now alone, and
with the long night still ahead, RV stared at the glow of a
single spark that remained in the fire-grate. He mulled
over what official station work he had yet to perform
before embarking on his current nightly vigil: that of the
surveillance of the house of Tom Duignan, his current
prime suspect who lived with his wife, Dottie, and their six
daughters, four miles north of the village. But that was
some hours away yet. No point, he reasoned, in

65

commencing observations until his suspect returned from his nightly card-game with Jim Joyce, a mile further up from Duignan's farmhouse on the side on Sliabh Cullen. In the meantime, he had to write his daily reports and he had to give some time to composing his application to HQ for a direct telephone or some form of radio link with Ballyglen. He also considered Guard Behan's defence of Miss Clara. He had to admit to himself, there was a grain of truth in what Guard Behan had said and indeed he himself also felt a great deal of sympathy for poor Clara's disposition. He was well aware of her difficult upbringing and he had, along with almost everybody in Ballykeogh, shown remarkable tolerance and understanding towards her increasingly idiosyncratic behaviour. Nevertheless, he was still highly annoyed whenever one of her "turns" got in the way of official police duty – as it had done this evening.

"All very well and good," RV thought, "when she acts up the way she does with local people who know her ways and what to expect from her. But what about strangers who come in from outside? What in heaven's name do they make of her carry-on? Well, it's downright embarrassing!"

He had lost count of the number of times visitors – mainly Americans – had come to the station to lodge complaints of how they were unable to gain entry to the post office to mail letters and make phone-calls. He well remembered the case of some unsuspecting German tourists who had ventured up to Ballykeogh. Not only were they not allowed inside the PO, the dumbfounded visitors had to suffer all kinds of verbal abuse from the unseen postmistress on learning their nationality, while she remained hidden behind her securely locked door.

"She some sort ov krazy voman over dare!" one perplexed and angry German matron exclaimed to the Sergeant. "She say she will not allow us entry to ze post office – no way! Ve ask why ever not? She say ve kill her fiancé vit our guns unt bomps! She say ve kill her fiancé but she make damn sure ve don't kill her! She some krazy lady over dare, for sure!"

These incidents – and there were many – took a lot out of RV who tried to placate the angry, confused tourists and tried to explain away, as best he could, the Ballykeogh postmistress's somewhat unorthodox behaviour. He then usually offered to intercede and take the visitors' mail to the office when Miss Clara had calmed down somewhat. It had not passed his notice that there were fewer German or American visitors to be seen north of Ballyglen these days and, quite frankly, it did not surprise him in the least.

Moving to the station-house window overlooking the school-yard, which adjoined the church and graveyard, RV swept his sleeve over the pane in a wide arc and peered out. A light rain was being whipped along underneath the street-light by a restless fidgety wind. Through the misty grey veil he saw a figure approaching. As he drew closer he recognised him to be his brother, RN, hunched against the driving rain, obviously on his way back to his quarters in Father O'Malley's house.

"Aahh . . . " RV said to himself, his breath misting the windowpane. "The little brother – skulking about in the dark, as usual. Always up to one thing or another – always busy – always on some church duty – and most of it after dark. Though how he fills his time during the day beats me. There could be more to my baby brother than meets the eye, I'm thinking."

RV never did understand his errant brother and why he had decided to return to Ballykeogh after so many years away. All those years missing, often reported dead or in jail and without as much as a letter or word to ease the heartache and distress of his heartbroken mother Cecilia.

His father, James, quite naturally, was equally distressed. His younger brother's behaviour had been downright shameful and callous. He made no effort to attend either Cecilia's or James's funerals and only wrote one short note inquiring if he had come in for anything in either of his parents' wills. Then one day some years back, out of the blue, in marched the brave RN as if he had been away for a short holiday to Killarney and expecting to pick up where he had left off.

When at last RN and RV did meet face to face and RV expressed these opinions to his brother, a bitter shouting match ensued, resulting in a coolness and furthering of the distance between them. But just where exactly had his brother been all those years? RV often pondered. How had he made his living during his time away? There were many rumours – and what reasons did he have for now making Ballykeogh his home when every able-bodied male for miles around had long since departed for London, Boston or New York? Surely the pay to be earned in Father O'Malley's employ could not hold a man of RN's restless spirit or nature in the village for too long. So what did keep him here in Ballykeogh? Once again, he admitted to himself that he did not understand his brother or the many facets of his somewhat shady mysterious life.

Most puzzling of all, however, was why his brother had become so involved with Father O'Malley and the Catholic Church. "Never had an ounce of religion as a lad. I wonder what change of heart he has experienced in his time away to take to the religion in this way?" He found it hard to believe that RN had a sort of "St Paul on the Road to Damascus" conversion. And to go over to Father O'Malley's lot too – poor Cecilia would turn in her grave. RV shook his head and returned to his desk. The last unattended spark spluttered in the fireplace. He would attend to the fire as soon as he had a cup of tea. The last spark expired as he settled down, a chipped cup of weak colourless tea in his hand, to complete his daily paperwork. He had yet much to do before setting out to cycle the four miles – all uphill – to Tom Duignan's place to begin his nightly watch on the farm. "Who knows," he thought as he sipped the tepid brew. "There might be a breakthrough. This might be the night I will finally nab Duignan in the act. He has to make his move *one* of these nights! And when he does, I'll be there – waiting for the scoundrel."

It was going to be a long lonely night and tomorrow was going to be an equally long and important day.

Chapter Four

Tombs O'Flaherty's mood was not good as he careered down the hillside towards Ballykeogh in his battered 1940s Packard hearse. Although, he had to admit, his visit to old Charlie Joyce had improved his humour greatly. Jim O'Flaherty was the local undertaker, and had been for many years now. Everyone called him "Tombs", although never to his face. Not that it would have offended the mild-mannered Tombs, who was of a pleasant and easygoing disposition, a man who took life as it was served to him. Apart from the odd undertaking job, Tombs O'Flaherty, a man in his late fifties, made his living as a stone-cutter and engraver. He had long since lost count of the number of funerals he had serviced and yet each time he found it more and more difficult to carry out these undertaking duties. He just was not cut out for this kind of work. He had felt this way about the job from the beginning but his father was also the village undertaker and, as is traditional in these cases, young Jim inherited the business, along with the nickname "Tombs", after his father's death. He took great pride and satisfaction in his stone-cutting and he knew he was good at his work. Stone had life and Tombs felt he could bring that life out in even the hardest of granite. These undertaking jobs took the spirit out of him, especially now that he was getting to the age when he figured that he himself might very well be his own next customer. This thought left him cold and empty inside. But somebody had to do the job and, for better or worse, that somebody, he accepted, was himself. But only for the time being, he always promised himself, when faced with another funeral to service. When the old Packard hearse packed in, he would not replace it and that would be that. O'Driscoll's Undertakers from Ballyglen could do the job just as well. In the meantime, Tombs would carry on and do the job and this coming assignment, from what he heard, was going to be his most important to date – not to mention the most financially rewarding.

The thought of money brought his attention to the present mechanical condition of the old Packard. "She could do with the brakes being completely overhauled, God knows!" he muttered, mashing down hard on the brake-pedal, pumping up the adequate braking pressure to reduce speed sufficiently to negotiate the sharp bend at the bottom of the hill below Ballykeogh.

Tombs' depressed state could be traced back to the moment he heard that Daniel "The Yank" Dwyer was dead and that, naturally, he was being hired to undertake the burial arrangements. Firstly he had to meet the eight-thirty train from Galway below in Ballyglen and collect Mr Dwyer's remains off the train. Mr Dwyer, he was informed, was to arrive in a lead coffin but would have to be transferred to an ordinary coffin which Tombs was to have in his hearse on meeting the train.

Mr Dwyer had left strict instructions that after his death he was to be carried home the final few miles in a coffin made from trees that grew around his home place. When the transfer of the body was complete, Tombs was to drive

71

back to Ballykeogh for the funeral Mass and the interment afterwards in the church graveyard.

Earlier that same evening, shortly after six o'clock, he had driven out to Charlie Joyce's place to collect the coffin, as instructed. Charlie Joyce was a small farmer-cum-carpenter and a good part of his income came from supplying Tombs with coffins. Business had been good for them both these last few years, what with all these sudden deaths. After the usual tour of Charlie's workshop and a detailed examination of all his coffins, Tombs finally decided on one of the more expensive caskets. This was, after all, not to be one of the usual run-of-the-mill funerals and instructions to Tombs dictated there was to to be no expense spared. After a fair amount of the usual haggling about the fineness of the coffin workmanship, the sheen of the polish, the quality of the wood and its resistance against the ravages of time, worm and the wet earth, a price was finally agreed on. To celebrate, Charlie drew out a bottle of pure white liquid from inside a coffin with his own name emblazoned on the lid. Uncorking the bottle, he passed it to Tombs who drank deeply and passed it back.

"That's a mighty fine drop, Charlie. I needed that! It's hit the spot, good and proper!"

"Does it every time!" Charlie burped and wiped his hand across his mouth. "I wouldn't keep anything but the best. We've RN to thank for that. Only for it we'd all be in one of those oul boxes long ago." He nodded towards the stacked coffins. "I'd be crippled with arthritis only for it. A tipple a day keeps the rheumatics away. That's my opinion anyway!"

"You know what it is, Charlie," Tombs said. "With the climate such as it is, the stuff should be issued free by the Government as a general panacea for a person's ailments."

"You're not allowed to touch the stuff by law," Charlie complained. "And the law's a funny thing, so it is, not allowing a body to make a drop of liquor in private."

"True for you, Charlie – a man's not allowed to make liquor in private nor water in public."

Charlie laughed. "That's a fact, Jim, but you be sure that the self-same boyos who tell you you're breaking the law to let a drop wet your palate are rarely averse to getting a bottle or two for themselves around Christmas-time. Especially when they hear that there's good stuff to be had."

Tombs nodded in agreement. "That's true too. With the exception of one man, I have to say. I'll no doubt meet the same man on my way back to the village. He'll be on his bike on his way up the hill to throw an eagle-eye on Tom Duignan."

"Ah, the bould Sergeant Mulrooney! Maybe it's one of Tom's daughters he's got his eye on. What do you think, Jim?" Charlie's eyes began to twinkle.

"Humph! He would need a full bottle of this stuff inside him to face one of those beauties, and that's a fact! No, our Sergeant has bigger things on his mind – like stopping you and me enjoying a drop or two when we wish to partake in the privacy of our own homes – a danger to no living soul." Tombs sampled another draught of the Pure Drop.

It was gone nine p.m. when both men loaded the coffin into the hearse and Tombs finally took his leave of the red-faced Charlie Joyce and started back to Ballykeogh.

Now, as the hearse laboured up the steep hill approaching the village, its cargo rattling loosely in the back, he felt the hair in the back of his head prickle. There was something about the sound of an empty coffin in the back of his hearse that always had that effect on him, though he could never explain why that should be. As he approached the edge of the village, Tombs decided he would drop in to the Golden Gloves and have just one quick one before retiring for the night. He reminded himself he would have to make an early start in the morning if he was to make Ballyglen in good time to collect the Yank's remains off the eight-thirty train from Galway. For the moment however, he wished to put aside all thoughts of his duties the following morning. He would continue to raise his spirits which, after his sojourn with Charlie Joyce, had improved considerably. The cold damp night air had sobered him somewhat and now Tombs felt in need of good companionship, some lively conversation and a hearty nightcap by a cheery fire. In the Gloves, situated at the northern edge of the village, Tombs knew he would find all these in abundance.

He pulled the Packard in by the kerb outside the pub, switched off the engine and tugged fiercely at the hand-brake. The hearse moved backwards with the fall of ground. Tombs swore and tugged harder. This time the brakes held and the hearse stopped moving.

"There!" he exclaimed. "That'll hold you for an hour or so." Stepping out of the hearse cab into the rain, he made a dash for the pub entrance.

As he pushed open the heavy oak door, he could hear from within the familiar voice of The Piper Hanratty. Tombs smiled and nodded knowingly. The Piper was giving forth on his pet conversational subject: " – a pair of 'em could have a good 15,000 descendants within a year. Within a year! Think of it. That's breeding for you and that's your Rattus Rattus for you! A fantastic species! The inferior designed Homo Sapiens isn't even in the running. I tell you, it won't be the meek who will inherit the earth, it'll be the vastly superior rat! Man will disappear – and he will be replaced by the Super-rat, who will rule supreme. Do you know that when given problems to solve in controlled conditions, the rat had no problem, even with the most complex task – and in fact got bored when faced with simple tasks. There's one thing, though, it can't cope with and that's poison. Y'see, the rat can't vomit. Otherwise he would be unstoppable!"

The Piper's audience consisted of John L O'Shaughnessy, publican, Erasmus O'Regan, retired schoolmaster and librarian, seated by a blazing coal fire, and Jamie O'Connor, poet and musician. From the looks on their faces they did not seem to share The Piper's excitement or be astounded by these facts. Stoically, they suffered The Piper's rantings on this particular topic frequently.

Erasmus looked toward the door, adjusted his wire-rimmed spectacles and called out: "Ah, Jim, we were expecting you to drop in. We have the makings of a game now. The Piper here has convinced me that if re-incarnation is on the cards, ultimately, a rat would seem the only available choice. I can't say I look forward to that possibility. I had hoped to come back as a tortoise or a dolphin." Erasmus gave Tombs a toothy grin and continued to suck vigorously on his crooked-stem pipe.

"Good evening to ye, gentlemen." Tombs waved at the men seated by the fire and made his way to the bar. "And you're still on about those filthy vermin, Piper?" He flashed a wry smile at Hanratty.

"Vermin! Vermin! Man is the world's vermin – not Rattus Rattus. Mankind refuses to give him any credit. Jealous, more than likely!" the Piper retorted loudly.

The Piper Hanratty was well named. Because of Seamus Hanratty's passionate and all-consuming interest in rats of all types, shapes, colours and sizes, he had long ago earned the title of the "Pied Piper of Ballykeogh", eventually reduced to simply "The Piper". Since he was a boy, The Piper had studied, and eventually took to breeding, rats until they became so numerous in and around the village a plague was feared. Rats brazenly rambled the streets and lane-ways, houses and out-houses and the sound of high-pitched squeals emanating from under floorboard and above ceiling-board was commonplace throughout the locality. When Sergeant Mulrooney had eventually to drive a cheeky and particularly large black-eyed specimen from sharing his porridge bowl at breakfast one morning, he decided finally that enough was enough. He had come to a decision – action had to be taken: The Piper's rats would have to go.

Very soon however, the rat had been replaced in The Piper's life by the study and breeding of pigeons. Soon they too reached plague proportions till every clothes-line in the village bent and swayed with great numbers of The Piper's new-found loves. Eventually, as with his rats, he was forced to part with his feathered friends and now he was confined to the study and the breeding of goldfish and other tropical fish. This pleased the much-relieved villagers who realised that should the goldfish reach plague proportions as had the rats and the pigeons, this would at least occur in the confines of The Piper's own living-room.

Regardless of all this, Rattus Rattus still held a special place in The Piper's heart and he never lost an opportunity to cut loose with a string of lesser-known facts and other trivia concerning the breeding habits, superior brain-power and complex social behaviour of this extraordinary rodent.

"Good evening, Jim. The usual, I suppose."

"The usual, John L. We have to ward off the damp and the misery of this place at all costs." Tombs stepped up to the marble-top bar, rested his arms on the cool stone surface and surveyed the dimly-lit surroundings. Apart from The Piper and Erasmus, seated by the open fire, the bar was empty but for Jamie O'Connell who sat quietly by the window in his usual seat, his red-setter dog lying by his feet. All present were nightly regulars in the Golden Gloves. For Tombs, as for the others, the Gloves was their favoured bar in the village – a home from home, so to speak. The bar itself had an aged ambience, atmosphere and character. Which was more than could be said for Big Tom McGarrigan's plastic palace at the other end of the village. Tombs liked this pub and the men who drank here. It was usually quiet, almost deserted, most nights of the week and the few regulars who did frequent the place could indulge in a quiet card-game of '45' while discussing topics ranging from the rise and fall of the Roman Empire to local history, from literature to sport and from The Piper's favourite subject to John L's favourite topic: Irish or Irish-American prize-fighter boxers.

The Golden Gloves was the property of John L O'Shaughnessy and a veritable shrine to his boxing heroes. The walnut-wooded walls of the pub were adorned with fading and age-yellowed photo-portraits of bare-fisted prize-fighters from the "great days of boxing" as John L referred to the years between 1880 and 1920. The boxers were tall, whip-cord, determined-looking men – Peter Maher, 'Gentleman' Jim Corbett, Bob Fitzsimmons, Jack Dempsey, Kid McCoy and the man who took pride of place in the centre of the mirrored bar, the legendary John L Sullivan, King of the Bare-fisted Fighters. Indeed, it had been commented on more than once that the proprietor of the Golden Gloves, with his slicked-down hair and handlebar moustache, did in fact bear a strong resemblance to his legendary boxing hero.

John L O'Shaughnessy had come to Ballykeogh fifteen years before and had purchased and converted an old barn at the northern end of the village into what was now the Golden Gloves. A first-time visitor to the Gloves could be forgiven for believing he had stepped into a New York or Bostonian drinking emporium at the turn of the century, such was John L's attention to detail in recreating the type and style of establishment his boxing heroes would have frequented in those cities. John L had arrived in Ballykeogh with a great deal of money which he said he had earned as a prize-fighter in America. No one questioned this but later it became known that the money was a legacy of a late wealthy aunt of his in New York, where, in his youth, John L himself had worked building the Brooklyn subways. Nobody ever learned his true Christian name. Here in Ballykeogh, he was known to one and all as John L, Irish-American ex-prize-fighter, genial proprietor and host of the Golden Gloves pub.

"I suppose you'll be airing your old top hat for your job in the morning, Jim?" John L said, passing Tombs a black pint of porter and a shot of Irish whiskey.

"Aye! The Yank. Good luck, John L!" Tombs nodded and raised the frothy pint to his lips. "I've just been up to Charlie's place to pick up the coffin. He'll be as safe as the gold in Fort Knox in it. It's as grand a coffin as I've handled for a while, I can tell you. The worms will need bits and brace to get at the bugger."

"I never thought I would see the Yank Dwyer back in Ballykeogh." It was Erasmus O'Regan, sitting with The Piper, who spoke. "And doing it in some style, I might add!"

"Coming home in a box is the safest way the Yank could show his face around here again," The Piper added.

Tombs moved to join his two friends by the glowing fire,

pulled a chair close and sat down. "You sound as if you had a run in with him too, Erasmus."

"You know as well as I, Jim, that there wasn't a man, or woman, within ten miles of here in any direction who didn't have some sort of dealings with Daniel Dwyer. And all of them turned out to be as rotten as last year's duck eggs. Oh, that Danno was a nasty piece of work all right. Came from bad blood, so he did. One of Piper's rats would have made a more trustworthy companion than Daniel The Yank."

"He had a bad streak, sure enough. But didn't he do his bit in the War of Independence? Wasn't he a handy man with guns and explosives and stuff like that?" Tombs inquired.

"Oh, he was that. A great man with guns and bombs – anything that caused destruction and mayhem. Hated to see the Troubles end, so he did. Loved blowing things up and just as likely to use them on his own side too, if it served his purpose." Piper chuckled heartily.

"Aye, he was one hard, cold-blooded bastard." Erasmus tapped his pipe on the fire-grate and added, "But as the Bard once said, 'All men are bad and in their badness reign'."

"I remember," Tombs recalled, "my late father telling me that Danno, whatever else he might have been, was as tough as old nails. My father used to tell one story about him. One freezing cold day in January several years ago, the father had to call out to the farm to tell Dwyer about a relation of his who had died and was being taken to the church that same evening. Danno had only one good shirt, his Sunday shirt, and that was hanging on the washing-line, frozen stiff as a board from the hard frost. But that didn't bother Danno, not a bit of it. He took the shirt from the line and forced himself into it, frozen and all as it was, put on his overcoat over it and headed off to the funeral with my father. Half an hour later later, in the warmth of the church, there was so much steam rising off him, it looked like he was about to burst into flame. Someone was about to chuck a bucket of holy water on him to extinguish him."

This tale drew laughter from the company.

"He was a hardy man, sure enough," The Piper offered, picking up a deck of cards from the table in front of him. "And I can tell you another thing – he was a fair hand at the cards too."

"Humph!" Erasmus snorted. "The man would gamble his own mother on the turn of a card or the spin of a coin. He had no love for the game, only for the gambling risk – and winning, whatever the cost. But I'll say this for the bastard, he had nerve! I heard tell he took bets one time on a game of Russian roulette below in Ballyglen. He put the bullet in the chamber, in full view, put the gun to his head and pulled the trigger – not once – not twice – but three times! Upping the ante each time! As true as I'm sitting here! It was the others who held him from pulling the trigger the fourth time. Their nerves just couldn't take it! That was the Yank Dwyer for you."

"I heard that story too, only I heard that Danno himself admitted later that the bullet was a blank," John L said from behind the bar.

"Still, he had the luck of the devil." Piper shuffled the deck of cards. "But his luck seems to have run out on him finally."

"Nevertheless, he's going to get a big send-off in the morning. I hear his old comrades from the IRA are going to fire a volley over the grave," Tombs said.

"It would not surprise me," Erasmus cackled, striking a match to re-light his pipe. "It would not surprise me one little bit if they fired directly into the coffin, just to make bloody sure the bastard is dead!"

"And it won't be blanks either!" The Piper added.

"Did you hear how he died? I'm wondering was it a natural death?" Tombs enquired.

"Hummph! Natural! No Dwyer ever died a *natural* death!" Erasmus chomped hard on his pipe. "No Dwyer ever deserved a natural death!"

"Well, one man who doesn't seem too upset by the Yank's death is his own flesh and blood, Jack," Tombs said. "I hear tell he's below in McGarrigan's since he got the news yesterday morning. Not exactly mourning, mind – celebrating would be a better word."

Erasmus nodded and said to himself, "Ah, young Jack. From the same bad seed, the same weak flesh and the same bad blood. You know what they say: *'Briseann an dúchas trí shúile an chait'*."

"You're right there! And just like the Yank, he has a long-term love affair with the jar. Black Jack could get halfway through a bottle of whiskey without even breaking the seal!" John L arrived with another tray of drinks.

"I can see why he would celebrate, sure enough. He's in for the Yank's money, or what's left of it! Isn't Black Jack the only living relative? Isn't the Yank's wife dead?" Tombs enquired.

"The Yank's wife!" Erasmus nodded. "A misfortunate soul. Died years ago – of a broken heart and broken spirit. I knew her before she married Dwyer – a good gentle lady from good stock. Why she hitched up with Danno, nobody around here could ever fathom. But the poet Longfellow said it well: 'The men that women marry, and why they marry them, will always be a marvel and a mystery to the world.' Who can tell why good women are drawn to the bastards of this world?" Erasmus shook his head and frowned.

"Well, just like his uncle Danno, Jack's a fair hand at the

cards too." The Piper held up the deck and waved it. "I hear it said he took a fair few pounds from Mr McCraven last night in a big poker game below at McGarrigan's. You can't beat breeding, can you? It's the same with Rattus Rattus, you know – their breeding habits are – "

"Ah, where's the art, the gamesmanship, the finesse or the satisfaction in poker?" Erasmus loudly interrupted. "Now take the 'Old Game' here. There's a game of cards that requires skill. Teamwork, a good memory and concentration too! Where's the intellect in playing poker, I ask you. All bravado – immature trials of will and nerve – boys trying to prove they are men. Now come, come, gentlemen! Enough of this. Let's play a decent card game – a hand or two of 45. Jim, we were waiting for you to appear – to make up the foursome for the game." Calling across to the silent Jamie O'Connell, he said, "And what about yourself, Jamie, will you join us by the fire for a hand or two?"

Jamie O'Connell sat, tugging absentmindedly at his unkempt beard and looking out into the October night, his thoughts pinned on withered leaves that drifted in the wind blowing up from the sea. Oblivious of the conversation across the room, Jamie had a tune running in his head and it spun and danced in his brain till he thought he would explode with the joy of it. He had taken his fiddle out of the canvas bag he always carried with him and now the tune cried out to him to release its spirit through the instrument's age-grained form.

Erasmus's invitation to join the game snapped him back to his present surroundings.

"What? Oh! A game . . . Right you are, Erasmus. I'll be over now," Jamie said, listening to the rain making its own timeless music on the stone and street and window-pane. He reached down to stroke Caesar, his red setter, lying by his feet, and looked again at his old fiddle. Under the soft glow of the oil lamp on the wall beside his table, the instrument seemed to vibrate with an energy of its own. He reached down and touched the strings gently, the melody of his favourite tune still burning in his imagination. The tune was "The Gold Ring", a tune he never tired of playing or hearing. It held a fascination for him which he could not articulate. He remembered his late father, who taught him the tune when he was still a boy, telling him how the tune was given by the Fairies as a precious gift to a wandering piper who, one moonlit night, found a gold ring they had lost. The piper returned the ring to the Fairy people and so overjoyed were they that they promised to reward him with the greatest treasure they possessed: their most valued tune. The piper sat with them all night learning the tune and when he came away from their world the next morning he could play it as well as the Fairies' best piper. He named the tune "The Gold Ring" and every time he played it, ordinary people sat entranced as the tune weaved its spell. It surely was a tune filled with a strange magic, Jamie often told himself; only the fairies could have written it. How many times did it tease and dance inside his head and lure his spirit on flights of fancy that were not of this world? Now again the tune lapped and tugged at the shores of his mind but he sighed and shook his head. Erasmus's call had broken the spell. What of it, he would play later, after midnight, when the fairy folk would be listening.

As a fiddle-player, there was no better than Jamie O'Connell within twenty miles of the village. Whenever there was a wake, wedding or soirée, Jamie was called upon to play. Once. a kindly man from Radio Eireann had come down to Ballykeogh with a tape-recorder and went back to Dublin with recordings of his fiddle-playing which were later played on the radio. For several months after the broadcast, Jamie was a local hero – the toast of Ballykeogh.

These days, few people listened to his music. There were no young people in the village and the modern dances in Ballyglen were all the go. Nobody wanted to listen to a ragged fiddler and his sad strange old tunes. He had no love for this modern pop music, though when he was in Dublin he had listened to recordings of Charlie Parker and of Django Reinhardt and could hardly believe his ears. Though the music sounded alien to him, inside he felt the same as he did that distant day in his youth when Johnny Doran, the famous travelling piper, had come to play at a fair day in Ballykeogh. Now Jamie played for the sake of the music itself and to soothe his sometimes troubled spirit.

Slowly, he returned the fiddle to the canvas bag which accompanied him everywhere. Though he could never even begin to explain it to the others, Jamie would not give up the contents of that bag for all the riches of the world. For in it were his riches, certain articles that gave his life both meaning and purpose. The bag contained a fiddle, which was his father's and his father's before him, a tin whistle and three tattered, well-thumbed books: a collection of William Blake's works, a copy of Plato's *The Last Days of Socrates* and a collection of WB Yeats's poetry. Between them, he knew, they could give a man insights into all he ever need know about life and a man's living of it – indeed about Truth itself!

He was happy enough in that knowledge, though he often despaired as to why these simple revelations were lost on so many others. Why mankind continued to ignore the essential truths when they were there for all to find was, he knew, the greatest stumbling block to man's happiness. If

Socrates was to come back in this age, he often thought, he would not be prepared to believe that in the two thousand years which had passed since he walked on the earth, mankind had progressed in spiritual development not a jot. "What a sorry lot we are," Jamie would say to Caesar, who wagged his tail in reply.

Since the death of his parents, Jamie lived alone to the north of the village, with only his red setter, Caesar, and a cat, Plato, for company and got along by farming a couple of cows and a few sheep and goats. He also did a bit of herding for a TD who was Minister of Finance and owned most of the cattle-grazing land on Sliabh Cullen though he rarely came down to visit. Jamie despised politics and politicians but the job brought in a few extra pounds, which helped through the lean times. As a young man, he had lived and worked for a while in Dublin but the hard music of city living was not the music his heart yearned for. Soon, he returned to this cloud-shrouded hill where, he knew, he would live out the remainder of his days. When mulling over his life since his return to Ballykeogh, he often recalled Blake's words:

"Great things happen when men and mountains meet.
This is not done by jostling in the street."

Jamie knew there was great truth and insight in Blake's words. Now there was a thinker, and a poet – and what an artist! How often he wished he could spend an evening in his company – or better still with both Blake *and* Socrates! Wouldn't that be the lively discussion? Perhaps they were together up above, eternally discussing some great notion or other. Jamie wished he could believe in a hereafter. Deep inside he sensed that all the existence there was, or could be, was right here on this earth.

Tombs often teased him by telling him that he should

prepare his soul for Eternity and have some important words carved on his own headstone. If booked now, in good time, Tombs would inscribe the words – at a discount. "So, Jamie, what do you want me to carve on your headstone?" Tombs would ask.

"As little as possible and not for a long while yet, if it's all the same with you, Jim."

"I suggest, Jamie," Erasmus had once offered, "that you take no chances. I would suggest that Tombs write: 'Lord, if there is a Lord, save my soul, if I have a soul'. That's what I want on my gravestone – just to be on the safe side."

Jamie laughed heartily and agreed. He liked Erasmus who, like him, questioned everything and possessed a lively philosophical turn of mind.

"C'mon over, Jamie," The Piper called out. "The night is slipping away,"

Jamie rose from his window seat and moved to join the others by the fire. As he did he glanced through the rain-flaked window to catch sight of a figure on the roadway. It was Sergeant Mulrooney going by on his bicycle, hunched against the drizzle, on his way to his nightly vigil.

"There goes the Sergeant," Jamie looked at the clock. "And spot on time, as usual."

"By Jove, the man spends so much time on that old bike of his he must have an arse like a clown's mouth!" Erasmus said, striking another match.

The others laughed and settled themselves around the card-table.

"Old Tom Duignan must be getting fairly fed up with Mulrooney's constant snooping at this stage," The Piper said, as he shuffled a well-thumbed deck of cards.

"Not half as fed up as Mulrooney will be when he finds out that Tom isn't the villain he has him marked to be.

And when he does he's going to be as mad as a wet hen!" Erasmus said, his pipe clenched firmly between his teeth.

"Bloody old fool!" The Piper said, chuckling at the Sergeant's fruitless investigations, and dealt out four hands of cards. The Piper never had much time for Sergeant Mulrooney, not since he forced Piper to eliminate his beloved collection of specially imported "Rattus Norvegicus". As he fanned his own hand of cards, he couldn't help hoping the old fool got a dose of flu or even pneumonia from sitting up there on the wet hillside night after night.

As The Piper thought his black thoughts, the door to the bar pushed open and the hunched wet figure of RN Mulrooney shuffled in, a bulky carrier-bag under his arm.

"By God, the Mulrooneys are out in force tonight!" Erasmus said out of the side of his mouth as RN saluted the gathering, brushed raindrops from his coat and went directly to John L at the bar.

"Evenin' John L, I've got your order," RN said and passed the laden bag across the bar to a beaming John L.

"Ah! good! I was beginning to run low. I hope this is as good a batch as your last, is it?" He bent to empty the bag and place the contents under the bar, well out of sight.

"It's a sweet batch, John L," RN whispered. "As good as I've produced in a good while, I guarantee you!"

"Fine, RN, fine – sure I know I can depend on you." John L filled a pint and passed it to RN, along with a number of folded pound notes.

"Thanks, John L," RN said, quickly pocketing the wad of notes. "You'll have enough to wet the mourners' whistles tomorrow, at least."

"There will be call for the Drop, I've no doubt. It should be a lively day, by all accounts," John L replied and set about polishing his large collection of whiskey glasses which had come all the way from a saloon his grandfather owned in Boston. Clutching his drink, RN moved to the end of the bar to where Erasmus, The Piper, Tombs and Jamie sat playing cards.

"From the looks of things, this isn't the first drink he's had today," RN thought, as he observed a red-faced Tombs swaying in his chair and trying to focus on his hand of cards. His tipsy condition did not, however, seem to impede his sharp attention to his game. Tombs and his partner, Erasmus, seemed to be on the winning side, so far.

"Were you below in the Dáil?" Jamie enquired of RN, referring to McGarrigan's Bar and Lounge.

"I was – just for one. It's going strong down there. They're all there – the self-appointed business moguls of the parish – all engaged in heated discussion. Politics, land and money."

"Ah yes! Politics, property and profits! The Holy Trinity! The True Religion of the true Gombeenmen!" Erasmus puffed on an unlit pipe.

"The way that loudmouth Tom McGarrigan goes on, you'd think he was the Taoiseach – or Tánaiste!" The Piper sneered.

"He fancies himself, sure enough, but then the whole bunch down there think it's they that run the country." Erasmus still puffed and sucked at his pipe.

"Well, they could hardly do any worse than the bunch of wasters who run the show at the moment," Jamie offered. "I mean, will you look at the way things are – the price of the pint, for instance – almost two shillings!"

"True for you, Jamie. The ten shilling note will hardly last the evening these days," RN nodded in agreement.

"A wiser man than I once said that politics is the diversion of the trivial man, who, when he succeeds at it, becomes important in the eyes of more trivial men. And that's my opinion too." Erasmus tapped his pipe yet again on the fire-grate.

"Isn't a cousin of yours married to a TD, Erasmus?" The Piper asked.

"Ah yes, I have to admit that is true. But we are living down the shame of it. I'd prefer if it wasn't discussed."

"The politician is a rare bird all right," The Piper agreed, laying a trump on the table with a loud thump.

"Aye! The only bird in the world who can sit on the fence and still keep both ears on the ground." Erasmus peered intently at his hand of cards.

"With his beak and brain up his backside!" The Piper guffawed loudly.

"You know what it is – they should elect a boxing man as Taoiseach," John L said, moving down the bar to join in the conversation. "A man like Jack Doyle, for instance."

"You mean Jack Lynch, the Cork hurler?"

"A hurler? A wild-eyed stick-swinger from Cork or Kerry? For Taoiseach? Don't be ridiculous! No, I mean Jack *Doyle*, the great heavyweight fighter! There was a man who could pull a political punch or two!"

"Ah yes! Jack Doyle, a great man in the ring, so they said," The Piper chipped in.

"And a better man in the bedroom, by all accounts," declared Erasmus, gathering in a trick just won.

"What about this new fella, Cassius Clay?" Tombs asked.

"Clay? The new 'Brown Bomber'? Style – but little substance," John L retorted.

"Cassius Clay! The very man!" The Piper said. "The first black Taoiseach of Ireland!"

"And why not?" said an indignant John L, twirling the end of his highly-waxed handlebar moustache. "Hasn't he as much right to the job as that long Spaniard de Valera –

or as much right any other Irishman! Wasn't Clay's grandfather an O'Grady from east Clare?"

"You don't say!"

"It's a documented fact!"

"You'll be telling us next that the Yank Dwyer was his uncle!"

"It's possible! Anything is possible!" A hurt John L went back to his glass-polishing at the far end of the bar.

The card game and the animated conversation continued, with Tombs ordering a round of drinks for everybody and calling for a double whiskey for himself. The game progressed, punctuated by further recollections of the Yank Dwyer, each one more outrageous than the other, and loud knuckle-rapping on the table at the taking of a trick and Erasmus's testy remarks at Tombs's increasing lack of concentration.

The lights of a car reflected in the bar's polished mirror. RN squinted through the misted window. He recognised the motor to be Father O'Malley's black Morris Minor. He groaned and walked to the bar and quickly finished his drink. "It's getting on. I'll have to be off, men." he said, wiping his mouth on his coat sleeve. "I have a few odd jobs to do before bed." Then to John L he whispered, "It's Father O'Malley! I'll slip out the back way. You know what I mean."

He nodded in the direction of the priest's car outside, which was noisily manoeuvring itself into a parking position in front of Tombs's hearse.

"Right, RN," John L winked. "You know the way. Good night to you now. See you in the morning at the funeral."

RN had hardly disappeared out the rear of the pub, when Father O'Malley came through the front.

"Of all the bars in all the world, he has to come into mine," John L hissed at the card players, waited for a response to his quip and when none came, shrugged and continued polishing the marble bar-top.

"Good evening to ye, gentlemen," Father O'Malley called out. "A damp old evening again, but I believe we're in for a spell of fine weather."

"Good evening to yourself, Father," Erasmus replied, after a long hesitant silence. "Fine weather in Ballykeogh – mmnnn. The odd dry day wouldn't go astray around here, that's for sure. Perhaps we're not praying hard enough." Through the smoke curling from Erasmus's pipe, a knowing wink slyly signalled his companions.

"You'll have a drink, Father?" John L enquired politely, surprised at the priest's presence in his bar. Father O'Malley hardly ever visited the Gloves, his usual haunt being down at McGarrigan's Bar & Lounge among his wealthier parishioners.

"Well, as I'm here, I'll have just the one. Thank you, John L," Father O'Malley said, removing his hat. He stood by the bar for a long while, rubbing his hands and looking across at the card-playing foursome.

"Nothing like a quiet game of cards to while away a dark night," he called to the men, who did not respond and continued to play in silence. Father O'Malley cleared his throat and said at last, "Ye will have heard, I suppose, of the recent passing of Mr Daniel Dwyer in the Bronx? Lord rest his soul." His right hand fluttered in front of his face.

"We have heard something to that effect, Father. Your deal, Jamie," Erasmus spoke again, after yet another long silence. "And his earthly remains are coming home to rest among us, I hear."

"That is the case indeed, Erasmus. It's a great honour. Mr O'Flaherty here has everything under control. I saw the coffin in the hearse on the way in. Mr Dwyer will be sorely missed. I didn't know him of course. He had already departed for America when I came to Ballykeogh, but I hear tell he was a great man – a great man."

Knowing looks darted like a shower of arrows around the card-table.

"A great man, did you say? Yes indeed, a man of rare qualities, sure enough, Father," Erasmus said in mock-solemn tones; then added for the ears of his table companions only, "And if the wages of sin is death, then the old bastárd's got the pay-packet he rightly deserves."

"Long overdue it was too," muttered the Piper.

"Mr O'Connell," Father O'Malley loudly addressed Jamie. "I wonder if I could ask a big favour of you? Mr Dwyer's dying request was that a graveside lament be played over his coffin as he is being laid to rest. RN – er – Mr Mulrooney assures me that you are the only man for the job. I was wondering if you would offer your services in the morning. It would be a fitting send-off."

Jamie eyed the priest for a long while, tugged his beard and slowly answered, "Well, Father, I'm rarely at my playing best that early in the day but seeing as how Daniel Dwyer was such a lover of music and the arts in life – " at this Erasmus snorted loudly, "I suppose the least I can do is go along with his wishes."

Jamie was more than a little surprised at Father O'Malley's request, as relationships between the two men had been strained, to say the least, for many years now.

On one of the many occasions that the priest had visited him, attempting to entice him to attend Sunday Mass, Father O'Malley had criticised Jamie's devotion to music. "It is," the priest said, "an unnatural devotion which will lead only to the damnation of your mortal soul."

"I play the fiddle, Father. I make music – not black magic concoctions in some deep cave."

"It is an unhealthy and Godless pastime, Jamie!" Father O'Malley had said. "And never brought anything but misfortune to anyone who plays or listens to it. It excites unhealthy desires and passions in men – and women – and tempts them to harbour unnatural desires, embrace false notions and drives them away from the one true religion. You fly in the face of your God with your music because you have made a religion of it. It will destroy you, my son! 'Music is the brandy of the damned'!" he quoted, not remembering exactly who had said that first.

"Father," Jamie's eyes flashed and his voice trembled with a cold anger. "It's my belief religions are like men. They are born, they grow and change and in the end they grow old and die. Music, on the other hand, like the God who created it, is eternal."

That Father O'Malley should make the charge that his music was the "Devil's tool" was both horrendous and insulting to Jamie. But he knew of many a musician who in the past had been driven either out of the country or into the workhouse by music-hating clerics. He tried to explain as best he could to the priest that he gained insights into some of the eternal truths and a clearer vision of his God through the playing one tune than hearing all of Father O'Malley's stumbling sermons put together.

Jamie's reading was then discussed.

"And those books – those heathen books of yours. Will you not put them from you and embrace the only book you need ever read in your lifetime? I'm talking about the Good Book – the Book of Life – of *Truth*. Written here are the Words of God – not the pagan ravings of some rabble-rousing Middle eastern fakir Socatees, or whatever the devil he called himself."

"*Socrates!* Father, his name was Socrates, the great Greek philosopher," Jamie held his ground, and his temper. "If it wasn't for great men of free spirit and great thoughts, like Socrates and the like, you and I would still be living in caves. And if the information passed down to us is reliable, wasn't Jesus Christ a rabble-rousing, middle-eastern magician himself?"

"You blaspheme! Jamie O'Connell, you blaspheme!" Father O'Malley's face grew purple. With that the outraged priest had departed and had not returned or spoken to Jamie until now.

"What time do you want me and my fiddle at the graveside, Father?" Jamie politely inquired.

"Well now, let's see. The remains should arrive in Ballyglen on the train from Galway at eight-thirty. Give an hour or so for Mr O'Flaherty to get the coffin to the church here in Ballykeogh. Then the funeral Mass will be celebrated at ten . . . " Father O'Malley paused, emphasising his words and looked hard at the card-players. "The funeral Mass at ten and the burial will follow Mass. Mr Hanratty," he added, smiling a weak smile. "I wonder if you could be called upon to assist RN with the digging of Mr Dwyer's grave? I'm assured there will be two others there to help you."

"It depends, Father, it depends," The Piper gathered in a trick.

"Depends on what, Mr Hanratty?"

"On the state of the back, Father. The oul' back is playing up a lot these days. Crippled, I am. It's the wet and damp – plays havoc with the bones. So we'll see, we'll see."

"Time gentlemen, please," John L said softly and began to extinguish the oil lamps. "I'll have to ask you all to move into the back room."

Without a word, the players picked up their cards and

94

drinks and began to file into a small room at the back of the bar.

Father O'Malley remained at the darkened bar, unsure as to what to do next.

"C'mon, Father," Erasmus called, sensing the priest seemed in no great hurry to depart the company. "Come and join us for a nightcap."

"Very nice of you to ask, Mr O'Regan. I don't know . . . it's late . . . I have to prepare my sermon for the funeral Mass. But I suppose one or two wouldn't do any harm. Just for a moment or two, then." Father O'Malley followed the men into the dimly-lit back room.

As the clock in the now-darkened bar-room of the Golden Gloves chimed midnight, a hush rolled down from the surrounding hillside and engulfed the entire village. The street-lamps hissed and sprayed a weak, silver-speckled light on glistening street flagstones. A hungry wind explored and rummaged in dark corners; occasionally lashing out with sudden viciousness at creaky doors, empty dustbins, rusted shop-signs and withered window-panes.

The village remained frozen in time until, at 2.25 a.m. exactly, the roar of Father O'Malley's Morris Minor sliced the night air like a keen blade through silk. Inside the car, the bleary-eyed priest called on all his senses and faculties in a effort to regain just enough sobriety to manoeuvre the car away from the kerbside. With car indicators and headlights flashing and blinking, he could not but help feel at ease with himself and the world at large – all thoughts of the morrow banished from his fogged-up mind.

"They may be Godless rascals," he chuckled heartily. "But they're lively company to while away an evening with, that's for sure!"

He hiccoughed as the car lurched under the sudden

acceleration and jerked back in reverse gear. Father O'Malley slammed back into the driver's seat as the Morris Minor's back-bumper connected sharply with Tombs O'Flaherty's hearse, parked less than three feet behind. The car leaped forward a few feet, halted and again reversed, this time connecting with the hearse's front grille with even more force than before. With a grinding and meshing of gears, Father O'Malley steered the car away from the kerb and drove away down the street, engine racing and labouring in low gear.

Father O'Malley out of the way, the company in the back-room of the Golden Gloves settled down to some serious drinking and card-playing, spiced with lively discourse and the occasional outburst when a good trick was won or Erasmus found cause to berate his now very drunk playing-partner, Tombs. None took heed as Tombs's hearse, its hand-brake cable snapped on the second contact with Father O'Malley's car, inched backward on the steep incline. Slowly at first, then gathering momentum with the fall of ground, the driverless hearse began to roll steadily down the hill away from the Gloves.

From inside the Golden Gloves came a new sound. Now Jamie's fiddle filled the warm smoky room with ringing bitter-sweet sounds as his fingers frolicked and danced on the strings and gave new life to the tune that had haunted his imagination earlier in the evening. His companions, Erasmus, The Piper, Tombs and John L listened, talked, laughed, smoked and drank long deep draughts of a clear white liquid.

Chapter Five

The streets of Ballykeogh at 2.12 a.m. did not look too good to Black Jack Dwyer, who had just emerged, red-eyed and doughy-featured, through the side door of the alley running by McGarrigan's Bar & Lounge; where, for almost thirty-six hours, he had wallowed in a warm and stupefying euphoria. A sharp steady drizzle stung his cheeks, lips and tongue. Slumped against the bar wall, a cigarette end dangling from his lower slackened lip, he squinted about him through red-rimmed pig-eyes and tried to adjust to his surroundings. The noise of the bar and the events of the last two days still roared in his throbbing head as he tried to focus on his immediate surroundings. The buildings up and down the lane and the rain-washed streets had taken on a queer, misshapen look under the ghostly street lights. He blinked and gripped the wall as he watched the houses gently sway and undulate before melting on to the street which now flowed, stone pavement rippling and lapping, beneath his feet. He dipped his foot into the flowing stone. It stopped and remained solid.

"Now keep still, you hoor!" Jack spat at the ground, "While I think where the hell I left my bike."

"*Grrrrr...*"

Black Jack's blood froze in his veins.

"Oh God, not that! Dear Jesus, don't let it be that! Not again!" he moaned, fear clenching his throat and voice. Pressing himself fast to the wall he peered in the direction of the unearthly sound.

There, glaring and growling at him from the ivy-covered wall opposite, was the head of a fierce-looking dog, hate spitting from its blood-red eyes and saliva dripping from its bared fangs.

"No, no! Not again! Blessed Mary, take it away," Black Jack sobbed, his eyes held fast in the hypnotising glare of the animal head, stripped of its skin, protruding from the wall opposite him. He closed his eyes tight, then slowly opened one and quickly glanced at the wall. *"Grrrrrr . . . "* In that instant the dog's head suddenly changed shape and doubled in size. Now its teeth snapped and bit the night as it attempted to reach Jack, his body frozen to the wall and paralysed with a sickly, gut-wrenching terror. As the misshapen head grew and reached closer, he forced himself out of his torpor, quickly reached down to grab a brick at his feet and flung it with all his might at the nearing apparition. Again, he gripped his eyes shut and waited. Silence. He slowly opened one eye, then the other. The animal's head had disappeared and he stared for a long while into the dripping ivy on the wall across the lane-way.

"I don't know what hell you come from, you Devil's cur – but you won't get me!"

He shivered in the night-air and glanced about him. Where exactly was he? Outside McGarrigan's Bar. Good. Now where was his bicycle? And when he found it, which way was he to point it to get home? From inside his overcoat pocket he drew a lemonade bottle full of a clear white liquid, uncorked it, took a draught, then replaced the corked bottle in his coat pocket. He lurched forward, halted, steadied himself for a moment in order to find his sea-legs on the shifting flowing pavement, then slowly tottered towards the main street.

It had been a long two days for Black Jack Dwyer. Early the previous day he had been engaged in chopping firewood in his backyard when the telegram bearing the news of his uncle Daniel's death was delivered to him by Tom Tobin, the village postman. Jack could tell from the look on Tobin's face that the telegram contained some weighty news, but he was not prepared for this particular news. He ripped open the envelope and the words screamed at him from Clara's carefully hand-written telegram:

"To Jack Dwyer, C/O Ballykeogh PO Stop. Daniel Dwyer Died Bronx NY. 10th Oct. 1964 Stop For Further Details Contact Mr Proctor Solc. Of Proctor & Grieves Ballyglen ASAP. Stop"

"I'm terrible sorry for your troubles, Jack," a solemn-faced Tom Tobin offered his hand in sympathy.

"Sorry? Don't be sorry, Tom. I've waited years for this! At last!" he hissed at the telegram. "At last! The bastard's played his last hand – and lost! I thought I'd never live to see this day!" Jack gave a whoop of joy and pumped the amazed postman's hand. "Come on, Tom!" He headed for the house. "This calls for a drink, by God!"

Black Jack's mind raced. He had plans to make and as soon as Tobin had his drink and was on his way he had to prepare himself to mix business with pleasure below in Ballykeogh. This was indeed news that called for a serious celebration.

After Tobin's departure, Jack hurriedly boiled water to wash and shave. Then forcing himself into his thirty-year-old, ill-fitting blue-serge suit – that once belonged to his

Uncle Daniel – he headed off towards Ballykeogh on his bicycle, feeling as light-hearted as he had felt in many a day. Riding downhill towards the village, four miles away, Jack still struggled to assimilate the facts in his racing mind.

"The brave bloody Danno," he shouted over and over to his bicycle handlebars. "Dead at last! I thought the bastard was going to live for ever! Dead! It's too bloody good to be true!"

It had been almost thirty years since Jack had last laid eyes on his Uncle Dan, but he still recalled the occasion as if it had occurred only last week. Jack was fifteen and doing a man's work at home on the farm. One bleak winter's night, he had awakened in the early hours to the sound of angry voices below-stairs. It was Jack's father Miko, and Miko's brother, Daniel.

"You can't do this thing, Dan! God damn you! If you do, the boy and I are sunk. Finished! We're all finished. How could you do it? For God's sake, it's the home place!"

"I can – and I will ! I'm bloody well going to sell the place! You watch me. This place belongs to me now! Mine to do with as I please. Get that into your skull, Miko. I'm not rotting on this barren rock for the rest of my days. You can, but I won't! Sold it's going to be and that's bloody well that!"

Up to that night, Jack had lived with his father and his Uncle Dan on the family farm, which belonged to Miko, being the eldest of the two brothers. Jack barely recalled his own mother, who had run away with a Polish trapeze artist and juggler who came with a travelling circus to Ballyglen. Her reasons for going were never discussed with Jack, though many years later he heard a story that while Miko was away at the Galway races his Uncle Dan had taken certain liberties with his brother's wife. Whether

100

Dan's advances were welcomed by his mother or not, nobody was prepared to say. Though there was much gossip and speculation locally, the whole affair was never again mentioned in the Dwyer household.

The farm had the makings of a comfortable enough living "for a man with a will to work", as Jack's father often told him and through the lean, hungry years they scraped a living from "this barren rock", as his Uncle Dan had called it.

"Danno is not for the hard work," Miko had complained to his son. "Danno is a man for the high road and the high life."

Miko had long since marked the measure of his errant brother. After the Civil War, Danno, who had been "on the run" in every county in the Free State, returned home to join Miko and his new wife on the family farm. It was not a peaceful or welcoming homecoming. Dan never fully settled, soon slipping into a life of quick shady 'deals', bitter local feuds and later, bouts of heavy drinking and gambling. After Jack's mother's sudden disappearance, relations between the two brothers remained cool and strained.

Things came to a head in the Dwyer household when, in the early hours of a December morning in 1935, Jack awoke to hear his father and Dan arguing loudly. Both men had returned from a horse-fair in Ballyglen and had sat by the turf-fire late into the night drinking and talking. In the wee small hours, a card game was suggested and the two men sat down to play poker. In a moment of drunken crazed bravado the stakes were laid and the stakes were high. Miko, losing badly, staked his entire farm on one final hand. When dawn broke over the bleak hillside and the Dwyer household, Dan, who had held most of the winning poker hands, also held the deeds to his brother's lands.

Three days later, Dan had sold the place to the O'Callaghan brothers, whose lands adjoined the Dwyer land to the north. A few days after that, Dan and the money disappeared, leaving Jack and his distraught father to fend for themselves with nothing but the dilapidated cottage and a few outhouses. Later, they heard reports of Dan's wild spending, womanising and gambling in Ballyglen before departing for Dublin City. There, it was reported, he got mixed up in an IRA gun-running operation, but due to a certain "deal" being struck with the authorities for information received, Dan was allowed to make good his flight to the USA.

From that day to this, nobody around Ballykeogh had ever laid eyes on Daniel Dwyer. He had, it was known, married a local girl he met in the Bronx but had abandoned her before the year was out. Some years later, he was reported to have been seen in Ballyglen with a new "wife" described in Ballykeogh as being "as black as a moonless night in March". A week after this reported sighting, Dan had once again disappeared without trace, leaving a trail of unpaid bills in his wake. The largest of these was owed to the Imperial Hotel where Daniel "The Yank" Dwyer and his black wife, Fifi, had lived royally for ten days before melting into the night. It was presumed he had departed once again to the Bronx, where he established his many and diverse "business" interests. Nothing more was heard of him – until now.

"And now the bastard's dead!" roared Jack to the rain-smeared sky, as he and his bicycle raced the last mile downhill to Ballykeogh.

Being the only living relative of the late Daniel S Dwyer, Jack reckoned he surely stood to inherit the proceeds from his late uncle's estates. Assuming of course that there

102

wasn't a gaggle of Danno's offspring in the Bronx waiting to pounce on the pickings. He swept away that thought and concentrated on the facts. Danno was not a family man and the telegram seemed to indicate that there was a will. Once legal matters were sorted out with this Mr Proctor, it would only be a matter of time, he figured, before he finally had his hands on Danno's cash. Then, Jack also reasoned, he could set about buying back the land that rightfully and morally belonged to him. He would repay the debt owed by Dan to his brother, who had died, a broken man, less than a year after the disastrous poker game with his wily younger brother.

Arriving in Ballykeogh, Jack went directly to the post office where he found Miss Clara to be in a surprisingly accommodating mood and so was able to quickly place a telephone call to Mr Proctor of Proctor & Grieves, Solicitors, in Ballyglen. From Mr Proctor he learned the details of his uncle's death in New York and of his last wish to be transported home to be laid to rest with his flesh and blood in Ballykeogh graveyard. He also learned that indeed his uncle had drafted a Last Will and Testament, which would be read following his interment. Mr Dwyer's remains were, at this very moment, Mr Proctor declared, being flown from New York to Shannon Airport where they would be taken to Limerick and put on the Galway train. From there they would taken to Galway and then on to Ballyglen where they were due to arrive at eight thirty on the morning of 16 October – the following day. Mr Proctor offered Jack his sincere condolences.

Jack left the post office in a state of elation and excitement. He was going to find it difficult to present himself to the village as a man who had just heard the sudden and disturbing news concerning the demise of a close relative. Trying hard to look as solemn and griefstriken as he could, he headed towards his usual haunt, McGarrigan's Bar & Lounge. Here he planned to drown his "grief" in the sympathetic and comforting company of those who, Jack knew, would surely gather there once the news of Danno's death got round the village. In McGarrigan's Bar the first to approach, a false smile pasted atop a massive double chin, was the proprietor, Big Tom McGarrigan, who grabbed Jack's hand and pumped it vigorously.

"We've heard the news, Jack. My sympathies. Poor Dan. Terrible! Terrible!"

A small group pressed around him, each one offering a hand in sympathy.

"Sorry for your troubles, Jack."

"He was a great man, Jack. He'll be a great loss."

"A rare man was Danno. A rare man!"

"You wouldn't find better the length and breadth of the land!"

"You're right there."

After much hand-shaking and back-slapping, rounds of drinks were ordered up by Jack who listened in silence as his dead Uncle Daniel moved closer to deification with the filling of every black pint and the emptying of every short glass.

The events of the last few days continued to rumble and jangle in his mind as Black Jack staggered up the incline towards the post office at the top of the village. He halted and, fumbling within his suit inside pocket, he drew out a large white envelope. He stared at the envelope for a long while before replacing it, muttering and nodding with satisfaction. While most of yesterday's events were lost in a mind-numbing alcoholic haze, Jack recalled with surprising clarity his meeting with Cornelius McCraven the previous night in McGarrigan's back room. He also recalled their subsequent game of stud poker from which Black Jack now held the winning pot of two hundred pounds in a white envelope inside his breast pocket. Poker was Jack's game and indeed it was poker which had earned him the nickname of "Black Jack" and helped him survive since his father had lost the family farm to Dan. He was, like his uncle, a born gambler but differed from Daniel in one respect. Jack was a dangerous loser. Jack's good fortune with cards was matched only by his bad fortune with affairs of the heart.

Mr Cornelius McCraven, Assistant Bank Manager in Ballyglen, checked in to McGarrigan's Bar & Lounge and sometimes guest-house without fail each Wednesday at ten p.m. Though his duties as bank manager and cashier to the Ballykeogh sub-branch did not commence officially until ten a.m. the following morning, McCraven liked to travel up to Ballykeogh the evening before and check into McGarrigan's Bar. There he could enjoy a few drinks, socialise with his best customers, make valuable new business contacts and when possible, discreetly meet and relax in the company of one of his many close women friends in the village. Had the dapper, immaculately-dressed and well-spoken Mr McCraven ever imagined what lay in store for him later that particular Wednesday evening he would, Black Jack speculated, have chosen to remain in Ballyglen with his wife and six children. Had Big Tom McGarrigan not informed him of the "quiet game" in progress in the back room, he might have finished his few pints quietly before retiring, to arise fresh and alert to begin his day's tour of duty in the Ballykeogh branch. However, fickle Lady Fortune, who led him into McGarrigan's smoke-filled back room where a number of stern-faced men sat around a table, was to desert him to stand for the rest of the night close to Black Jack Dwyer's shoulder. Six hours and many poker hands later, a haggard and pale-featured Cornelius McCraven faced Black Jack across the card and glass-strewn table in a room reeking with pipe and cigarette smoke, stale beer, sweat, fear and damp wallpaper.

Mr McCraven tried to stop his hands from trembling, but could not. He nervously filled out a large measure of poteen from a whiskey bottle and gulped it down.

"Well, *Mister* McCraven?" Black Jack stressed his words.

"Well what, Mr Dwyer?"

"You should be more careful who you play poker with. You owe me a total of two hundred pounds, by my calculations. How do you intend to pay me?"

"Look, Mr Dwyer. I only have only twenty pounds cash on me. I wasn't prepared for this! Take the twenty, and I give you my word you will get the rest bye and bye."

"Not good enough, Mr McCraven. Not good enough at all!"

McCraven's eyes darted about the room as he tried to figure an angle on his predicament. Running a sweaty finger around his collar, he said, "Look, I'll be back in Ballykeogh again next week – I could get you some money then."

"Look, McCraven!" Black Jack's eyes narrowed and sparked with deadly threat as he leaned across the table to within a few inches of McCraven's twitching face. "This wasn't a game of friendly whist with your granny! You played poker here. You lost. You owe me two hundred pounds! That's a sum I don't intend to wait a week to collect. Find a way to pay up – now. Or perhaps . . . " he leaned back, a sneer playing about his thin lips. "Perhaps a word or two in Sergeant Mulrooney's ear about the goings-ons between yourself and that little mouse of a wife of his wouldn't be out of order."

McCraven paled visibly at this and glanced at the other smirking players at the table who were obviously enjoying McCraven's plight.

"Let's act like gentlemen, Mr Dwyer. There's no need to be too hasty. Look, I'll tell you what. Come up to the bank tomorrow at close of business, say three p.m. or so, and you will be paid – in full, I promise you."

"For your sake, Mister McCraven, I hope so. I bloody well hope so. Tomorrow at three in your bank – I'll be there."

At exactly 3.10 the following day, Black Jack Dwyer stepped out of the bank, patting his right-hand breast pocket and smiling broadly.

Things couldn't be going better. His Uncle Daniel dead, two hundred pounds in cash in his inside pocket and the promise of a great deal more to come – once Mr Proctor and his partner in Ballyglen sifted through all the legal mumbo-jumbo of Danno's Will.

"Right! This calls for another drink!" Jack squared his shoulders and turning in the direction of Big Tom McGarrigan's Bar & Lounge almost stumbled into Sergeant Mulrooney's wife. She walked quickly and without speaking to the bank side-door which opened to admit her inside.

Eleven hours and three times that many drinks later, Black Jack zig-zagged his drunken way towards his bicycle, which he now remembered having left outside the post office the previous day. Through the clinging mist he saw that a light still shone through one of the post office windows. Probably Miss Clara's bedroom, he thought. This thought was replaced by another, as black as his name and as evil as his soul. Then, out of the corner of his eye, he imagined he saw a faint light glimmering across the road in the graveyard adjoining the church. Holding his breath, Jack peered towards the graveyard, all thoughts of Miss Clara banished from his mind. There! Yes, it was a light all right! Moving in and out between the gravestones on the southern side of the church.

"Saints in heaven preserve us this night!" Jack intoned (as his mother had taught him to do on occasions such as this) and crossed himself twice. His mind flooded with the old people's tales of strange unearthly lights roving around cemeteries in the dead of night before and after burials. "Oh, God, maybe it's the soul of Uncle Dan?" Jack felt an icy chill again clench his entire body. Leaning against his bicycle for support, he drew the lemonade bottle from his inside pocket and raised it to his lips. New courage burning its way to his belly and bloodstream, Jack roared in the direction of the light, "Don't you worry, Danno, you black bastard! I'll see to it you get put down good and deep in the morning and no amount of skulking around the gravestones will stop that!"

With his words echoing across, the light disappeared.

Gathering himself for the effort of manoeuvring himself onto his bicycle, Jack switched control to some deeper instinct that came into play to handle difficult situations such as this. The bicycle moved to position itself at an angle of forty-five degrees underneath his shapeless rear end. For what seemed like an age the bicycle performed a difficult and incredible balancing act before finally propelling itself and its rider forward on the correct course for home with nobody but Mrs Flanagan's night-prowling tomcat to witness this supreme defiance of the natural laws of gravity. From outside the post office until the sharp left-hand bend fifty or so yards below the Golden Gloves it was practically all down hill. After the bend to the left the road swung sharply right, before climbing away up Sliabh Cullen in the direction of Black Jack's cottage, four miles away. Four miles of tough uphill pushing and pedalling – though this never much bothered Jack, as he had never undertaken the trip while sober. Not in the last thirty-five years. Not since that summer night in 1929 in fact, when, as a boy turning man, his father had taken him for his first serious drinking session in Ballykeogh.

Tonight, Black Jack Dwyer was as inebriated as he had ever been in all those thirty-five drunken years of cycling home in the wee small hours when most decent folk were safe in their beds. His bicycle seemed to have things fairly well under control as it gathered speed past the Gloves at the edge of the village. As the bicycle careered past the Gloves, its rider failed to take notice of Tombs's hearse, parked outside, containing the coffin chosen to hold the earthly remains of Jack's uncle Daniel. The rider paid no heed to Father O'Malley's Morris Minor or to the light in the back room of the Gloves or heard the music coming from within. Neither did rider or bicycle paid heed to the sharp left-hand bend below the pub as Jack's mind flicked on and off between last night's poker game and deep sleep. Without warning, Jack and his bicycle parted company, leaving both sprawled, though undamaged, on the soft wet grassy verge by the roadside.

For a long while Jack lay perfectly still, enjoying the surging waves of warm sleep which swept over him. His inebriated brain informed the waking part of his mind that he had just fallen out of his bed. He sighed, closed his eyes, and remained in this position until at last the cold wind and drizzle brought his true situation home to him with some force. Coming fully awake he sat up and, now panicked, pulled the lemonade bottle from his coat pocket. "Thank God nothing's broken!" He patted the bottle gently before replacing it in his pocket. "Now where's that bloody bike of mine?"

He sat up and peered about him, re-adjusting his eyes to the murky dark. As he struggled to his feet to search for his bicycle, which had hurtled on ahead into a hedge some yards away, he heard a low hissing rumbling sound coming from the direction of the Gloves. Staring up the road towards the pub he saw a bulky black shape slowly emerging out of the misty dark and heading directly for where he stood positioned on the bend. He tried to put a name on this shapeless outline as it fast approached him but could not. Then, as it was almost upon him, he recognised it. It was Tombs O'Flaherty's hearse! What in God's name was Tombs up to, reversing his hearse, its engine off, down the hill? In the same instant he saw, inside the hearse, the outline of the coffin through the glass.

"Christ, maybe Danno himself is in the coffin? Maybe he . . . " Jack's voice trailed off as he watched, in frozen awe, events roll up in front of his saucer-eyes as in a slow-motion silent film.

On and on the hearse came, on and on until, with a crunching thud, the vehicle came to a sudden halt within feet of him, its rear wheel having mounted an outcrop of sharp rock on the roadside. With a metallic clang the back door of the hearse snapped open on impact. The coffin, shaken free from its moorings, continued its forward momentum in the direction of a dumbstricken Jack.

His last thought before the airborne coffin connected with the side of his head was that Danno had surely cursed him from beyond the grave and had returned to destroy the last living Irish member of the Dwyer family. His mind urgently signalled that he should take immediate avoiding action. His limbs, however, refused to respond to the signals. Try as he did to dodge the on-coming coffin, he was firmly rooted to the ground on which he stood.

In the briefest of moments before oblivion, Jack watched with horror the flying coffin take on the leering features of his uncle Daniel then change into the monstrous dog-head of the fiend, its jaws opened as wide as the night itself, which he had earlier encountered.

"God damn you! I'll meet you in hell! You bastard, face to face! We have a few old scores to settle!"

Kerrack! The leading edge of the coffin made contact with living bone. Jack pitched forward and slid over the road's edge and continued on down the steep mossy bank until he and the coffin came to rest at last in the marshy bog eight feet below the point of impact. The exploding shooting stars in his head began to slowly give way to a heavy, silent – though extremely comforting – blackness as he slipped into deep unconsciousness.

This day, for Black Jack Dwyer, had come to a sharp sudden end.

Chapter Six

"Clear off, you cretinous canine!" Sergeant Mulrooney spat at the scraggy sheepdog who had just urinated on his muddy boot.

"Yecch! Filthy mutt!" he snarled and lashed out at the animal with his soiled boot. The dog yelped and slouched away into the dark. The high-pitched bark brought the Sergeant out of the trance-like state into which he had lapsed since taking up his position overlooking Tom Duignan's farmhouse. From underneath his cape he drew a flashlight, switched it on and illuminated his watch-face. "Two o'clock! Two o'clock in the morning! I've been out here freezing my behind off since ten and that crafty Duignan hasn't made one wrong move."

He stretched each long leg in turn and began to massage his rear end in an effort to banish the numbness of over three hours sitting still in a cramped position on a cold wet stone. Having cycled up the hill from the village, RV had arrived at ten o'clock and positioned himself – as he had each night for over a week now – in a tiny clump of hazel-bushes which grew on the craggy slope overlooking Duignan's solid two-storey farmhouse. It was, he had reasoned, the best possible observation post, given the circumstances. From this advantageous lookout position

RV could monitor all the nocturnal comings and goings to and from the house, without himself being observed.

As he scrutinised the silent house, he uncorked his flask and poured the contents into the cap-cup and drank slowly from it. "Pea soup! That woman and her pea soup! She knows how much I detest pea soup!" He grimaced. "Hardly a suitable beverage to sustain a soul who has to sit for hours on end in these Arctic conditions." Making a mental note to mention this to Hannah, he spilled the remainder of the greenish liquid on the ground and scowled as Tom Duignan's mongrel returned to sniff the thick mixture before trotting off in the direction of the farmhouse.

"Ah well!" RV yawned, stretched and sighed. "Might as well call it a night. It's a war of nerves, that's what this is. Only I'm not going to be the one to break. The crafty old codger will have to make his move sooner or later and when he does – and he will eventually – I'll be here to nab him – red-handed!"

RV was still utterly convinced beyond all doubt that Tom Duignan was manager of the illicit poteen still. All the evidence now pointed at Duignan as the prime suspect. The facts, after all, were undeniable. Had Duignan not increased his crop of barley and potatoes – essential ingredients for the making of poteen – this last season when every other farmer in the locality was cutting back in production? Had he also not improved his farmhouse dwelling and outhouses? And the road leading to the farm? There was money coming from some source, RV was sure of that, and poteen *must* be the answer. "There was always something – well – highly suspicious about the man. Shifty eyes and guilty look about him. Hell's fire!" the Sergeant reasoned. "He is the culprit!" Detailed and prolonged investigations had, more or less, removed all the other local farmers from his initial list of possible suspects. Years of methodical sleuthing had cleared all of them – with the exception of the man now under surveillance for some time. Sergeant Mulrooney was convinced Tom Duignan was his man.

As he crept silently to where his bicycle lay concealed in a ditch by the roadside, he felt a great sense of frustration creep over him. He desperately longed that both his diligent detection work and his nightly vigils would bear fruit. He had felt hopeful of a catch tonight and now, yet again, he had to face back to the station-house empty-handed, frustrated, utterly exhausted, cold and wet.

"Perhaps Duignan's been tipped off he's being watched?" RV considered that possibility. He shook his head, "No, impossible! Guard Behan is the only other person who knows of this entire operation."

Duignan was a clever operator surely, but, RV knew, like most criminal types, he would show his hand eventually. And when he did, Sergeant Mulrooney would be there to bring him to book. All those long and lonesome night-watches would not be in vain.

A few times earlier tonight, during his damp vigil, RV had thought he was on to something, but each proved to be a false alarm. Mrs Duignan had twice come out the back door – once to throw out tea-leaves and later to empty a chamber-pot of its contents over a low privet hedge close to the house. RV noted how she had paused for a moment to stare intently into the darkness in the Sergeant's direction, before returning to the house.

"Peeping Tom, indeed!" RV muttered in disgust.

At 11.28, one of Tom's moon-faced daughters returned from a visit to a neighbour's house further on up the hill. RV could hear loud voices from inside the house as she went in the back door. At 11.50 precisely, the prime suspect himself came through the door, a lighted flashlight in his hand.

"This is it! At last!" RV's heart pulse-rate rose sharply. "He's on his way to the still!"

Shadowing Duignan at a safe distance, RV followed him to a field some distance from the house. There the suspect set about examining a cud-chewing cow, obviously close to calving. At 12.10, the suspect returned to the house and went inside. RV watched the lights in the house being extinguished one by one, until once again he sat alone with his hopes as flat and as damp as the stone on which he sat.

"Ah well! Better hunting tomorrow!" He cheered himself with the thought of the comparative warmth and comfort of the station cell where he would try and snatch a few hours of well-deserved sleep before Guard Behan came on duty at eight o'clock. He remembered too that he would be officially required to attend the Yank Dwyer's funeral in the morning. As he sped away from the Duignan place, a night-bird called high above him and he began to hum a few bars of Beethoven's "Pastoral" Symphony. He was always reminded of the magnificent "Pastoral" whenever his duties took him out into the countryside.

Perhaps it was the sweet scent of damp earth mixed with the perfume of mountain-heather in full bloom, lush hazel trees and the moaning of the wind in the blackthorn bushes that overwhelmed his senses and conjured up the piece in his mind tonight as he gathered speed, heading downhill toward Ballykeogh.

"I wonder what great works the Master could have produced, had he lived here on the side of Sliabh Cullen?" RV mused. "Or would he too have turned out to be a good-for-nothing poteen-making sleeveen like some around here?"

He was humming his way into the Pastoral's "Storm" passage when his bicycle-light caught the outline of a vehicle, parked, he thought, at an unusual angle. As he rounded the bend before the road swung sharp right up to the village, his cycle-light revealed the scene in more detail. He braked and, dismounting from his bicycle, slowly moved closer to examine the vehicle.

"Good grief! It's Mr O'Flaherty's hearse! He's crashed!" RV cast aside his bike and taking the flashlight off the cycle, walked quickly to the driver's side of the hearse. The badly-dented open door revealed an unoccupied driver's seat. He flashed his light inside. Empty! He then directed the light-beam on the glass-strewn ground around the hearse, then underneath the vehicle and up and down the road. Nothing! There was no sign of Mr O'Flaherty in any direction. RV's mind raced, sifting through the facts. Tombs's Packard hearse had been parked earlier outside the Golden Gloves. Fact! He had observed it – as he observed all things – while on his way to take up his night-watch. The hearse, he had noted, contained a coffin. Fact! He had seen the coffin-handles glint in the reflection of the street-lights and his flashlight's strong beam. Now, here was the hearse, badly crashed, no coffin and, worse still, no driver.

"By heavens!" RV exclaimed aloud. "Now there's a puzzler for you!"

He moved to the back of the hearse and stared for a long while at the open back door, before moving to the grass bank at the side of the road.

There, lying at the foot of the incline that sloped away from where he stood, caught in the beam of his flashlight, was an empty coffin, its lid thrown off. RV immediately launched himself into action, clambering down the slippery incline to where the coffin lay on its side like a huge open mouth gaping at the night-sky. Just as he slid to within a few feet from where the coffin lay, his right hand came to rest on something soft among the dead leaves and bracken. His probing fingers traced the outline of a nose, mouth and stubbly chin. "Jesus!" he recoiled as if he had been hit by a powerful electric charge and leapt to his feet. "My God! It's – it's a body!"

RV's flashlight beam came to rest on the still prone figure of a fully clothed man, very obviously not that of Tombs O'Flaherty, lying face-up and open-mouthed less than six feet from the open coffin. RV stood transfixed in both shock and amazement. Slack-jawed, he gazed first at the body then at the coffin nearby.

"It can't be!" his mind raced. "But it must be! It can be no other! It's the corpse home from the Bronx – Daniel Dwyer – the Yank himself!"

He must have misunderstood Guard Behan regarding the funeral arrangement details. Mr O'Flaherty must have already collected the Yank Dwyer's body from the 8.30 p.m. train in Ballyglen earlier that evening – though RV could have sworn Guard Behan had stated the planned pick-up time to be 8.30 the following morning. Regardless of how he had interpreted the information, his own eyes now confirmed the actual situation. Here was Tombs's hearse, here was the coffin and here, returned again to his native soil, was the body of Daniel "The Yank" Dwyer.

Steadying his tumultuous mind and trembling hands, he moved close to examine the condition of the still figure, his flashlight playing on the ashen features. He was left in no doubt. Sure enough, it was the Yank Dwyer. RV could see the obvious family resemblance to his nephew Jack.

"Better-looking though – and well preserved too, for his age," RV thought. "Big city living in foreign parts does wonders for a man's looks – even dead men's looks."

Dropping to his knees and brushing away leaves and

rushes scattered over the body, he considered its twisted position on the ground.

"I hope there are no bones broken as a result of – " he cut off in mid-sentence on remembering the prone figure was already dead before this accident occurred. "What am I saying!" he added nervously. "This misfortunate man is beyond the pains and ills of this world now! Lord rest his soul!"

He continued to stare at the corpse until it crossed his mind that Tombs O'Flaherty was still missing. He could very well be in a similar condition close by. Rising to his feet he flashed his light about him and called out, "Mr O'Flaherty! Mr O'Flaherty! Tombs! Can you hear me? Are you out there? Answer if you hear me! Mr O'Flaherty!"

RV listened to his voice echo in the distance. He strained to hear some response but all was silent. His flashlight beam settled on a gnarled group of dead tree-trunks towards the centre of the wetland where he stood. He froze, his slitted eyes following the sweep of his lightbeam as it settled on the tangle of ancient growth, now looking like some primeval octopus trapped for eternity in the clinging marsh-mud. For an instant, it seemed as if something had moved within the twisted web of dead wood. He shook his head. Nothing. Just a trick of the light. From across the marsh, an eerie owl-hoot resounded to the beating of his own heart in rhythm with the falling rain.

RV's mind raced. "He's probably wandering about out there somewhere in a dazed condition or maybe he's . . . " He looked again at the body at his feet. He dismissed the thought. He had to think, and act, quickly. He also realised that he had to find help and find it soon.

"I'll deal with finding Tombs later. Firstly, I have to solve this little problem." He brushed some weeds and leaves from the body.

One dead body was enough to cope with for the time being. "What a welcome home for poor Daniel Dwyer!" he thought. "To come this far in one piece – all the way from the Bronx – and to end up tipped out in this godforsaken bog like a sack of spuds – and he not a half-mile from his resting place." His flashlight arced from coffin to corpse.

Turning his back on this macabre scene, he clambered with some difficulty up the steep incline to the road. Panting with the effort of the climb, he paused to consider the best course of action. Who was he to turn to for assistance at this time of night? It was now 2.30 in the morning and every decent, law-abiding person for miles was fast asleep in their beds. Nevertheless, help had to be recruited. He could not just walk away and leave the Yank's corpse lying in the marsh until morning. He knew there was only one course of action open to him. He had to ensure that the body be re-coffined as soon as possible and removed from this place to the church in the village, where it would rest until morning. Regardless of this tragic mishap, Daniel Dwyer would still get as dignified a funeral as was possible under the circumstances. But who to turn to for assistance with this tricky and sensitive task? Guard Behan was his only hope. He would cycle to the other end of the village where Guard Behan roomed with Mrs Callaghan, rouse him, return here and sort out this whole affair.

He was about to set off in the direction of the village, when the sound of a motor-engine caught his ear. He could hear it approaching from the north side of the hill. Soon the vehicle lights were cutting cone-shape amber slices in the mist. As it rounded the bend, RV stepped into the middle of the road and raised his right hand.

A black Austin van, containing two occupants, came sharply to a halt. Inside the driver gripped the steering wheel, blinked frantically and turning to his passenger, stammered, "Chr-Chr-Christ! It's a b-b-bloody Guard. What'll I do?"

"Do nothing and say nothing, that's what you'll do!"

"B-b-but it's the law! "

"Just shut up and drive on."

The gear box crunched loudly as the driver fumbled with the gear-shift. The van jumped forward, its engine revving fiercely, only to come to a halt, motor stalled, inches from the Sergeant's feet.

RV walked to the driver's side of the van and shone his flashlight first on the face of the startled driver, who peered back at him and then on the passenger, who stared straight ahead.

"Good morning to ye, men." RV addressed the pair. "Having a spot of trouble with your gear-box – or maybe your brakes?"

"G-g-good morning, Guard," the driver answered nervously, rolling down the van window. He blinked in the flashlight beam before turning to his passenger who now leaned across the driver to bring his face into the beam of light.

"And a good morning to you too, Inspector. What is it we can do for you? We're all up to date with tax – and insurance."

The passenger's voice sounded distinctly northern, RV thought. "Yes, I can see that. The fact is you could not have turned up at a better time. There's been an accident here." He waved his light in the direction of the crashed hearse. "I could do with some assistance here. If you could help out, I would be grateful – it would save me a lot of time and trouble. If it's not putting you to too much trouble that is?"

The driver continued to blink and looked again at the

man with the northern accent, who seemed to be the spokesman for the two.

"An accident! Is that all? To be sure, we'll try and give you whatever help you need, Inspector. Nobody injured, I hope?"

"That's grand – this is a bit of an emergency," RV replied. "No, nobody injured – just dead. Follow me and I'll show ye what's to be done."

The driver hesitated and gave his companion a frantic look. "Wh-wh-what'll we do?"

"We do as he says, of course!" the man with the northern accent hissed. "Grab a torch from the tool-box and follow him. Let's go!" Then loudly calling out to RV, "Righto, Inspector. We're right behind you."

RV had already descended the slope by the time the two men had reached the road-edge. Now they stood overlooking the grisly scene below.

"H-H-Holy Mother! What in God's name is that?" the driver stammered, as his eyes took in the sight of the lid-less coffin and body lying nearby.

"Don't worry, men," RV called up to the amazed pair. "It's not as bad as it looks. The poor devil never felt a bit of the drop, so he won't feel being hauled back up. C'mon down here. I'm going to need you both to help me get the body back in the coffin where it belongs and then get the coffin back up on the road. Then we can decide what to do next. Let's get cracking!"

While the two men slid reluctantly down the incline, RV tried to explain, as best he could, how Mr Daniel Dwyer, one-time native of this parish, had come to be in this predicament.

"These," he said in solemn tones, "are the mortal remains of Mr Daniel Dwyer, originally from this parish but lately of the Bronx, New York, returning to Ballykeogh to rest among his forebears. This, sadly, is what you might call an unscheduled stop on that long journey. I'm afraid to say it's up to us to see that he gets to his destination with some dignity and honour."

RV admitted to the two men that he was still somewhat confused with regard to certain aspects of this situation. How long had the coffin and Mr Dwyer's corpse been lying there before he came on it? Minutes? Hours? He could only speculate. How was it the hearse was faced uphill? And what of the driver, Mr O'Flaherty?

"The poor devil may be wandering in a confused and concussed condition further into the marsh. He's nowhere about, at any rate, I've checked." RV informed the men. "However, as soon as we've seen to Mr Dwyer here, we can attend to the missing Mr O'Flaherty."

A strange silence descended on the trio as they stood over the body of the man they took to be Daniel "The Yank" Dwyer. Only the sound of the wind moaning in the bushes and the plish-ploshing of the raindrops on the undergrowth could be heard above the beating of their hearts as they gazed at the lifeless figure at their feet. Somewhere in the distance a night-bird shrieked, causing all three to jerk in startled surprise. Just then, the clouds parted allowing a munched-apple moon to filter an eerie misted light on the still gathering.

"Oh Jay-Jay-Jaysus!" the driver gasped in a high-pitched voice and crossed himself as he stared at the mottled, ghastly features of the corpse at his feet.

"Get a bloody grip on yourself, man!" the man from the north hissed through clenched teeth.

RV sprang to take command. "Right!" he said confidently. "I figure the best way to go about this is, first, we haul the coffin up on to the road. Then we bring up Mr

Dwyer, replace him inside the coffin then take the coffin up the hill to the church. After that, our troubles are over!"

The man from the north had an idea. "Inspector, we have a rope in the van above. We could use it to drag the coffin and the corpse up the ditch, maybe?"

"Great idea – just the ticket," RV agreed. "Hop up and throw the rope down, would you? In fact, better the both of you go up and do the pulling. I'll fix things this end. And by the way, it's 'Sergeant' not 'Inspector'."

"Sergeant – oh, right you are – Sergeant. We're on our way."

Minutes later, the man from the north appeared at the top of the incline and tossed a thick – though slightly frayed – rope down to the waiting RV. After much manoeuvring, he attached one end of the rope to the coffin, secured it, and tossed the other end up to the man from the north. Soon the coffin and coffin-lid were towed up the slope and on to the grassy roadside. The rope was once again thrown down to RV, who made a loop and, with some difficulty, slipped the loop over the the corpse's upper torso and fastened it under the armpits.

"OK, men," he panted at his waiting helpers and tossed the rope towards them. "I've secured this end of the rope. Let's get Mr Dwyer up out of here. Haul away! Careful now!"

Inch by inch, the body moved up the slippery slope while RV guided and shouted encouragement to the two men tugging on the rope. "That's it, men! We're almost there. Only a few more feet to go and we're home and dry! Gentle now! Gentle! Eeeasy does it!"

"What was that?" the driver stiffened and released his grip on the rope.

"What was what?"

"That s-s-sound! I heard a s-s-s-sound – from the body! It m-m-moaned! I heard it! I s-s-swear I did!"

"Don't be daft! A dead man is a dead man! And this one is deader than most," the man from the north snorted. "Now shut up, get a grip of this rope and keep pulling."

At last the corpse lay on the roadside by the coffin, surrounded by RV and his panting helpers. It had begun to rain again.

"Well done, men!" RV said, placing his flashlight on the road beside the body. "That wasn't so difficult, was it? So far so good! Now to get him into the coffin. Each of you take hold of a leg. I'll take this end," he placed his hands underneath the corpse's armpits, "and we place him down in the coffin."

As the body was being lowered into the coffin, the man from the north whispered, "Begod, that's the first time I've seen Wellington boots on a corpse!"

"So he has!" RV glanced at the corpse's legs, annoyed at himself for not having noticed this peculiar detail. "It must be some strange American custom – or maybe he wanted it to be this way." Returning Irish-Americans sometimes acted very strangely.

At last, the body lay in the coffin and the men stood gazing at it.

"What now, S-S-Sergeant?" asked the driver, still panting from his exertions.

"Now we get him out of here. You go and get your van up here and we can load the coffin in the back. Then I'll ask you to take the unfortunate man up to the church. After that, our work is over. Father O'Malley will handle things from there on."

The driver boarded the van and reversed it as close as was possible to the coffin. The van in position, he then opened the back doors and proceeded to clear a space for their unusual cargo.

"Ye are in the building trade, I see," RV observed,

peering at the various tools, tool-boxes and implements in the van's interior.

"Building trade? Oh – er – y-y-y-yes, the building trade! That's what we do, all right, S-S-S-Sergeant – the building trade!" the driver blurted, moving two shovels to the front of the van.

"By the sound of ye, ye don't come from this part of the country at all. Where are you from yourself?" RV inquired, watching the driver as he shifted a folding ladder to the side of the vehicle.

"Ah – ah – Wa-Wa-Waterford, Sergeant. I'm from county Waterford."

"I was thinking as much – from the accent," RV said, then turning to the other man asked, "And yourself?"

"Me? Oh – ah – Derry – I'm from Derry myself," the man from the north replied, his eyes firmly fixed on the coffin.

"Derry – I was thinking that. Ye have a job on around here, I suppose?" RV queried.

"Aye, we have that, Sergeant . . . " The man from the north hesitated, then added, "We've a job on at the bank."

The man from Waterford froze and waited for his companion to continue.

"We've got a small plumbing and re-wiring job to do there. We were going to go at it good and early, in order to be out of the people's way by the time the bank opens for business in the morning."

"Good idea! And you're quite right too," RV nodded. "The early bird etcetera. I can often get more work done in one hour at night or early in the morning than I can in the whole of a working day. Funny that, isn't it? Right! Let's load up and get out of here. We could catch our death standing around here at this time of the morning."

"Except for Mr Dwyer there," the man from the north muttered.

"OK? Let's get to it. All ready to lift? Watch out for the lid. The screws came off in the fall."

With all three lifting, the coffin was raised and slowly slid forward to come to rest in the van's cramped interior.

"That's grand! Grand altogether!" RV whispered. "Don't worry about the end sticking out – just tie the rope across the back doors. Ye haven't got far to travel with it. Drive on up to the church and wait for me there. I'll have a further quick scout around here for some sign of Mr O'Flaherty, then I'll follow you up on the bike." He turned and headed back down the incline to the marsh to seek out the possibly concussed, badly-injured, unconscious or perhaps even dead Tombs O'Flaherty.

The two men climbed into the van together and turned to stare at their strange cargo. Eventually, the driver started the motor and gunned the vehicle up the hill towards the village.

"Jay-Jay-Jasus! What a m-m-mess. He'll c-c-cop us for sure!"

"Now listen!" the man from the north snapped, his voice metal-hard. "Don't lose the bloody head! All we have to do is play along with the Sergeant. He doesn't suspect a thing. He's too busy worrying about all this crack to be suspicious. Anyway, haven't we helped him out of a spot and done everything he's asked of us? It's probably a reward he has in mind for us. Listen! All we have to do now is take your man here," he jerked his thumb in the direction of the coffin, "up to the church, dump him and then be off about our business – "

"But what if the Sergeant – "

"If nothing! Look, I know this old boy. He hasn't recognised me, even though I worked here a few years back in the building of the bank. As far as he's concerned, we're here to do a wiring and plumbing job so as soon as we dump the stiff, we go about our job as planned. It's that simple!"

"I hope you're r-r-right."

"I know I'm right. And for Christ's sakes, keep your bloody nerve! Ever since we bumped into the Sergeant back there, you've been a nervous as a cat in a room full of rocking chairs!"

"Well, what do you expect! I've seen nothing so far tonight but c-c-coffins, dead men and bloody p-p-policemen. That's enough to try the nerves of a man of s-s-steel!"

"Well, keep a grip on yourself from now on. Play along and we'll do rightly. Only let me do the talking. It would only take one wrong word for to get the Sergeant smelling a rat. And just remember, this time tomorrow, if we keep our wits about us and do the job we came here to do – we'll be up to our necks in champagne and the good life, mark my words."

The van swung into the gravel drive in front of the church door and came to a stop. The hair on the back of the driver's neck again began to prickle. He strained his ears to listen. There it was again! That low moaning sound! Coming from the back of the van – coming from inside the coffin?

"Did you h-h-h-hear it? You must've h-h-heard *that*!" his eyes bulged in fear.

"Hear what?" said the man from north impatiently.

"I thought I heard – oh n-n-nothing, nothing at all. Just the wind in the t-t-trees."

The driver switched off the engine and the two men sat in the darkness, speaking in low voices, to await the arrival of Sergeant Mulrooney.

Chapter Seven

"It's all a matter of organisation," RN said to himself as he made his way his way between the ivy-covered wall and the tangled web of tombstones scattered about the unkempt graveyard. "Organisation and planning," he repeated as he flashed his torch about the uneven ground. On leaving the Golden Gloves some hours before, RN had returned to Father O'Malley's house where he had his rooms. There he collected another laden carrier-bag, then walked down the street to McGarrigan's Bar & Lounge where he slipped unnoticed into a cubicle, off the main bar, that served as both snug and off-licence. Here RN passed over the bag and its contents to a sour-faced McGarrigan, who complained loudly.

"That last batch you delivered wasn't up to much at all!" he whined. "A few of the regulars complained. And it isn't as if I'm not paying enough for the stuff." Still grumbling, he passed a wad of folded pound notes to RN, who – as he meticulously counted them – coldly informed McGarrigan that he was under no obligation to buy "the stuff" from him and that if he thought he could obtain a better, or cheaper, batch elsewhere he was perfectly entitled to do so.

"That McGarrigan's a sour, mealy-faced, penny-pinching son of a bitch!" RN muttered as he headed back to his rooms after making the delivery. "Not at all like John L. There's a real gentleman!" He made a mental note to drop a few extra items to John L come Christmas.

Arriving back in his room, he set about making a strong cup of sweet tea for himself before settling down to wait until it was time to go about his night's labours. Shortly after 2 a.m. he decided that it was time to go to work. Before leaving the house he checked that the coast was clear. The town was as silent and deserted as a Christmas Day afternoon – though it bothered him that Father O'Malley had not yet returned home.

"Probably back with his cronies at McGarrigan's," he said as he crept out and down the gravel pathway by the hedge to the graveyard wall. Slipping over the low wall, he began to make his way over the tufted, undulating graveyard surface. As he gingerly picked his steps between the tightly packed gravestones, he heard a wild shout coming from the street. He switched off his torch, halted behind a tomb and held his breath. Remaining in that position for a long while, he carefully peered around the corner of the tomb, hoping to catch sight of the shouter. Through the wafting waves of drizzle he made out the figure of a man struggling to mount his bicycle.

"Only one of McGarrigan's drunks on his way home." RN breathed a sigh of relief and continued to move through the graveyard until he came to a spot by the northern wall. Here he halted, dropped down on both knees and again strained his ears and eyes for any sound or movement other than his own. Satisfied that all was once again safe, he began to roll away a layer of thick, grassy sod by his knees, revealing a timber course underneath, a little bigger than an ordinary manhole. This he removed with ease and switching on his torch, he shone it down the opening, illuminating the inside of the black hole. The torch's beam fell on a number of stone steps dropping away sharply from the opening to another larger entrance at the foot of the tunnel, some six feet below the surface. Moving quickly, with the sense and ease of a man who had performed this action many times in the past, RN lowered himself down into the dark opening. Once inside, he pulled the timber cover over his head to seal the entrance, descended the stone steps and went through the portal the bottom of the steps.

Flashing his torch about him, he surveyed the room in which he now stood. Though "room" was not quite the word to describe this place, as he stood in a burial vault, twelve feet by eight feet wide and seven feet high, once the hallowed resting place for some forgotten local dignitaries and now the hub of operations for RN Mulrooney's tightly organised, highly efficient, extremely lucrative poteen-making business.

RN smiled contentedly. This was the illicit operation his brother RV had been combing the length and breadth of the countryside in search of. This was the mystery poteen still that had given his brother all those sleepless nights on useless wild-goose chases and bitter days of crushing frustration. Here it was, not an ass's roar from the Garda Station, the centre of RN's poteen-making empire, secure and unknown to a soul except himself, twelve feet beneath the lush green carpet of the graveyard surface. And, unless some local laid claim to the vault, here it would continue to lie, undetected and undisturbed, the finest poteen still in the country.

RN could not but congratulate himself each time he stood in this place to admire his handiwork. It had been a stroke of pure luck that he should stumble across the unknown vault in the first place. But it was a stroke of pure genius on his part to come up with the idea of converting the vault into a working poteen still and then putting his idea into action. That was just a few short years ago and it was now from this subterranean chamber that RN supplied the county and beyond with the finest drop of the mountain dew to be tasted west of the Caspian Sea. So once Erasmus informed him, at any rate.

RN recalled how the still came into being. Not long after arriving in Ballykeogh and obtaining employment as sacristan from Father O'Malley, RN had set about devising some plan that would make life in this God-forsaken spot a little more tolerable and, more importantly, a little more lucrative. Having eventually taken over the day-to-day running of the church's financial affairs, RN had financially invested and speculated, manoeuvred and connived until he had acquired, on behalf of the church, several parcels of land along this side of Sliabh Cullen. This property would, he knew, one day pay dividends, but still his restless spirit longed for a more exciting and active venture which would give greater scope to his varied and undeniable talents.

"Chance and Lady Luck," RN often reminded himself, "favour those who are best prepared to receive them!" And so he prepared himself and patiently waited for a suitable scheme to take root in his fertile, creative imagination. For a business to thrive, RN rightly reasoned, it was necessary to attract people to your place of business. Clearly, what was needed here, he felt, was a greater flow of people to the church. Once he had achieved that, he could then develop other lucrative sideline ventures. But how to proceed and where to get these throngs of visitors? All Ballykeogh had ever seen was mass emigration as the young had deserted the locality in droves towards the freedom, glamour and prospects to be found practically anywhere away from this place. So how was he to attract huge numbers of people to Ballykeogh? He seriously considered orchestrating some event which would signify the working of some supernatural power – in short, a miracle. He toyed with the idea of creating a tear-producing Saint Patrick, whose chipped statue dominated a corner of the church, or a weeping painting of the Virgin or some other religious icon, but had to abandon these ideas due to the fact that similar efforts had been tried in the midlands and ultimately failed owing to the general reluctance of the clergy to play along with the schemes. Anyway, Father O'Malley would never willingly endorse any such undertaking, he was certain of that. He would have to put his thinking cap on and come up with a plan that need not employ any talents but his own.

Finally, RN 's belief in the maxim that "Chance favours those who are prepared" paid off. One day, while rummaging through some old church papers he came across an old 19th century plan of the graveyard. On close inspection he discovered the presence of two subterranean burial chambers. He had not until that moment known of their existence and, to his best knowledge, neither did Father O'Malley. The vaults were situated side by side by the northern wall of the graveyard, twelve feet below ground level. The entrances, he discovered, to the vaults were covered over with heavy stone slabs which themselves had been covered over by countless years of grass and weed growth. His curiosity immediately led him to investigate and after some searching, he discovered the stone-slab vault entrances. He could hardy wait till dark to explore his find. How keen was the surge of excitement he had felt on removing one of the stone slabs to reveal the entrance tunnel below. How his heart and blood had pounded as he descended the narrow passage to enter the chamber leading off the tunnel. Now he knew how

Howard Carter must have felt on discovering the long lost tomb of Tutankhamen. In this tomb, however, there was no fabulous treasure to be found, only the rotted remains of old coffins and the crumbled white bones and grinning skulls of the men and women they once held.

He was about to reveal his find to Father O'Malley when a daring idea began to blossom in his mind. Here, under his very nose, lay what he longed and hoped for – the answer to his dreams and schemes. Here was the very place from which he would establish and run his long-dreamed-of poteen still. Having acquired the knowledge during his time in Lisdoonvarna, all he had lacked to put his poteen-making art into practice was a working fermentation-still. And now he had found the ideal location for such a venture. He could hardly believe his good fortune. Once he had overcome some of the obvious problems – such as clearing the tomb of its grisly contents – all he had to do was convert the vault into a working still. Then he would be free to brew away to his heart's content. There were also minor problems; for instance, how to get the distilling equipment down into the vault without the whole village knowing about it. This he achieved by stealthily working in the dead of night. The other problems he tackled with the same zest and creative ingenuity. Firstly, there was the problem of smoke emitted during the distilling process and how to get rid of it. Secondly, how was he to neutralise the pungent aroma of the fermenting poteen-mash? The first he solved by driving a tunnel from the vault to connect with a sewage pipe which ran into a tank behind the bank, on the other side of the graveyard wall. He then directed a smoke-funnel from the equipment down the tunnel. This way he could pipe smoke directly from the still into the sewage system, thus cutting down the chance of being detected due to any suspicious smoke-signals emanating from beneath the graveyard surface. Next was the problem of the tell-tale smell. This problem he never quite overcame, though he soon discovered that the use of a gas-fire and the burning of large quantities of church incense during distilling operations had some effect in lessening the acrid and identifiable aroma of poteen in the making. This latter plan would have to serve his purpose until a more efficient method was discovered. More than one visitor to the graveyard, however, had some difficulty in identifying or explaining the true nature and source of the strange smell which seemed to emanate from nowhere in particular and cling to the very gravestones themselves.

To his delight, RN's initial experiments proved successful. So much so, he was greatly encouraged to persist and develop the venture. Now, five years later, he had ironed out most of the problems and had perfected this ancient and noble trade. From deep within his vaulted still, RN was now producing a rich, creamy-white and exceedingly potent blend of poteen which was being sought after far and wide. So successful had his operation become, he now had plans to expand into the neighbouring vault in the very near future. With the sharp rise in business of late, more space would definitely be required if he was to keep pace with demand.

"One day," he would often fantasise, "the entire graveyard and churchyard will be a network of tunnels and underground operational vaults – with workers and overseers – all producing the Pure Drop on a huge scale!"

But for the time being, he told himself, one step, and one day, at a time. He had other, more grandiose, plans. Ultimately, he dreamed he would develop an internationally popular "Health Resort". A Spa, similar to Baden-Baden in Germany or Lisdoonvarna in Co. Clare, where paying visitors could partake of a special blend of mineral waters, known only to RN: a panacea which would contain certain magical ingredients only to be found in Ballykeogh. RN hoped to outline these plans to Father O'Malley within the next few days. But for the moment, he had to work overtime to meet the ever-increasing demands of his many customers – whose thirst increased with the passing of each day.

"Right, let's get down to business," RN muttered to himself.

He reached up to a stone ledge, just above eye-level on the vault bricked wall, and took down a Tilly lamp and a box of matches. Soon the vault was bathed in an illumination as powerful as that of any electric-light. Placing the hissing lantern back on the ledge, he let his eyes adjust to his surroundings. At the far corner of the chamber sat three large drums: one metal and two wooden. The metal drum and one of the wooden barrels constituted the main part of the poteen-producing apparatus while the remaining wooden barrel held clear spring water. Next to the barrels, lining the walls on both sides, sat a couple of earthenware jars, two buckets and next to them, several plastic containers filled to the brim with poteen. Placed above them, on a slab on which once lay the original inhabitants of this place, sat a number of empty bottles and containers, waiting to be filled and on their way to their various destinations.

RN rubbed his hands and said aloud to the empty bottles, "Right, my lovelies! I'll soon have new life in you. Just be patient!"

He tended to speak his thoughts aloud down here, to be company for himself during the long hours he toiled at his solitary task. In the early days he had worked nervously in the vault. After all, it was a tomb which had once housed who knows how many dead and more than once he felt his flesh creep at the slightest imagined movement, rustle or sound. More than once he imagined he was not alone down here and more than once he had to partake of his own produce to bolster his flagging nerve and spirit. Though God knows, he had now worked down here often enough to consider the place a sort of home-from-home or, at least, his "office". Still, the dank taste and atmosphere of the tomb lingered on and affected him from time to time and so he spoke to himself and often lilted a tune, to keep the spirits high.

Popping one of Mrs Flanagan's lozenges into his mouth, he moved to the metal drum and gazed down at the fermenting mixture. Leaning over the drum he inhaled deeply, his eyes shut. "Ahh . . . yes. Excellent! Almost ready, almost ready," he said with satisfaction. Nine days before, RN had begun this present fermentation's working-cycle, mixing the potatoes, oatmeal, sugar, yeast and hot water in the metal drum-cum-brewing-vat. Twice a day since, he had visited the vault to add yeast and top up the mixture with three or four gallons of boiling water – which he boiled in a large kettle on a gas ring there in the vault – in order to keep the mash as close to the ideal fermentation temperature as possible. "Ninety-eight point four degrees!" his teacher in Lisdoonvarna had drilled into him. "Keep the mix at ninety-eight point four degrees and you've got the makings of the purest of the pure."

The old man would have been proud of his pupil, RN often thought. Unlike his teacher, however, who could verify the correct temperature just by inserting a finger into the fermenting mix, RN had to use a thermometer. Nevertheless, he wished the old boy had lived to see this operation in action and taste the results.

From day six of the eleven-day cycle, RN had

submerged the earthenware jar filled with boiling water in the vat twice a day, keeping the mash as close as possible to that magic ninety-eight point four degrees F. Now at last, the powerful-smelling mash was ready for its final stage of processing which consisted of adding several gallons of cold clear spring water to the metal drum. This done, the vat was then sealed with bread-dough, which baked hard in the boiling process, before the gas fires were set underneath it. When the contents of the vat came to the boil, the steam was siphoned off through a copper worm-pipe down through the barrel full of cold water into the container that patiently collected – drop by precious drop – the raw poteen, or 'singlings' as it was called.

RN had considered waiting one more night until the Yank Dwyer was buried and the excitement in the village had died down, before getting this important stage under way. But each day was as crucial and precious as each silver drop oozing from the copper worm and so RN decided that – funeral or no funeral – he had no option but to get the final stage of the fermentation under way.

As RN set about his work, the sound of a car, its engine revving frantically, seeped into the vault from the world above.

"Well, well! The brave Father has decided to call it a night," he said, recognising the sound of Father O'Malley's Morris Minor as it negotiated its inebriated way up the drive on the other side of the graveyard to the house. "Listen to that racket! He'll wake half the bloody village!" He frowned and looked at his watch, which read two thirty a.m. precisely.

He sighed, shrugged and continued with his work. With the priest home, and, hopefully, the village still asleep, he could proceed in peace. His next task involved going back up to the surface to connect a water-hose to an outside tap at the back of the sacristy and running the hose down into the vault. With the same silent stealth as when he entered the vault he emerged to connect the hose to the tap and turn on the water. He then returned to the vault and proceeded to top up the vat containing the mash and both timber barrels with cold water. The barrels now filled, he went to the surface once again to disconnect the water-hose, coil it and pack it away out of sight.

Back in the vault, he set about preparing the gas-ring fires and setting them underneath the fermentation vat. He decided that a low heat would be sufficient for the time being and set the gas-flame accordingly. The sound of the gas rings hissing along in harmony with the Tilly lamp produced a low rumbling hum which filled the vault with a cheery sound. It was a sound which filled RN with satisfaction. He felt good, so good he decided to treat himself to a hot poteen.

"Now to test the last batch," he said, placing a saucepan full of fresh water on a gas jet and waiting for it to come to the boil. "All I need down here now is the old easy chair, the bedroom slippers, and I'm at home!" he chuckled as the gas-fire's flaming halo cast prancing, spidery shadows on the dank russet walls. Even with the gas fires burning, the place was continually damp. It was a palpable damp which clung to the walls like ivy and billowed over his body like an invisible shroud to burrow into his blood and pinch his bones. It was, RN thought, an evil damp, the damp of the grave. But, he sometimes mused, no worse than his own room up in the priest's house. "This," he beamed at the generous helping of hot poteen he poured into a chipped tin mug, "is the only central heating you'd need, wherever you are. Aaah!" He sipped the clear liquid, held his breath, wiped his mouth, patted his stomach, rubbed his hands and released a long hiss of satisfied breath.

"That's powerful stuff! Wouldn't that bring a corpse back to life!" Remembering where he was, he crossed himself and drank the remains of the hot toddy in one long gulp.

His next task before taking off home to his bed was to fill the waiting empty bottles with poteen. He was weary, but he felt well satisfied with his night's work. Going to one of the cans containing poteen ready for bottling, he emptied the contents into a plastic bucket into which he then submerged each lemonade bottle until it was brim full. As he filled and corked the long line of bottles, he hummed a tuneless "Begin The Beguine", envisaging the not too-distant day when he might put his very own label on each bottle produced here. A mark of quality. Some stamp or other which would tell the world that here was a bottle of poteen of some distinction and one not to be confused with any of the other inferior distillations. "'Chateau Mulrooney'? 'Mulrooney's Premier Poteen' perhaps?" he mused. "That'd be one for the history books." A cork popped on the final bottle. "There!" he said. "That's the next order complete." He checked his watch. "Three fifteen. Time is moving on. Better wrap up here and get away to my bed. There'll be an early start for the Yank Dwyer business in the morning."

Before he left the tomb and its apparatus to the magical workings of nature and science, he needed to leave a quantity of the incense he had earlier procured from the sacristy burning in a couple of old Benediction thuribles. A couple of extra helpings of burning incense would not go astray, he figured, given the activity expected in the graveyard in the morning. His nose began to twitch with irritation as the thick heavy odour of the church incense wafted about his face. In ten minutes it would be unbearable down here. The smell of fermenting poteen mash was one thing, but the stench of that combined with the pungent incense was enough to make the strongest stomach turn over.

Eager now to be away from this place, RN turned his attention to a makeshift work-table on which lay the half-filled bucket of poteen and a number of filled lemonade bottles. He was about to ladle the contents of the bucket back into the airtight container when the distant sound of a motor engine cut through into the hissing stillness of the vault. Sensing the vehicle's nearness, he froze instantly, cocked his head and strained to focus on the sound from above ground.

"Strange," he thought. " A car around here at this time of night."

By the sound of it, it was approaching the church. Could it be Father O'Malley going out on a sick call, perhaps? He shook his head. He could recognise the sound of Father O'Malley's Morris Minor anywhere and this was not the priest's Morris. His pulse quickened as he sensed possible danger. He had to investigate immediately. Moving out of the chamber and up the steps leading to the tunnel entrance, he raised the timber cover a fraction and peered out in the direction of the village street. A pair of car headlights cut twin cones of cold light through the softly falling drizzle, bathing the church front and a few gravestones in a pale ghostly glow. As the vehicle approached up the pathway to the church, RN's mind raced. This could be big danger! Could this be his brother RV and a squad-car full of his police cronies from Ballyglen, finally on to his operation and making their swoop? While his imagination and blood raced as he struggled to compose himself and prepare for the worst, the vehicle came to a halt. The driver switched off the engine, giving the night back to the rain and the wind.

In the silence it seemed to RN that the thumping of his

own heart could be heard by the occupants of the parked vehicle. He continued to listen and wait, fully expecting to hear the advancing search party bear down on his secret lair, but no one came. For what seemed like an eternity, he remained absolutely still, occasionally peeking out in the direction of the parked motor-vehicle. He had to make a move and make it soon. He knew he could not remain down here in this tunnel like a trapped rabbit. He had better get up on the surface and check this out.

In one lightning movement he lifted off the tunnel cover and sprang through the opening, crouching low as he replaced the covering of timber and the carpet of grass. Swiftly and silently, he moved like a shadow through the graveyard to take up a more advantageous position by the front corner wall of the church. Stealing a glance around the corner, RN choked back a sigh of relief to see – parked by the front door of the church – not a police patrol car crammed with guards as he had imagined, but a small van, its glowing tail-lights revealing a long, bulky object protruding out its rear end. From his hidden position RN could hear the low tones of its occupants conversing. If they weren't the law, then who in heaven's name were they? And what were they up to here at this time of the night? As he racked his brain for probable answers, a tall, dark familiar figure on a bicycle emerged out of the darkness and came to a halt by the stationary van.

"Christ!" RN hissed under his breath. "It's the brother! What's he doing here?"

"You made it up here OK, I see." RN heard his brother say to the van's occupants. "So far, so good! You boys hang on here while I go up to to the house and fetch Father O'Malley. Then we can get Mr Dwyer to his proper place inside the church."

Dwyer! The Yank Dwyer? What was he talking about?

141

The Sergeant laid his bicycle by the church wall and set off in the direction of the priest's house. As he disappeared into the night, both the driver and passenger stepped out of the van and walked to the church door. RN's mind worked with reptilian quickness. He knew that as soon as RV got to the house and roused Father O'Malley, the priest would immediately go to fetch RN and discover that he was not in his room. It would be difficult to explain later if he make no showing at all. He had to act now and take the bull by the horns. Taking a long. deep breath, RN stepped from his hiding-place and walked towards the two hunched figures by the church door.

"Good morning to ye both," he hailed and waved his torchlight. "What can I do for ye?"

The figures by the doorway jerked as if gripped by some invisible hand.

"Jeez!" the taller of the two men gasped. "You almost gave me a heart attack coming up on us like that!"

The smaller man's eyes blinked furiously and bulged in stark terror, a cigarette dangling from his slackened lower lip.

"I'm sorry 'bout that," RN said. "I was working late in the sacristy back there and heard your van pull in. I was wondering what could be the trouble at this time of night, so I came round to check."

The two men continued to stare at him in silence.

"Are you in trouble?"

"Oh, no trouble," the taller of the two men spoke at last. "Well, not really. The Sergeant there," he waved a hand at the night, "flagged us down coming in to the village. There was an accident down the bottom of the hill and we're helping him sort things out. He's gone for the priest."

"An accident! What accident?"

The man gestured toward the long box poking out of the back of the van. "Well, it's this here coffin, y'see. We came across this hearse – crashed at the bend of the road down there. There was a coffin – and a body – and the Sergeant asked us if we would get both up to the church here – and here we are. It's some fella named Dwyer, according to the Sergeant."

"Dwyer! Are you sure? Are you sure that's his name?"

"Aye! So the Sergeant tells us. That's the poor devil's name, right enough. And it says so on the lid of the coffin. Take a look for yourself."

RN moved to the rear of the van and directed his torchlight on the tiny nailed plate on the coffin lid.

"Daniel Dwyer. Died The Bronx, New York. Oct. 12th 1964. RIP." RN read aloud. The men were right. This was the infamous Yank Dwyer himself. RN tried to reason it out. The Yank Dwyer wasn't due in Galway until the following morning! Yet here he was. How, and more importantly when, did Tombs get the remains back to Ballyglen? He had not mentioned a word about this change of plan earlier in the Golden Gloves. As RN recalled, Tombs's hearse was parked out front when he went in to the pub earlier that night with John L's supply of poteen and yes, there was indeed a coffin in the hearse. Tombs must have already been to Ballyglen at that stage, collected the remains off the Galway train and immediately returned the Ballykeogh. But why did he not mention it earlier in the Gloves? That was most unlike Tombs. And how on earth did he end up crashed at the bottom of the hill? This was all thoroughly confusing. The only man who could shed any light on the whole affair was Tombs himself. But where was Tombs?

"Where is Tombs – er, that is, Mr O'Flaherty, the hearse-driver?" he asked the men.

"No sign of the driver high up or low down," the man with the northern accent answered. "The Sergeant figures he's wandering about down beyond in the marsh there – in a daze from the crash. As I said, 'twas all over by the time we came on the scene."

RN shook his head in confusion, trying to comprehend the unfolding story. He was, however, deeply relieved that the situation was now far less dangerous than he had first imagined it to be. "Well, no sense in getting wet standing around here. Let's get the coffin inside the church. I'll nip around to the sacristy and switch the lights on and get the door open. I won't be a jiffy." Leaving the men, RN headed off in the direction of the sacristy.

A few minutes later, a single light came on inside the church and the church door creaked open. RN emerged and signalled to the waiting men. "OK men, let's get Mr Dwyer inside." RN and the two men set about lifting the coffin out of the back of the van and into the church. As they carried the coffin through the front porch, RN got his first good look at his two helpers. Strangers, both of them – though the taller one who did all the talking looked familiar. He had heard that northern-accented voice somewhere but try as he could, no name came to fit the face or voice, yet he felt certain he had seen the man before. The smaller of the two men, his face drawn and pale, remained silent.

Inside, a single electric bulb hung over the altar at the far end, casting its weak light about the church interior.

"Right," RN said. "We'll put him down here."

As they lowered the coffin to the floor at the rear of the church, the lid slid away to reveal the body inside. The two strangers crossed themselves and with RN stood for a long time gazing down on the still yellow mud-stained features of the body inside. Strands of pea-green marsh-weed clung to the corpse's matted hair and clothes.

"So that's the famous Yank!" RN whispered. "Home at last." He could not help but notice the Yank bore a strong family resemblance to that loutish nephew of his, Black Jack Dwyer.

After a long while, the man with the northern accent spoke softly. "Isn't it a funny thing – death. There he is – cold as stone and yet he looks like he could rise up and walk away any second."

"What did Shelley say? *Death is the veil which those who live call life: they sleep, and it is lifted.*' We will all have to lift that veil one day and at the end of the day there's only two ways out of this old world – up in one of those Sputnik tin-cans and down in a box, like Dwyer there!" RN philosophised.

"Well, whatever a-a-about a 'veil', have you ever seen W-W-Wellington boots on a corpse before?" the smaller of the two men whispered.

A look of amazement spread over RN's face. The corpse did indeed have a pair of muddied patched black Wellington boots into which was tucked the crumpled pants of a blue serge suit.

"These Americans have strange ways of dressing their dead," the man from the north muttered.

"You're right! Very strange, right enough." RN shook his head. "Well, we can't leave him like this. We will have to get him out of that gear and into a proper burial shroud before Father O'Malley sees him like this. Father O'Malley would never allow a body go to the grave dressed in a suit and Wellington boots. He often says that when the Final Trumpet blows, at least *his* flock will be properly attired to meet their heavenly Judge and jurors."

"A-A-Amen to that!" the shorter man said, his words echoing through the church interior.

"Wait a sec!" RN clicked his fingers. The two men jerked again, startled by the suddenness of the noise. "There's a shroud in the vestry. I'll fetch it. We can slip it on Mr Dwyer before the Father arrives and sees him in this state." RN set off towards the altar and the sacristy door at the far end of the church.

"This p-p-place is giving me the c-c-creeps, I'm t-t-telling you!" the shorter man whispered to his partner, "How in G-G-God's name did we get mixed up in this b-b-bloody business! Let's get out of here while we can!"

The man with the northern accent glared at his companion with a look of iron. "Pull your bloody self together, man! We have to see this through. We're in this through no fault of ours. We'll be out of here in no time and we're not turning back for anybody. Alive or dead!" he glanced quickly down at the open coffin. "Just keep a cool head and hold your tongue!"

At that moment RN arrived back carrying a moth-eaten, yellowed night-shirt. "This will do as a shroud. Let's get the Yank into it – but off with these Wellingtons first," he said, and lifting each of the corpse's legs he tugged off each rubber boot in turn. "Whee! What a pong!" He turned his head away as his nostrils were assailed by the overwhelming stench of rotting socks and sweat.

"OK, now to get his jacket off. Then we can slip the shroud over his shirt. Here, help me lift him up to a sitting position. It'll be easier that way."

The men hesitated, looking furtively at each other, then bent forward to assist RN in raising the body to a sitting position. As they lifted, the shorter man drew back, exclaiming loudly, "S-S-Saints protect us! He moaned again! I tell you, he moaned! The b-b-bastard's alive!" His voice echoed through the shadows.

146

"Stay calm! Stay calm now!" RN spoke with the authority of a man who knew how to take charge. "Don't panic. I've some experience in this area. It's not uncommon for corpses to make all kinds of sounds. It's the air trapped in the lungs escaping that makes that sound. It often happens when the body is being moved. It's the last sound they ever make, and that's for sure."

The explanation did not seem to fully convince the smaller man, who – ashen-faced and blinking furiously – stood with his back to the wall and looked on while RN and the man from the north removed the corpse's jacket. The man folded the jacket and placed it on a nearby pew seat, his fingers brushing against an envelope in the inside pocket.

"How long has this one been dead?"

"Why do you ask?" RN grunted, struggling to relieve the corpse of his pants.

"Well, look at him, will you! You say he came all the way from America – and yet he's as warm as you or I! He should be stiff as a board by now."

"Oh, you mean *rigor mortis*!" RN paused. "You're right! I have to admit this is the most flexible six-day-old corpse that I've ever handled, now that you mention it! But *rigor mortis* only lasts a short while and in any case maybe he's full of some newfangled embalming fluid or some-such. There's no end to what science can achieve these days, you know. Yes! I'd lay a bet that's what it is all right."

"I suppose you're right."

"I know I am. I got a mighty whiff of pure alcohol from him just now and that's the finest embalming fluid money can buy."

The man from the north bent forward over the body and sniffed. A cutting aroma pinched his nostrils. In the stale, wafting scent he clearly detected certain elements:

147

Brylcreem hair-lotion, shaving-cream, human sweat and cow-shit. He also detected the tang of moth-balls and cat-piss. He leaned closer and sniffed again. Yes, there was a powerful overlay of essence of alcohol also present in that acrid mixture of indelicate perfumes that now fairly overpowered him. "Yes. I see what you mean. He's rightly pickled in alcohol, to be sure."

RN continued to struggle with the body in his efforts to get the shroud over the head and shoulders. "Would you give me a hand here," he called. "This is bloody awkward."

After much pushing, pulling, tugging and shoving, the body, dressed in the moth-eaten night-shirt, lay in peace once again, suitably dressed for its last journey to the grave.

"Now to put the coffin lid on as well as we can and get the coffin up on these stands," RN said. As he placed the lid firmly on the coffin he noticed that a large chunk had been chipped off the bottom end.

"Must have been damaged in the fall, I suppose. Not to worry, we can cover it with a black cloth in the morning."

With the coffin resting securely on the stands, RN proceeded to place a tall funeral candle-stick at each corner. As he settled the final candle-stick in place he heard the sound of voices from outside the church door. It was Father O'Malley in loud conversation with Sergeant Mulrooney.

"It's all very confusing, I must say, Sergeant. All very confusing indeed. What you've told me does not correspond at all with the information I received yesterday from Ballyglen. It just does not add up. How can Mr Dwyer's body be here? Why didn't Mr O'Flaherty mention it, I wonder? I was with him below in – " Father O'Malley broke off in mid-sentence, remembering whom it was he was addressing. "What I mean to say is that Mr O'Flaherty was to collect Mr Dwyer's coffin from Ballyglen at eight-thirty in the morning. That was the plan. And now you tell me that the coffin – and Mr Dwyer – are here! In Ballykeogh! In my church! I don't understand a bit of it!"

Father O'Malley swept into the light, followed by Sergeant Mulrooney. For a moment RN's eyes met and locked with those of his brother. RV removed his cap, curtly nodded and looked away. RN could see that Father O'Malley had dressed hastily: his black mackintosh raincoat over his plain flannel pyjamas. RN could also see, from his red-rimmed eyes and dark scowl, that the priest was not in the best of humour.

"Ah! RN. There you are! What on earth is going on here? Your brother has just dragged me out of bed at this ungodly hour to inform me about – " he blinked in the light and waved his arm in the direction of the coffin, " – about all this! Who are these two gentlemen? Can you tell me what in heaven's name is going on here?"

For several moments, everyone looked at each other in silence.

"Well?" Father O'Malley repeated.

"Well, from my understanding Father, it's just as the Sergeant has told you," RN answered. "There has obviously been some confusion regarding the whole business. It seems Tombs – Mr O'Flaherty – must have collected Mister Dwyer earlier in Ballyglen, driven back here without informing anybody, had this unfortunate accident but thanks to the Sergeant – and these two men – the Yank – er – Daniel Dwyer's remains have finally come home."

Father O'Malley wagged his head, hiccoughed, stifled a belch and said in his pulpit voice, "Well, I have to say this is all beyond me at the moment. But what's done is done. Now I must ask that we get on our knees and say a decade of the rosary for the repose of the soul of our departed brother and for his safe deliverance home to us here in Ballykeogh."

RN, followed by the man from Derry and the man from Waterford, filed reluctantly into the nearest pew and knelt down. Sergeant Mulrooney, his head lowered and his eyes fixed on a spot on the church floor, nervously fingered his cap and stepped back into the shadows by the porch door to await the completion of the prayers and litanies.

Prayers over, Father O'Malley got stiffly to his feet, went to the coffin and liberally splashed it with Holy Water from the nearby font while making the Sign of the Cross, muttering unintelligible Latin. Then turning on his heel, he headed for the door. "RN, you finish up here, won't you? That's all we can do for Mr Dwyer tonight. I'm sure the Sergeant here will have the whole mystery unravelled by morning, won't you Sergeant? Standing around here won't answer questions, that's for sure. I suggest that we all get away to our beds. Mass will be at ten o'clock. Sharp. I expect to see you all there. Goodnight to you all!"

"Yes, Father. Goodnight, Father," RN called after the priest. Turning to the others he said, "The Father is right. There's nothing more we can do here. Ye've done a powerful night's work, surely! There's great credit due to ye. I've no doubt that Dwyer's relations will show some gratitude for the work done this night – if you know what I mean." He winked at the two men. "So I'll expect to see you both at the funeral."

"Aye. Well – maybe. We'll see," the man from Derry replied. "We have a tight schedule to keep. But you never know. We'd better be away. We have an early start in the morning."

"Before you go!" Sergeant Mulrooney stepped out of the shadows. "There is just one more favour I have to ask of you men. Would you see your way clear to tow the hearse from where it is, up to the street here? It may well be the cause of another accident if it's left where it is and it would look fierce bad altogether if the funeral goers came across it in that state in the morning. It just has to be shifted. I'm sure you understand."

The two men looked at each other and then at their watches. The man from Derry sighed, "Oh well, I suppose we could do that for you, Sergeant."

"That's great." The Sergeant donned his cap. "I'll see you both back at the site of the accident. I'll take the cycle and see if I can catch a glimpse of poor Mr O'Flaherty on the way." And followed by his two unnamed helpers, he moved to the door, nodding a silent "goodnight" in RN's direction.

RN relaxed and felt the strain of the last thirty minutes or so drain away, leaving him very, very tired indeed. "A quarter to four! Almost dawn. I'd better get a few hours shut-eye." Picking up the dead man's crumpled jacket and pants, he headed towards the sacristy. He had had a long and eventful day and he was utterly exhausted. Tomorrow, he knew, would be just as eventful.

Chapter Eight

Out in the village street, in front of the church, RV attempted to mount his bicycle in his usual, individual fashion. As he swung his right leg over the angled frame, he was dive-bombed by a squadron of bats, squeaking frantically, en route to their lair hidden deep somewhere in the ivied churchyard walls. At the same moment, he was attacked by an acute stabbing pain, deep in the marrow of his right knee-cap. Wincing, he massaged the throbbing trouble-spot.

"Aahh! I'm getting too old for this game!" he grumbled.

Was it any wonder, he thought, that he was now beset by all manner of aches and pains? All this chasing around the countryside on his bicycle almost every night, winter and summer, in all weathers and sitting on wet, cold stones on long fruitless vigils. And now, to top it all, tonight he had to lug a coffin and corpse from the marsh. No wonder his bones were complaining. No question about it, this was getting to be a task for a younger, fitter man. If only Guard Behan would show a little more sense of duty, a little more professional application and a little more enthusiasm for the job of ridding the area of the *real* criminals – especially the illegal liquor-makers – rather than serving summonses to harmless old ladies, RV might feel more confident in delegating some of this back-breaking night-work to him. He decided he would have to have a serious discussion with Guard Behan in the next few days.

As the blood began to find its way back to his right knee, he began to long for a hot drink and to sit and rest for a moment or two in a warm, comfortable spot. He glanced at the grim outline of the Garda Station and wished he could be back there, stretched out on the single hard bunk in the station cell. Even one of Guard Behan's cups of tepid tea would now be as ambrosia to his flagging spirits.

The van, with the two strangers inside, roaring past him on its way back to the accident site, brought him out of his musings. The comforts of the station would have to wait until the hearse was towed to the church-front and the missing Tombs O'Flaherty was discovered to be safe and sound. Sergeant Mulrooney was resolved not to rest until his present mission was completed.

Tombs's disappearance was indeed a mystery. Could it be possible that after the accident he had wandered back up to the village, still dazed and in shock, and gone directly to his own home? RV decided to investigate this possibility. Pushing his bicycle across the street to where Tombs's house stood, almost directly opposite the church and next door to Mrs Flanagan's shop, he peered over the tall hedge. The house was in darkness and RV could see no other signs of life about the place. Going to the front door, he rapped loudly and called out.

"Mr O'Flaherty! Are you there? Are you inside?"

Silence. He rapped again and waited. Nothing. He went to the cottage window and peered inside. A shy autumn moon darted from behind a cloud and, for a brief moment, was reflected in the glass. As he stood there, it flashed across RV's mind that all he needed was a saddled horse "chomping on the ferny floor" to feel he was the subject of the De La Mare's ghostly poem "The Traveller". He felt a shiver creep and tingle down his spine at the image he had conjured up but quickly drove it from his mind. This was no time to let his tired mind start losing concentration. He took a deep breath and walked briskly back to his bicycle. Wherever Tombs was, he was not here. That meant the poor devil must still be down in the marsh. He had no more time to lose. He had to get back to the accident site as quickly as possible and take another good look around while the two men hitched the van to the hearse for towing back up to the village.

As he cycled past the Golden Gloves on his way down the hill, his mind dwelling on the different fates which might have befallen the hapless Tombs, the sound of a violin – high and mournful – wafted by on the wind. He slowed the bicycle and listened. The sound seemed to be coming from the Gloves. There it was again – and then – silence. He shook his head. It must have been the wind playing a trick on his over-tired imagination. Yes, that was it. He was plain exhausted. What a night! Tracking down the elusive poteen still, hauling a dead man and coffin from the swamp, Tombs still missing in the marsh and now fiddles in the wind! He would be glad when this night was over. Perhaps it was time he should consider taking a little holiday. It would the first since his honeymoon. Hannah would like that. She had been nagging him to take a holiday for years, but how could he leave his responsibilities, with only Guard Behan to look after things at the station in his absence? Until RV had nailed his prime suspect, Tom Duignan, and his accursed poteen-still, he could never relax and enjoy a holiday away from here, no matter how well-deserved that holiday might be. Then, and only then, could he relax and bask, confident in the sure knowledge that he had restored proper law and order to Ballykeogh and environs and could safely leave Guard Behan in charge.

As he arrived at the bottom of the hill, RV found the two men had already hitched their van to the hearse and were ready to commence towing the vehicle up the road to the village street.

"Ah, good men!" he called out. "I'll take a final look around the marsh here to see if I can locate some trace or sign of Mr O'Flaherty, You carry on and tow the hearse up to the village and park it outside Mr O'Flaherty's house – that's the house next to Flanagan's Grocery Shop, opposite the Garda Station. That's all I'll be asking of ye both and I'm grateful for all ye've done so far tonight. It was lucky that ye came along when ye did. Thanks again and goodnight to the both of ye."

He was tempted to mention the fact that the van's motor tax disc was out of date – a fact which had not escaped his trained eye – but under the circumstances he decided to let it pass. Anyway, he thought, if the vehicle was still to be found anywhere in the village tomorrow, Guard Behan was sure to pounce on it. Guard Behan never missed a trick when it came to untaxed vehicles, guns, dogs and radios.

"Oh, no problem, Sergeant, no problem at all. We were glad to be of some assistance. Goodnight to you too, Sergeant!"

The man from Waterford revved the motor hard.

"Oh, and by the way," RV added, "If ye're doing a job in the bank grounds, I would advise that you park the van at the back of Reilly's Garage. It's right next to the bank and it'll be well out of the way there. The street should be jammed by early morning with traffic arriving for Mr Dwyer's funeral. Well, goodnight and thanks again."

An uneasy smile crossed the driver's face.

"T-t-thanks for that advice, S-S-Sergeant. That's probably w-w-what we'll do. G-g-goodnight, Sergeant."

RV watched as the van, its engine labouring under the stress of the double load, inched away from the side of the road and began a slow crawl up the hill to the village.

"Right, Mr O'Flaherty, let's see if you're to be found around here." Switching on his torch, RV moved off and clambered down the wet slippery grass bank leading to the marsh to recommence his search for the missing undertaker.

Arriving in the village street and parking outside the house the Sergeant had described to them, the two men unhitched the van and hurriedly drove off in the direction of the yard adjoining O'Reilly's Garage. They were hardly turned into the yard, some fifty yards down the street, when three figures emerged after the back of the Golden Gloves Pub, one slumped between the other two.

"Issh – hic – isshasshreetchleer?" an unsteady Piper Hanratty garbled to his equally unsteady partner, Jamie O'Connell.

Jamie closed one eye and tried to focus on the dimly lit street. "It'ssh OK. C'mon!" His red eyes watered in the sharp sting of the night. Between the two men slumped Tombs O'Flaherty, now comatose from an inordinate intake of poteen in a very few hours.

"Lessh get 'ol Tombsy to hish bed – hic – heesh had a fair – hic – skinful an thash for sure – hic!" The Piper staggered under the weight of his portion of his unconscious drinking companion.

"Haven't we all. Here, you grab his arms – I'll take the legs and off we go!" Jamie steadied himself to set about the task and tucked Tombs's legs firmly under his arms.

Stopping, staggering, swerving and swaying, the drunken procession snaked its way down the deserted street and at last disappeared around the back of Tombs's house. A moment later, a wild howl of pain from Mrs Flanagan's surly old tom cat rent the air. This was followed by an even louder yell from The Piper Hanratty. As much as The Piper loved all manner of rats, he despised and detested all manner of cats – and from the sound of things the feeling was mutual.

A predawn wind began to freshen, swinging in now from the west and bringing with it a fresh light rain that smacked of salt and the Atlantic. For those who were often out and about, this time of night was often one of the loneliest, most forlorn times of the twenty-four hours, full of dark unnamed fears, unspoken truths and great wells of hopelessness. It was a time when good men looked deep into their own souls and there were few men here who would plunge into that abyss – with perhaps the exception of Sergeant Mulrooney – without the cushioning effect of great quantities of RN's nut-sweet poteen.

These were the thoughts which tumbled in Jamie O'Connell's mind as he emerged alone from Tombs O'Flaherty's house, having deposited the senseless hearse-driver and the soon-to-be senseless Piper Hanratty on a bed inside the house to sleep off their excesses. Crossing the street, he headed back to the Gloves, where he slipped quietly in through the back door to rejoin Erasmus, John L, his fiddle and his dog Caesar.

"There's going to be a few sore heads in Ballykeogh in the morning," he said to Erasmus as he eased himself into a seat by the glowing fire, "and I'm going to have one of 'em."

"Not unless you go to bed, my boy." Erasmus cut a thick slice of plug tobacco and rubbed it between his palms.

"Not unless you allow the body to regroup and fight back. Sleep is the curse of the serious imbiber. Now fill up your glass, rosin up your bow, play me 'The Wind That Shakes The Barley' and give thanks to your God you're not waiting in a coffin below in Ballyglen for Tombs to collect you in the morning."

At exactly five twenty-five a.m., Sergeant Mulrooney and his bicycle slowly shuffled up the pathway to the bleak grey-stoned Garda Station. He was cold, hungry, drenched to the skin and utterly exhausted. His search of the marsh had proved fruitless. He had probed the wet reedy marsh surface and the surrounding hazel clumps and ash groves with meticulous care. Yet there was neither sight nor sound of the missing Tombs O'Flaherty. Any further search would have to be postponed until a proper search party could be organised in the morning. In the meantime, he had to rest his weary, complaining bones. Entering the station, he headed for the single lock-up cell, which, thankfully, tonight housed no offender, removed his tunic jacket and lay down on the hard cot. His head had not settled on the pillow when the droning bees of sleep swarmed into his tired mind, blotting out entirely the waking sting of consciousness.

Outside the station, the street, village and hillside were given back to night and the squabbling wind, rain and dark.

Chapter Nine

The long night reluctantly released its grip on the sleeping village of Ballykeogh and retreated before a hazy persistent dawn. Slow grey ribbons of tattered light filtered down over the village, ushered in with a flapping of swan wings, as they flew their dawn patrols in from the sea and on over Sliabh Cullen towards the rising sun. Somewhere at the northern end of the village, a cockerel crowed his dawn call, answered by a lone fox yelping high up among the heather on the hillside. Ten miles below in the valley, in Ballyglen, the morning had dawned crisp and fine, with the sun looking as if it it might show itself for the best part of the day. Here in Ballykeogh however the sun's rays struggled to pierce the thick wall of mist and rain that seemed determined to engulf the village for eternity.

Throughout the village, the living slept as soundly as the dead, with the exception of the man from Derry and his cohort from Waterford. Deep in an underground graveyard vault, situated next to RN's vault-cum-poteen-still, both men commenced labouring at the task of driving a connecting tunnel between the vault and the bank which was immediately outside the graveyard's north-side wall. They had parked their van in the yard at the back of

O'Reilly's garage. From here, they easily crossed into the church graveyard through the plot of ground behind the bank building. After poking around a while in the grey dawn light, and several consultations with a tattered old map which Derry drew from his hip pocket, they found, at last, what they sought – the entrance to the vault.

"Right! Let's get to work!" Derry's eyes glittered with excitement.

The two men worked quickly and silently. Having moved the heavy stone slab from the surface to reveal the entrance tunnel, they set about transporting the required tools and equipment – two short-handled shovels, a number of timber planks, a storm-lantern, a bag of other sundry small tools (including a saw and hammer) and a flask of hot tea – from the van down into the vault.

Derry watched as Waterford struggled to get the last of the planks down the narrow tunnel entrance. For the first time that night, Derry was beginning to lose some of his ice-cool composure. "C'mon! C'mon!" he barked at the slow-witted Waterford. "Get a bloody move on! Time-wise, this is not going according to plan. We've got just over four hours to get this job done and out of here. By ten o'clock the place will be crawling with people – not to mention the law!"

"I'm going as q-q-quick as I c-c-can. It's not my bl-bl-bloody fault that we got mixed up with the S-S-Sergeant back there, is it? Nothing this night but c-c-coffins and dead men, Guards and p-p-priests! And now here we are – going down into a bloody g-g-grave ourselves!" Waterford retorted, hurling the last piece of timber down the entrance tunnel to the vault, six feet below ground.

"Well, if we follow the plan from now on, dig the tunnel, get what we came here for and get the hell outta here, we can make up for lost time, I suppose." Derry grumbled as the men entered the pitch-black tomb.

According to Derry's detailed plans and considered calculations, the most northern corner of the vault extended underneath the graveyard wall by three feet; this point being four or five feet, at most, from the back corner of the bank. All they needed to do, Derry had calculated, was to drive a connecting tunnel the four feet between the vault and bank building. From this point they would break through the foundations and through the floor of the back room which the Branch Manager used as his office. Here – a red X marked the spot on Derry's map – Mr McCraven kept the bank's small strongbox which held the entire cash takings. Once they had broken through to the office, it would only be a matter of minutes before the strongbox, full of yesterday's cash deposits, was removed – first back to the vault and then to the waiting van, where they would depart the scene of the crime without attracting any further attention. It was to be, as Derry had earlier proudly informed his accomplice, the "perfect bank hoist."

"Right!" Derry snapped, placing the lantern on a ledge. "Let's get to work. I'll do the first fifteen minutes digging, you do the next, and so on, till we break through. You make sure the earth I dig is pushed well back from the tunnel. And see to it the light doesn't go out."

While Derry hacked away at the brick wall, Waterford looked nervously about the dank vault. In the far corner lay a small pile of bones and some old rotten coffin-boards. Waterford shuddered and tightened his grip on his shovel. He couldn't help but notice that the place reeked with a very strong smell. Not decomposing bodies, surely? Apart from the few bones and coffin-timber, the vault was empty. He sniffed the damp air. It was as if someone was burning old socks. He had never smelt anything quite like it before. It was not a pleasant aroma, he thought, screwing his face in disgust. He decided not to dwell on the bothersome smell and concentrate instead on the job on hand.

"Begod!" he called to his digging partner, "You f-f-fair put the wind up me b-b-back there when you told the S-S-Sergeant we were off to do a 'job' at the b-b-bank!"

"No problem! I wasn't worried," Derry puffed as he hacked away the soft crumbling earth and pushed it behind him. "I know that old boy from way back – when I worked here building the bank, as I told you. He never recognised me. I figured it was a smart move to tell him we were going to do some sort of job at the bank. That way if he spotted us shifting tools and so forth, he would think we were at our 'rewiring' job, or whatever, and take no further notice of us. And so he won't, either. You have to admit, that's practically as good as police protection, while we get on with the job in peace." Derry laughed and wiped away drops of grimy sweat from his swarthy face with his bare forearm. He rested his shovel for a moment. "Cripes! This is hot work. Here! You take over for a bit."

"Righto." Waterford spat on his open palms, grasped his shovel and faced the growing hole in the wall. "You're a ch-ch-chancer, right enough," he humoured his boss. "Maybe getting mixed up in the d-d-dead b-b-body business back there was all for the best, after all."

"Maybe. Maybe. Though I hope that sacristan boyo didn't recognise me. I saw him giving me some queer looks while we chucked that corpse about back there in the church. He used to supply us with the hard stuff when we worked on the bank building site. And a right fine drop it was too, as I remember. Anyway, what matter?" he added cheerfully. "What if he does cop me? We'll be long gone and knocking back brandies on that mail-boat from Rosslare – rich men, the both of us – before your man – or anyone else, for that matter – discovers what's happened here."

Both men laughed heartily and Waterford continued to dig. "I think we could do with a t-t-tunnel support here." Waterford stood back from the gaping hole and rested on his shovel while Derry fitted the timber tunnel support into place. They stood back to admire their handiwork. "It doesn't look t-t-too safe. Are you s-s-sure this lot won't f-f-fall in while one of us is in there?" A fresh look of panic washed over Waterford's sweating features.

"Don't worry!" Derry said, confidently. "It'll hold up till we're well out of here. And I've got a little something in my bag to help cover our tracks. When we leave here there won't be too many clues left, that's for sure."

"Why's that?

"Because gelignite doesn't leave clues. "

Waterford laughed heartily and rubbed his hands together.

"But we better be outta here before the funeral starts! We don't want them slinging Dwyer down here on top of us while we're still at work. We've seen enough of that poor devil already tonight!"

As Waterford continued to hack away at the tunnel face, Derry once again drew out the operation plans from his hip pocket and peered at the crumpled parchment by the light of the storm lantern hanging on the wall of the vault. He was in no doubt this tunnel would bring them directly underneath the bank's foundations, as calculated, and after that, the taking of the strongbox would prove to be as easy as taking sweets from a baby. His blood quickened in his veins at the thought of it. It was such a daring, simple but brilliant plan and he had masterminded the whole plot. Filled with new vigour and determination, he grabbed his shovel.

"Here! Let me at that!" He pulled the sluggish Waterford back from the hole. "We'll be here till Christmas at the rate you're going."

Waterford shrugged and stepped back, happy to let his partner take the brunt of this back-breaking labour while he took a much-needed breather. While Derry attacked his work with the spirit of a man possessed, Waterford moved to the other side of the vault and stood by the ever-growing mound of earth and rubble coming from the tunnel entrance. His nose informed him that the stench, reeking now of yeast – yet strangely both repugnant and attractive – was still around and if anything, stronger, he figured, than before. What the devil was it? And where was it coming from? What if they were digging into some ancient graves and disturbing the sleep of the long-dead? His skin crawled at this thought. Filled with some of his partner's eagerness to be finished and away from this place, he grabbed his shovel and began to push back the diggings from the ever-growing hole in the vault wall.

As the work in the tomb continued in determined silence, the world outside brightened up considerably, with the rain easing off to a soft silvery drizzle. No one yet moved in the village street, with the exception of Mrs Flanagan, who had sleepily come to the front door of her shop. She anticipated a day of extra business – funerals always meant good business and the Yank's funeral was sure to generate more than usual. She yawned, pulled her shawl about her shoulders and looked up and down the deserted street, hoping to catch sight of Lucifer, her missing tomcat, or anything which could be used as stimulating shop gossip when the rest of the village came to pick up their morning papers, wads of plug-tobacco, strong cigarettes, Sloan's Liniment, tins of Andrew's Liver Salts, cough-lozenges or small unmarked bottles of a clear white liquid which Mrs Flanagan furtively fetched from a box well-hidden under the counter.

Chapter Ten

From the murky troubled well of fitful sleep in which he floundered, RV heard a voice coming from a place high above him, calling him back to wakefulness. Each time he reached up the funnel of sleep to focus on the voice, his subconscious urged him to ignore the nagging sound and tugged him deeper into the morass of all-forgetting unconsciousness. For a brief moment, the irritating sounds from above him faded. Then, at once, the voice telescoped down to sit on his left shoulder and pull him, slowly and forcibly, back to his hard cot in the small cell at the back of the station.

"Sergeant! Sergeant! Wake up! It's 8.50. Wake up!"

RV opened one eye and focused on the swimming form of Guard Behan bending over him, a chipped mug of tea clutched in his hand.

"Begod Sergeant! I thought I'd have to get the cold water to bring you to this morning. You were out for the count."

RV struggled stiffly to a sitting position and took the mug. He sipped his tea, grimaced and drew his tired frame up from the bunk-bed. "What time did you say it was? 8.50? You're fifty minutes late for duty, Guard. You're supposed to come on duty at eight o'clock sharp! Not eight-o-five or eight-twenty-five or eight-fifty." RV regarded Guard Behan with a frosty eye.

"Ah yes, Sergeant. I know that, but the landlady was late herself with the breakfast this morning. How was your own night?" Guard Behan angled for a change of subject.

"My night!" RV exclaimed, the previous night's events crowding back into his mind. "My night! You wouldn't believe it!" With the threads of sleep still tugging at his mind, he still wasn't sure if the whole thing wasn't but part of a fantastic dream. He stretched himself and went to his desk. From the drawer he took a key and going to the smoke-faced pendulum clock on the wall, he began to wind it with the unconscious ease of a man who had performed the task many, many times in the past.

As RV wound the clock, Guard Behan, growing increasingly wide-eyed and slack-jawed, listened intently to his account of last night's nocturnal adventures. "I don't believe it!" He shook his head in amazement. "You're telling me the Yank Dwyer came back in the middle of the night! I don't believe it!"

"True as you're standing there. He's back all right. I've seen him with my own eyes – lifted him out of the marsh and coffined him with my own hands. He's in the church next door as we speak. Look at the time! I'd better get a move on if I'm going to make it back in good time for the funeral service."

"So, that's why you look like you've been chasing ferrets through a forest of holly-bushes," Guard Behan remarked, a sly grin curling on his lips.

RV glanced at his crumpled, muddied uniform and gave a grunt of self-disgust. If there was one thing he hated more than any other, it was an untidy dishevelled uniform. Now, here he stood, looking like he had indeed spent the night in a forest of holly bushes, while Guard Behan looked spick and span. It was, RV felt, both irritating and embarrassing for him to be like this, especially in front of his subordinate.

Guard Behan was about to inquire if the Sergeant's night-watch on Tom Duignan had yielded any new leads, but decided it best, for the moment at least, not to mention it. Things, he reasoned, were bad enough. What his superior needed now was humouring. "It's no wonder you're tired out, Sergeant. Look what you've been through! You go on home and freshen up. I'll see to things here till you get back."

Nodding in tired agreement, RV picked up his still-wet cape and moved towards the door. "I'll do that. You see if you can raise Ballyglen on the phone and inform Sergeant Kelly at the station that Mr Dwyer's corpse arrived here OK. There's no need to bother him just at the moment with any details of the accident. I will be making a full report on the matter later on."

The station clock began to strike nine as RV stepped out the door into the swirling mist. Pushing his bicycle down the path and out on to the street, he felt some of the dull ache of tiredness wither away in the face of the tingling freshness of the morning air. He had an hour to get home, get washed and shaved, have breakfast, change into a clean uniform, get back to the station and then present himself at the funeral of Daniel Dwyer.

As he free-wheeled down the hill, he was filled with a comforting numbness at the sight of the smoke curling lazily skyward from the chimney of his cottage and the thought of Hannah busy inside preparing his breakfast. His stomach rumbled in anticipation. He had forgotten how hungry he was. He sighed, wishing he didn't have to go back to the village again this morning, wishing the funeral was over and wishing he could go directly to his bed and sleep for an age.

Going around to the rear of the house, he entered by the back-kitchen door to be greeted by the warm smells and sounds he knew so well. It seemed an age since he had left the house last evening. So much had occurred since then and he felt again the pangs of pain and weariness gnaw at his bones.

"Is that you, Rudy?" Hannah called from the bedroom.

"Who else?" he said, grumpily. "I'm late – due to Guard Behan not coming on duty on time. You wouldn't believe the night I've put down! I've barely got time to get ready and get back for the funeral service." RV slumped in his armchair.

"You poor dear! Your breakfast is in the oven and I've pressed and laid out your best uniform. I knew you would need it. You have to look your best today." Hannah came hurriedly into the kitchen dressed in the hat, gloves and frock she usually wore going to church on summer Sundays. "I'll be going on up to the village. I have a few things to get done before I go to the church. I want to get there early. I'll see you there – or back here afterwards. Bye, dear!"

Before he could respond, Hannah was gone, leaving a faint trace of perfume in her wake. This was not at all like Hannah, getting all dolled up like this for a funeral. RV sighed. He hadn't even had a chance to relate his night's adventures to her. "Women!" he sighed again. "I'll never understand them if I live to be a hundred."

As he filled his shaving basin with boiling water from the iron kettle singing on the range, he was tempted to put on a Beethoven record to raise his spirits, but decided against it. It would, he felt, be somewhat insensitive to regale himself with music, considering the body of Mr Dwyer lay not half a mile away. And after all, what would the locals coming into the village for the funeral think, if they heard music booming from the house. He and the Master would have to wait until this affair was all over.

Washed and shaved, he began to feel more alert, though the cracked mirror could not disguise the two red-rimmed eyes set in hollow cheeks staring back at him. It was then he remembered the missing Tombs O'Flaherty. "Good God!" he thought. "He completely slipped my mind!" In the excitement of telling Guard Behan the details of the other events, he had forgotten entirely about poor Tombs, still lost somewhere out in the marsh. He had better put a spurt on himself, get back to the station and get things organised. Guard Behan could begin an immediate search, while he, in his official capacity as Sergeant of Ballykeogh, would attend the funeral service. Now that it was daylight, perhaps some clue as to the whereabouts of the unfortunate Tombs would be found which would lead to his quick and safe return.

Sitting down to his breakfast of porridge and salty rashers, RV could take no relish in the repast. Try as he could, he could not shake off the disturbing vision of an injured Tombs O'Flaherty still wandering, or lying, deep in the marshland adjacent to the site of the accident. Pushing the half-eaten meal from him, he got up from the table and quickly donned the uniform that lay, crisp, fresh and neatly pressed, across a chair next to the glowing range.

As he left the house, he decided to leave the bicycle and walk up to the station. The way he was feeling right now, the old Armstrong would only slow him down and anyway, the walk might help put a bit of life back into his weary bones. At the front gate, he was hailed by two men on old Raleigh bicycles, straining on pedals against the push of the hill.

"Good morning to you, Sergeant! It's a grand sort of day for a funeral," one of the men called.

RV recognised the men as being from below in the valley, now no doubt on their way to the funeral Mass. Returning their salute, he could almost feel their sense of excitement and anticipation. Ballykeogh was a place where, as it was said, "Nothing ever happens except what you hear happens". There was little activity to break the humdrum monotony of everyday life. Events such as a funeral or wake gave most of the menfolk the excuse to stop work and come into the village to spend the day in one of the two public houses "drinking the health" of the deceased. That they possibly had never known, or cared little for, the departed was of no importance. Tradition dictated the importance of everybody in the locality attending every funeral. The important thing was to be *seen* to be there. As the men pushed on up the hill ahead of him, he could hear their gay banter and full-throated laughter ripple back on the breeze.

"Anyone would think it was a wedding they were off to," RV muttered as he trudged against the fall of ground. Their easy laughter stung him like a nettle and the sour-apple of envy and irritability rose in his craw. Why could these people not see life for the serious business it really was? Why was life not as simple for him as it was for them? Why did the weight of the world have to rest on his shoulders while these men seemed to greet each day without a trouble or care in the world? It just did not seem fair or just. At times like these, he felt that some unknown power had decreed that he – RV Mulrooney – should carry that cross of responsibility in order to atone in some way for the sins of the whole community. Even Father O'Malley did not have to endure such a heavy burden. "Well," RV squared his shoulders, "This is no time for soul-searching. Work to be done – duty to be carried out!"

Quickening his step, he followed the two men up to the village hidden in the clouds.

As he stepped through the station doorway, the combined aroma of carbolic soap, mothballs and shoe-polish assailed RV's nostrils. Standing by the table inside the door, which also served as an enquiry desk, was the diminutive figure of old Ned Finnegan, turned out in the one and only suit of clothes he ever possessed, purchased in 1940 for his own wedding and now several sizes too large for him. Ned and Guard Behan were engaged in a loud, animated discussion. As RV moved closer to the wiry seventy-year-old, the smell of strong whiskey was added to the other aromas.

"Ah! Sergeant. You're just in time," Guard Behan called out. "Mr Finnegan here wants a word with you. He won't deal with anyone but yourself, so he says."

"Well now, Mr Finnegan," RV declared, moving behind his desk. "We don't see too much of you about the village these days. What can I do for you?"

"Don't go out much – not since the missus passed on. I was wondering . . . " Ned tried not to look the Sergeant in the eye. "I was wondering if – ah – if you had found that missing donkey of mine yet?"

"What donkey was that, Mr Finnegan."

"What donkey? My donkey! The donkey that went missing on me, that's what donkey! I reported it at the time."

"I don't recall any report of such a beast going missing!" RV noticed that Ned sported several shaving nicks from which drops of blood had dripped on to his attached white shirt-collar and his black egg-stained tie.

"It's gone all right. Stolen, more than likely. It wouldn't surprise me if Black Jack Dwyer rustled him and sold him off to pay a gambling debt."

"Please don't make unsubstantiated accusations, Mr

Finnegan. When did you report the alleged theft of your donkey?" RV opened the station report book and began to thumb through the pages.

"When did I report it? Let's see now. Yes, I remember! Back in nineteen and fifty-two it was. I came to this very station to make my complaint. 'Twas yourself that took my statement. Now I'm wonderin' if you had any news on his whereabouts – and as I was passing I – "

"Nineteen-fifty-two!" RV slammed the report-book shut with a bang. "Mr Finnegan, what is it you want from us, exactly?"

"Well, I'll tell you, Sergeant. I'm wanting the loan of a shotgun, is what I want. Only for a few hours. I'll have it back to you safe and sound by mid-day latest."

"You want us – to give you – a gun?" Guard Behan laughed loudly at Ned's outrageous request. "You're joking, of course! It looks to me as if you're already in possession of a dangerous weapon in that blackthorn walking stick you're carrying. If we gave firearms to every Tom, Dick, Harry or Ned Finnegan who walked in here and casually asked for one, what kind of town would we have at all? On top of which, you've no licence to either own, carry or discharge such a weapon."

"Guard Behan is absolutely correct, Mr Finnegan," RV added. "Your request for a gun to be released to you is totally out of the question."

"I'm not about to rob the bloody bank wi' it!" Ned's voiced piped high in obvious irritation regarding – in his opinion – his not unreasonable request. "I'm in the Guard of Honour for the Yank's funeral. I need a gun to let off a volley or two over the grave of our old comrade. Jacko Flannery and Willie Sweeney have a shotgun and a .22 rifle between them. I have no gun. How can I be part of a firing squad if I don't have a shooting piece? Will you tell me

172

that?" Ned's voice cracked with the urgency of his dilemma.

"I hope Jacko and Willie are in possession of current gun licences?" Guard Behan licked his pencil-top and wrote something in his notebook. Having paused for a moment to analyse the situation, RV came to a possible solution. "Now look, Mr Finnegan. I appreciate your problem, but we have only one pistol here in the station and we're bound under law to retain that firearm under supervision of a member of the Force at all times. So, I'm afraid I'm going to have to refuse your request. However," he lowered his voice as if to impart a matter of some importance to old Ned. "Could I suggest something to you?"

"What's that?"

"If my memory serves me, you are the oldest member of the firing squad, are you not?"

"Aye, I am that."

"Well then! Could I suggest to you, that being the senior man, and therefore the most high-ranking member of the squad, in effect, you're the Captain of the Brigade. You should be the one to give the order to fire the volleys. And you won't need a firearm for that!"

Ned thought for a moment, then pulled himself as erect as his years would allow and beamed a gap-toothed smile. "Begod, that's a fact, Sergeant. I am the senior man, right enough, and I'm the man to give the order! I'm grateful to you, Sergeant. I'm sorry I troubled ye. If you hear any trace of that old donkey of mine, you'll let me know, won't you? Good day to ye both." With that, Ned turned on his heel and left the office, a spring in his step and a roguish gleam in his eye.

"Can you beat the spunk of the old goat!" Guard Behan looked after the aged soldier, hurrying off to attempt to recapture some of the surge and glory of his raging youth. "Can you beat him! He comes in here bold as brass and asks us to hand him over a gun and ammo. And, you know, from what I hear, there was never any love lost between those old-boys and the Yank." He chuckled, but was silenced by a withering look from his superior.

"Did you call Sergeant Kelly in Ballyglen?" RV enquired.

"No, Sergeant. Sorry, Sergeant. Couldn't get to the phone. I can't raise Miss Clara at all this morning. I've tried a dozen times, but not a budge out of her. She must be having one of her turns. She's really not fit to run that post office – her licence should be revoked. Anyway, when she wouldn't answer, I wrote a note and gave it to the van man from Ballyglen who delivers the papers to Mrs Flanagan. He said he would have it to Sergeant Kelly within the hour or so."

"Clara will break our hearts," groaned RV. "I'll have to write to head-office. Make a note would you, Guard. *Something must be done re: the intolerable communications situation currently hampering normal police duties in Ballykeogh. Urgently request direct phone line to station-house.*' Got that?"

"Got it."

"Good. Now pay attention, Guard. I have a most important assignment for you." RV put on his most authoritative voice and face.

Guard Behan's spirit rose, only to fall as quickly as RV revealed the facts surrounding the disappearance of Tombs O'Flaherty following his unfortunate crash at the foot of the hill. Guard Behan was to proceed immediately to the scene of the accident and thoroughly comb the entire area for any clues that would lead to the missing undertaker.

"He may well be suffering from severe concussion – prostrate with exposure or even worse!" RV added. "So be

174

off with you. And if you come across anything, report back to me at once. I'll be in the church."

As Guard Behan set off, silently and sullenly, on his mission, RV gazed through the window on to the street outside. It was almost ten, time for Mass, yet apart from Mrs Flanagan and Willie Sweeney heading in the direction of the church gate, the street was deserted. Usually, with less than ten minutes to go before Mass starting, small groups of men would congregate by the church gate and across the street to discuss the weather, cattle, sheep, crops, football and politics – these discussions often continuing inside the church – while the women, heads covered and pious-faced, went inside to take up their usual pew-seats. Today, however, with the funeral service for Daniel Dwyer about to commence, not a soul was to be seen.

"Strange." RV's gaze swept up and down the bleak empty street. "Very strange indeed."

Chapter Eleven

Only a few more feet and they were through. Only a few more feet of sodden, black clay hacked away from the tunnel-face and pushed to the opposite side of the vault, and they were through. Derry's estimated four feet of tunnelling between the vault and underneath the bank was grossly miscalculated. They had burrowed almost six feet of tunnel and still they weren't there. Another foot at most, Derry now calculated, and they would be under the floorboards of the bank Manager's office at the rear of the building. Their earlier involvement with the Sergeant and the corpse and now the strain of four brutal hours of digging in the vault's oven-hot and stifling atmosphere was taking its toll. Both men were exhausted. Their faces, drained grim and sweat-streaked, showed utter fatigue. But they had to press on. Nothing must stop them now. After all the waiting and planning, another foot of earth pushed away from this hole and the Prize was theirs for the taking.

It was Derry's shift inside the tunnel. For each bucket of earth shovelled back into the vault, it seemed to him a bucket of his sweat also went with it. But still he attacked the black unforgiving earthen wall like a man possessed. The fifteen minute shifts were now reduced to five minutes per man. Any longer working in the thin, stale air inside the tunnel drove them back to gulp deep lungfuls of the relatively cooler, healthier air inside the vault. Waterford crouched by the opening, taking each bucket of earth passed back to him by Derry, and emptying them on the ever-growing mound of soil by the opposite wall. One by one, the tunnel supports were carefully put in place and the work slowly progressed towards completion.

"I can't see w-w-why," Waterford had remarked to his partner, after an hour of laborious digging, "we couldn't have just b-b-burst down the bloody d-d-door of the bank and walked off with the m-m-money – instead of h-h-having to go through this la-la-lark!"

"Look," Derry growled. "Why can't you get it into your thick skull that we're professionals! We're not a couple of milk-behind-the-ears corner boys out to snatch pensioners' handbags, you know! We're professionals! We have professional criminal standards to maintain and as such we must conduct the operation in some style. That's the professional way. And," he tapped his inside pocket with two grubby fingers. "I didn't spend night after night working on my plan for nothing. It's a bloody good plan – a foolproof plan – and it's going to work! The plan says we tunnel and so we tunnel! This time, crime will pay. Now get on with the digging."

"It had b-b-b-better be worth it, th-th-that's all I can say!" Waterford grimaced at the menacing black hole before resuming the dig.

With only inches now to go, Derry felt new energy course through his blood. He could almost taste and smell the money with every bucket of earth.

"How's it g-g-going in there?" Waterford called, to be answered by Derry's legs and rear-end waggling through the tunnel opening with an urgency which gave him his answer. Their back-breaking labour was about to come to a welcome end.

"We're there!" Derry hissed excitedly, his eyes glowing like burning coals in a patch of streaky black ash. "We're there! Smack under the bank, as per plan. But I hear noise of movement up there. It must be that cursed bank manager, come in early. We're just going to have to sit it out till he's finished whatever he's at and gone."

"The bl-bl-bloody b-b-bank manager? Christ! Wh-wh-what's he doing there? It's only n-n-nine thirty or so and he's not due t-t-till eleven!"

"I don't know what the blazes he's doing there, do I? But he is. And while he's up there, we sit tight until the all clear. Then we push through the floorboards and collect!"

"If there's a-a-anything st-st-still there to collect. What if your man w-w-walks off with the st-st-strongbox?" a note of panic tainted Waterford's voice.

Derry jerked his head sideways and, with eyes darting tongues of flame, gave his pessimistic partner a withering look. "That's a chance," he spoke in low measured tones, "we're going to have to take, isn't it! Now keep your voice down – and listen."

The two men sat on the mound of tunnelled earth and drank deeply from the flask of coffee which they passed to each other. The silence of the tomb once again quickly settled on the vault as its desecrators sipped coffee, smoked and strained to hear the muffled sounds filtering down the tunnel from the bank manager's back-room office.

Not ten feet from the vault in which Derry and Waterford toiled, Mr Cornelius McCraven, completely unaware of the existence of either the men, the tunnel or indeed the vault, sat at his office desk wearing the look of a man who bore in his breast some dark, terrible secret. Having spent a restless night, he had risen early and come to the bank where, he knew, he would have time to himself to think and make plans. Every few minutes or so he glanced at his watch – it now showed 9.23 – rose from his desk, walked across the room to gaze out the window then walk back to his desk and sit down. He pushed aside the large accounts ledger he had studied since arriving and lit another cigarette, his sixth so far this morning. He began to toy nervously with the golf trophy he had won in Ballyglen some years before, while throwing expectant glances at the side-door of the small back room he used as his private office. Cornelius McCraven showed all the outward signs of a man under considerable strain and stress. He had been in this condition since exactly three-ten p.m. yesterday afternoon when he had removed the sum of £200 from the bank's strongbox, in order to pay his gambling debt to Black Jack Dwyer. Since then, his mind could find no peace as he anguished as to how to find a solution to the predicament he now found himself in. From the moment the smirking Black Jack had departed his office the previous day, McCraven realised he had, once again, put his banking career in jeopardy. For this was not the first time Mr McCraven had recourse to unofficially removing moneys from the bank's coffers in order to pay gambling debts. In the past, he had always managed to wriggle out of such sticky situations by quickly repaying the relatively small sums owed, thus keeping the books balanced. This time, the sum of money owed was beyond his reach. This time, as he well knew, it would take more than just a spot of quick thinking or smooth talking to his superiors to manoeuvre out of the tight corner he found himself in. Unless he could right this sticky situation, without having to admit the matter to his unsympathetic superiors, his days in banking, he well knew, were numbered.

But what Lady Luck took away with one hand, she gave back with the other. The possible answer to his dilemma had presented itself in his office only a few moments after Black Jack Dwyer, with £200 in used notes stuffed in his inside pocket, had departed. The moment Hannah Mulrooney stepped lightly into his office, McCraven felt she had been indeed sent to his aid by the gods – in this, his greatest hour of need. As they talked about the weather and the coming funeral, McCraven's mind struggled to catch an idea which raced in his brain. He knew – it was, after all, his business to know – that Hannah Mulrooney's deposit account held in the region of £150, and if she could be persuaded to draw from the account and lend him that sum, his problem was as good as solved. In this way, he could put the £150 against the missing sum, then make up the deficit in some other way. It was not, he knew, an ideal plan but at the moment it was the only workable plan which came to mind.

Taking the bull by the horns, McCraven had blurted out his predicament to a dumbstruck Hannah. He told her of how, in the course of a little business deal, he had been cheated out of a large sum of money by that blackguard, Jack Dwyer, and of how Jack had threatened him with physical violence if he did not immediately hand over the cash. As he did not have that kind of money on his person, he explained to Hannah, he had no option but to remove a large sum from official finances. It was, he admitted, a terrible, unthinkable, totally unprofessional thing to do, but what other choice did he have? If this transgression should be revealed he would lose his job, or worse still, be convicted and sent for a term in jail. What should he, or his family, do? There was however, he added, a possible solution. Inviting Hannah to sit, McCraven removed a bottle of sherry and a glass from his desk drawer, filled the glass to near-overflowing and handed it to her. Sitting next to her on the tattered horsehair-filled sofa, he asked if he could suggest to her a way in which she could help solve his small problem. He then asked if she could perhaps see her way clear to lending him the sum of two hundred pounds. In the same breath, he confessed to her his deep and personal feelings for her. For this long time now, he gushed, he had harboured for her a love – nay, a passion – and now that they were finally alone he had to unburden himself of these heart-felt emotions. Hannah, completely taken aback by both McCraven's financial difficulty and by his declarations of love for her, could only mumble weakly that she would have to think the whole thing over. Flushed from her sherry and McCraven's outpourings, Hannah quickly left the office, promising she would return and let him have an answer first thing in the morning.

Now, as McCraven waited patiently for Hannah's arrival, he hoped he had judged her correctly. If not, then he really was in a rare stew. Over the many years she had come to the bank as a customer, he had noticed her shy smiles and blushes in response to the honeyed balm of his flattering, and sometimes extremely flirtatious, banter. Now he was about to find out if she felt for him as he figured she did. He cracked the golf trophy down hard on the desk. How could he have been so stupid as to have allowed himself to be taken for a ride by that drunken poker-playing oaf, Black Jack Dwyer? He knew Dwyer to be a ruthless card shark, yet he sat down to play poker with him knowing his own chances of coming out on top were slim to nil. What in God's name had gotten into him the other night? What on earth was he trying to prove? Why didn't he stay in the bar, enjoy his drinks and flirt with McGarrigan's dowdy wife? He shook his head and continued to thump the table. He had been in sticky situations before but this one was serious. Two hundred pounds! Two whole months' salary! A huge sum. A sum he did not personally possess and now the bank accounts were down by the same sum. Because of all this, he had been forced into saying things to Hannah Mulrooney, things which he knew only too well would later lead to further complications. But what was he to do? What alternatives did he have? He would have promised Hannah a one-way ticket to Tír Na nÓg if it would help extricate him from this present pickle. He wished, though, that he hadn't gone overboard with the love and passion bit. Mild flirting with her in the course of normal bank business was one thing – he did it with all the women who came into the bank – but now, in order to ward off this impending disaster, he had been forced to take this harmless flirting a stage further. Hannah was an attractive woman, he had to admit that. He had had tea out with her on a few occasions and even drinks on a couple of evenings earlier that summer, but as for getting involved with her in a serious way! He shook his head. A harmless tryst with no further complications, yes, he would not pass up that opportunity, but with a wife and six children in Ballyglen, McCraven knew only too well what the consequences of a more serious long-term involvement might be. Still, he had taken the first steps down this road and he would have to walk that road to whatever end if he was to solve his present financial problems. If pouring on the honeyed charm was necessary to get Hannah to open her arms, and especially her bank account, to him, then he would do what had to be done to melt her unsuspecting heart.

A footfall outside and two soft knocks on the door

brought him to his feet. Hannah! McCraven drew a deep breath and steadied himself. So much depended on what might transpire between them in the next few minutes. Crossing the room, he opened the door to receive his expected visitor. "Hannah! My dear Hannah. Come in, come in! I was beginning to think you weren't going to make it. But you did – you did! Here, let me take your coat," McCraven gushed, taking Hannah in his arms and kissing her full on the lips.

Flushed and embarrassed, Hannah drew away and glanced nervously at the window. "I really shouldn't be here." She patted her hair into place, while McCraven slipped the catch-lock on the side-door. "Rudy," she continued, "my husband, is finishing his breakfast below at home and he's bound to be along any minute now, so I really can't stay long. We only have a few moments."

"My dear sweet Hannah!" McCraven bared a set of gleaming, though false, teeth. "We can have all the time in the world, if only you will agree to leave this place and come away with me. You know how I feel for you. Did you think about what I asked you yesterday?'

"Yes, I have, Mr McCraven – but it's not an easy thing to – "

"Cornelius – Hannah, please call me Cornelius. Hannah, if you have in your heart any feeling for me at all – and I know you have – you will have considered what I asked of you yesterday and give me – er – loan me – the money in your account. It would only be for a short time. Once I set the bank records straight, we can go away from here and be together, as we were meant to be!" McCraven took her in his arms and sprayed her neck and face with cheap words and hot kisses. "I desire but two things, my sweet, to sort out this unfortunate and unplanned mess and to take you away from this place. We can escape from it all – you from the Sergeant, me from this dead-end job in this hole of a bank, and make a fresh start in the city. You were meant for better things, Hannah. You can be something – somebody – with me, darling, but not here – not in Ballykeogh. Say you'll help me, Hannah! Say you'll come away with me!"

"Come away with you?" Hannah's pulse raced and her blush deepened. "Leave Rudy? And Ballykeogh? Oh, Mr McCraven – I mean Cornelius, do you really mean it? Oh, yes! Yes! I mean no. No! I couldn't. Oh Cornelius, I don't know what I mean. I don't know what to say. This is all too sudden!"

McCraven took her hand in his and smiled his most syrupy of smiles. "I realise that all this is indeed a bit sudden. But you must have known of my feelings for you over the past while? I know that you feel the same – don't you? I've dreamed so often over the past months of us both leaving and starting a new life – together. Say you'll make my dreams come true, Hannah? We can do it – but first I have to sort out this little irregularity here at the bank. That is why, my dearest Hannah, I am desperate for your help. Say you will, Hannah? Otherwise, I'm sunk!" His eyes implored hers as he raised her hand to his lips and kissed her trembling fingers.

"Oh, Cornelius, I feel my head's in a spin! I like you dearly – yes! You're a very attractive man – but I'm married – to Rudy! He's not the answer to my dreams, God knows, but he's a good man, an honest man. I can't just up and leave him! What we have isn't everything I wanted from life but I can't just throw all our years together to the wind and go away with you! This is happening too quickly! I think . . . I think . . . Oh, I don't know what I think."

"It's sudden for both of us, I know. We can talk about going away together later – when you've given it a bit more thought. But please say you will loan me the money,

Hannah? Please say you will?" Cornelius grasped both her hands in his and fervently kissed them.

"Of course you can have the few pounds in my account, Cornelius. But you said you needed two hundred pounds and I have only one hundred and fifty or so."

McCraven stood deep in thought for some time, his forefinger stroking his pencil-line moustache. Hannah looked at his long eyelashes and she sighed an inaudible sigh, thinking how like Clark Gable he looked at this moment and not at all like her dour husband, Rudolph Valentino. "You could," he heard himself say, "ask the Sergeant – your husband – for the extra fifty pounds. You could say you needed it to buy clothes, or materials for the house or suchlike. He wouldn't refuse you and you could tell him it would only be for a few days. If you have an ounce of feeling for me, Hannah, I beg you, do this for me."

"This is all so sudden – so confusing!" Hannah said, glancing furtively towards the door. "But I'll do it for you. Now I really must be going, Cornelius. I have to get to the church before Rudy gets to the station. I don't want him to see me here."

McCraven could hardly contain himself. He could never quite understand, no more than other men who knew him, what this fatal attraction was that he held for most women, young or old. Whatever it was, he had it and this morning it was paying off handsomely. "Thank you, my darling Hannah! I knew you wouldn't let me down. Everything is going to be wonderful for us – once this business is sorted out, I just know it will!" He pulled her to him and kissed her full on the mouth. Hannah felt herself melt to his embrace and gave herself fully to the moment. Lips to lips, heartbeat to heartbeat, body to body, they moved as one to a silent rhythm until they sank down together on the sofa.

In the tomb at the other side of the bank wall, Derry and his accomplice waited patiently to recommence their excavations. They tried to make some sense of the sounds filtering down the tunnel from the room overhead. They heard the sound of voices. One male – the manager? And another, lighter in tone – another man? A lady customer, perhaps? There was then a short silence, followed by the sound of shuffling and thumping – as if furniture was being re-arranged in the room – followed by sighing, moaning sounds and then, once again, silence.

"What's g-g-going on up there?" Waterford stared down the black tunnel.

"I don't know – but if we don't get our hands on what we came for and get out of here soon, our goose is cooked!"

Time was now of the essence, both men realised. Every second counted, if they were to reach their goal, tidy things up back in the vault and make good their escape before people began to arrive in the town for the funeral.

Chapter Twelve

In the ten years she had worked as housekeeper to Father O'Malley, Mrs Scully had only known him to be late for breakfast on one or two occasions. Each morning, at seven-thirty sharp, Mrs Scully arrived at the priest's house to begin her normal housekeeping duties, the first being the preparation of breakfast for Father O'Malley and, for these last five years or so, his sacristan, RN Mulrooney. While RN munched his way through a large plate of egg, sausage, black and white pudding and fried bread, breakfast for Father O'Malley consisted of a mug of sweet milky tea – as he waited until he had said his daily Mass before tucking into a similar repast. Usually, he was up before eight o'clock, at the latest, as week-day Masses commenced at eight-thirty sharp.

On this particular morning, Mrs Scully cocked an ear for any sound of life coming from upstairs. None came. She tut-tutted and wagged her head. "Here it is – almost eight-thirty and not a stir out of him. Or Mr Mulrooney!" She had sensed all was not normal even before she put her head through the door this morning. On the way up the drive, she was shocked to see the lawn-border of flower-beds trampled flat, with tyre tracks running through the Red-Hot Pokers, Carnations, Dahlias, Flock and Roses, which she had so carefully tended. A stone flower-pot by the garden seat was knocked over and the Father's Morris Minor, its driver's door ajar, had mounted the front door-step.

Flicking her cleaning rag at imaginary cobwebs and patches of nonexistent dust, Mrs Scully continued tut-tutting to herself, while considering rousing them both if they did not show in the next few minutes. She was about to hail them from the bottom of the stairs when a bleary-eyed RN shuffled from the upstairs bathroom, down the stairs and into the kitchen, where he took all his meals, and slumped on a chair by the kitchen table.

"So! Ye decided to rise!" Mrs Scully said curtly, with more than a hint of sarcasm in her voice and replaced the kettle on the range.

RN rolled one red eye in her direction, looked as if he was about to reply but decided to remain silent. He opted instead to stare in deep concentration at the shining cutlery laid out before him on the table.

"Is himself up?" Mrs Scully enquired, swilling out the brown crock tea-pot with boiling water and dumping the old tea-leaves into a bucket by the range. "He has a funeral Mass to say this morning at ten. Has he – have ye – forgotten that?"

"Don't worry, Mrs Scully." RN's first words of the day sounded like jack-boots crunching on thick ice. He cleared his throat. "We haven't forgotten. It's just that we both had a long hard night. 'Twas past four this morning when we both got to our beds." RN yawned, lit his first cigarette of the day, inhaled deeply and began to relate the night's events to Mrs Scully who tut-tutted and crossed herself and listened, her eyes growing large in amazement and astonishment, as the strange tale of Daniel the Yank Dwyer's home-coming slowly unfolded. "And that's why we didn't get to bed till cock-crow." RN stirred three spoons of sugar into a large mug of tea.

"God rest the poor man's soul! What a way to start his time in eternity." Her eyes rolled towards the ceiling and she crossed herself again. "And the both of you having to go through all that! And in the dead of night! Lord bless us!"

A door opening and closing on the landing, footsteps and a series of loud hacking coughs, informed Mrs Scully that Father O'Malley was at last up and about. Picking up the already prepared silver breakfast-tray, she went into the dining room to attend to the priest, leaving RN to fend for himself in the kitchen.

A few minutes later she returned and said glumly, "Tut-tut! The poor man is not looking himself at all! He looks," she lowered her voice and spoke out of the corner of her mouth, "like a man who's had a few too many last night – as well as having to cope with poor Mr Dwyer."

"Very possible, Mrs Scully, very possible. It was not an easy night for any of us, you know."

RN had just eaten his fourth slice of deep-fried black pudding when Father O'Malley came slowly into the room. He looks dreadful, right enough, RN thought.

Father O'Malley's sunken eyes strained to remain open under the pressure of his puffed blood-shot lids and sagging eyebrows, while his fleshy jowls had taken on the colour and texture of flaky, pasty dough. He stood for a long time, as if trying to recall what it was he had come into the kitchen to say. "Ah, RN," he said at last. "I'm off down to the church. I want to make sure Piper Hanratty and a couple of McGarrigan's men turn up to dig the grave. I'm sure Mr Dwyer's nephew, Jack, will be along soon, to see that things are in order. Follow me down, will you, as soon as you finish your breakfast."

189

"Rightho, Father. By the way, when Jack Dwyer arrives, I think it might be best not to trouble him with the full facts as to how his uncle arrived in the church several hours early. Though I'm sure the whole village knows about it by now!"

"Not tell Jack? Oh . . . yes, I suppose you have a point. No need to cause the bereaved any more unnecessary suffering. Try and be as quick as you can, will you. We have a busy morning ahead of us."

Mrs Scully handed Father O'Malley his black coat and hat and proceeded to follow him down the hall to the door, brushing him down while complaining loudly about her trampled flower gardens.

"The man looks like he should be in bed. We don't want another funeral in the village before we have to," she said as she bustled back into the kitchen to begin to wage war once again on invisible spider-webs and unseen layers of dust.

"Don't worry, Mrs Scully. He'll survive." RN rose from the table and prepared to follow Father O'Malley to the church.

"Mr Mulrooney!" Mrs Scully called after him. "Is this your suit lying here on the chair?" She held a crumpled suit-jacket at arm's length.

"Not mine," RN called back. "It belongs to the corpse. We took it off him in the church before we coffined him."

Mrs Scully dropped the jacket as if shaking off the Devil's handshake and took two steps backwards. "God between us and all harm!" she exclaimed, picking up a pair of tongs from the range top. "Clothes from a corpse! I'm not having a dead man's clothes in this hallowed house." Picking up the coat with the tongs she stood for a long while and considered what she should do with the garment. Then she moved to the range, opened the fire-door, stuffed the coat and pants inside, crossed herself again and slammed shut the door. She was soon back at her endless dusting and sweeping and paid no attention to the spitting and crackling as the flames licked around, and finally devoured, the fat envelope containing a neatly-folded wad of used five, ten and twenty pound notes, tucked inside the breast-pocket of Black Jack Dwyer's moth-eaten blue serge suit-jacket.

Winter's coming was no longer a promise. It had arrived. In hushed conversation the swishing hedges, leafless trees and telephone wires knew it. So too did the wool-packs of rolling cloud, gathering to slide down the hillside towards the defenceless village. Since dawn, restless sea breezes had swept the streets clean of the silver mist which had draped Ballykeogh since dusk the previous evening. In an hour or two, the whole village would once again be lost inside the clouds, while the real world rolled back down the hill to Ballyglen. RN hunched his shoulders against the sharp, damp chill and dug his hands deeper into his pants pocket. Though weary from last night's activities, his spirits brightened at the thought of the day ahead. This was just the kind of day, he knew, when the men, and some of the women, of the townland would be even more determined than usual to seek relief in the sunshine, light and liberty distilled in the poteen he would supply to all. His mind conjured up the sight of row after row of lemonade bottles – brimful with a fresh batch of his best brew – lined up below in the vault; their contents ready and waiting to find a way into the blood to fire the souls of those who would sample it that day.

What with the extra business to be picked up because of the funeral, RN knew he was bound to have a good day, sales-wise. He was bound too, he felt, to have a good day socially. It wasn't every day, after all, that a man like the Yank Dwyer came home to be buried. As the full potential of the coming day gripped his imagination, his mood improved, his step brightened and he began to hum a tuneless melody.

This mood was dispelled with the same suddenness, however, on seeing Father O'Malley, with Micho Farrell trailing behind, heading up the path in his direction. As he drew close, RN could see the priest was obviously in a state of agitated excitement, not to mention bad-tempered, as he still battled with a monumental poteen-induced hangover from his sojourn at the Golden Gloves the previous evening.

"He's let me down! He's let me down badly! That so-and-so rascal, Piper Hanratty promised me faithfully he would be here this morning to dig Mr Dwyer's grave and here it is, long past nine o'clock and not a sign of the man. Is there anyone left in this place who will live up to their word? Is there anybody a person can trust at all these days?" Father O'Malley panted. His face had taken on a bluish tinge in the sting of the morning. "RN," he added. "There's only one thing for it. You will have to dig the grave. I met Micho outside McGarrigan's Bar and he's agreed to help with the dig, haven't you, Micho?"

Micho Farrell stared sullenly at the ground and muttered under his breath.

"By the way, where is Mr O'Flaherty? I see his hearse parked over in front of his house. Was he with you in the church last night? I'm afraid things are still a bit hazy for me this morning." Father O'Malley rubbed his eyes and temples.

RN could see that the full weight of last night's events in the church were only just beginning to dawn on the priest. "I'm afraid he wasn't with us, Father. There's not a trace of the man at all. Not since the Sergeant found the hearse crashed at the bottom of the hill. I think the Sergeant has a search party out looking for him."

"Is that a fact! The poor man, I hope he hasn't gone and injured himself. It's a mystery, sure enough, but the Sergeant will sort it out, I've no doubt. Now the thing is, RN," he pushed aside the matter of the missing Tombs O'Flaherty, "in an hour or so, the place will be packed with all kinds of important people up from Ballyglen following the funeral cortege. It would be very bad form entirely if things here aren't organised. So, you and Micho get on with digging of the grave while I run down to McGarrigan's for – em – a few more men to help you out here."

"Well, Micho, are you ready for a bit of digging?" RN enquired.

The press-ganged Micho, his face as long and taciturn as an Easter Island statue, made no answer and continued to stare at his boots.

Father O'Malley stepped close to RN and whispered, "Are there many gone in to the church?"

"Nobody other than your usual clients. I haven't seen any Ballyglen faces pass in yet, at any rate."

"Unusual! Yes indeed! That's most unusual! They should be arriving by now. And by the way, I tried to phone the Parish Priest in Ballyglen to let him know that Mr Dwyer's corpse arrived here safely and everything is ready but Miss Clara can't be raised at all this morning. Still, I suppose they're on their way up here by now. Well, I better go and prepare myself for Mass. I won't know until the other priests arrive from Ballyglen whether the Mass will be Requiem or Low. I hope they turn up soon. I'll leave you men to the work. I've no doubt but there will be a drop or two in it for the both of you when the grave's dug.

See you in the church." Father O'Malley turned and headed for the village street and McGarrigan's Bar & Lounge.

RN looked at Micho, who returned his glance with dull empty eyes. RN waited for a comment from his workmate. None was forthcoming.

"Right!" RN spat into his hands. "Let's find a couple of shovels and get to work on the grave. The sooner we start, the sooner we finish."

Chapter Thirteen

Stirring a third spoon of sugar into his cup of tea, RV gazed absentmindedly out the station side-window. From this vantage point, he had a full view of the empty street leading to the church gate and the churchyard itself. A light drizzle drifted like confetti before a soft breeze, to glisten on flagged pavements, stone roofs and half-hidden spider-webs. A stray dog ambled towards the church gate, sniffed, cocked a leg and urinated on the wheel of a bicycle parked by the church wall before wandering away towards Flynn's butcher's shop. RV shifted his gaze to settle on two figures wielding shovels beyond the graveyard wall. He watched with growing interest his brother RN, along with Micho Farrell, commence work on a grave, no more than a stone's throw over the wall separating the graveyard from the station.

"Now, there's one for the books! The little brother actually working!" RV had rarely witnessed RN engaged in any form of manual labour – certainly not since he arrived in the village over five years ago. Though even now, as RV observed the activity across the graveyard wall, he could see that it was Micho Farrell who was doing the dig while RN stood leaning on his shovel while watching the work in progress.

"Typical!" RV muttered. What was it about his brother that bothered him so? Try as he might to establish normal relations with him, RN seemed to go to any lengths to avoid direct contact with him. Why did he act so cold and distant? Was RN not, after all, flesh of his flesh, blood of his blood? Sometimes, when RV came on his brother unexpectedly, RN looked positively guilty if not downright suspicious. What did he have to hide? Even now, across the graveyard wall, as he stood leaning on his shovel over Dwyer's grave-to-be, RN peered nervously about him as if waiting or watching for somebody or something. Come to think of it, his brother did seem to spend a great deal of time mooching about the graveyard. RV shook his head. "Yes," he said, not for the first time, "There's a lot more to the little brother than meets the eye."

After some time watching the grave-diggers, and the usual handful of Mass-goers entering the church, RV went to his desk and sat down. He could not decide whether he should attend the funeral Mass service proper, or wait for the interment only. He felt embarrassed and awkward at the prospect of having to attend any service not of his religious persuasion. But this, he assured himself, was after all an official assignment and so he was duty-bound to put in an appearance. In a way, he wished he had detailed Guard Behan to attend the Mass while he continued the search for Tombs O'Flaherty. But the Big Brass from Ballyglen were bound to be in attendance, so he had no choice but to attend the church in his capacity as Sergeant of Ballykeogh. He decided he would wait until the Mass was well under way before slipping in the back door. That way, at least, he would be seen to have done the "correct" thing. In the meantime, he still had his daily report sheet to fill, while the details of last night's occurrences were still fresh in his head.

RV was busy composing a suitable opening statement when the church bell tolled once – twice – three times. He put his pen down. There was a moment's silence, then three more peals. He felt a cold shiver run the length of his spine. Strange, he thought, how the very same church bell sounded dull and mournful when tolled for funerals, yet light, gay and joyful when rung for Christmas, Easter or wedding celebrations. "Funny thing – the mind," he mused as he re-directed his attentions to the tedious task on hand of filling out the ever-required duty report forms. He was still engrossed in his composition when the station clock struck the ten-thirty chimes. "Time to be getting along to the church," he told himself. The writing of this report was proving tricky. Try as he might, he just could not get the intricate complexities of both his nocturnal watch on Tom Duignan's place and the Daniel Dwyer affair into the proper formal language required. He pushed the report from him, yawned, stretched and stiffly arose from his chair. "It'll have to wait." He donned his cap and cape. "It'll just have to wait until later – when I'm fully rested."

Immediately on stepping outside the station door, it became apparent to RV that the number of vehicles parked in the street outside the church, or for that matter, anywhere in the village, did not signify the large gathering of mourners expected at the Yank's funeral. Where were the usual collection of bicycles? Where were the cars from Ballyglen? Or from further up Sliabh Cullen? Mass was already under way, yet the place was deserted. He could only surmise that the mourners, visitors and other interested parties would turn up in time for the actual burial service. On reaching the church door, he hesitated for moment. Then, as gently and as silently as he possibly could, he pushed open the door leading off the porch to the back of the church. Inside, the uneasiness he had experienced earlier returned. He felt like a man who had slipped unnoticed into some family living-room to eavesdrop on their private conversations.

From the altar, Father O'Malley's voice echoed over the heads of the kneeling congregation. *"Confiteor Deo omnipotenti . . . "*

RV moved quietly to the nearest pew at the rear of the church and sat down. His eyes, now accustomed to the poor light, squinted around him. Directly opposite, across the central aisle, Daniel Dwyer's coffin rested on two rough-hewn coffin-stands, surrounded by four ornate brass candlesticks, each one holding a large yellow lighted candle. A faded tattered tricolour, which RV correctly guessed had been placed there by one of Dwyer's old comrades-in-arms, lay draped across the casket. Judging from the size of the congregation, he was correct in his assumption that the great number of expected mourners had not materialised. His eyes searched for, and found, the figure of his wife Hannah seated about half-way up the aisle on the women's side of the church. In front of her, sat Mrs Flanagan. Next to her sat Mrs Flynn. Mrs O'Reilly was also there, as was her husband Sam O'Reilly across the aisle on the men's side. Directly in front of O'Reilly sat the three members of the guard-of-honour and firing party: Ned Finnegan, Jacko Flannery and Willie Sweeney. Willie Sweeney had not been seen out of doors these ten years or so and had been rumoured dead on at least three occasions. RV guessed he must be well over ninety, if he was a day. Yet here he sat, a shock of grey hair spiralling in several directions and a rasping smoker's cough racking his body, waiting to pay his last respects to his old comrade. As RV continued to put names to the backs of greying heads, he could see no trace of Dwyer's nephew, Jack, among the assembled locals. He could also see that there was not one person present from Ballyglen. Strange, very strange indeed, RV thought, pondering on the possibility that there must have been some misunderstanding with regard to the date or time of the funeral service. He felt again a wave of annoyance and frustration sweep over him at the realisation that this situation could have been avoided through one simple phone-call being placed to Ballyglen. However, Miss Clara's increasingly erratic and wholly unprofessional behaviour, had once again rendered that act virtually impossible. Something would definitely have to be done about her, RV reminded himself. He would have to take action as soon as possible.

As Father O'Malley droned on with his Mass of funeral Latin, RV realised that the service had only just begun. He surmised that Father O'Malley must have been equally confused and surprised at the poor turn-out and had delayed as long as he possibly could to commence the service.

RV was contemplating slipping outside to wait for the service to end, when Father O'Malley turned to give his sermon. For a long time he gazed silently down from the altar, first at the waiting congregation then at the door, with a look of both disappointment and expectancy.

Then, with much shuffling and coughing from the congregation, Father O'Malley cleared his throat and began to deliver his eulogy for the late Daniel Dwyer. Waxing Shakespearian, he began by saying how some men achieve greatness and how others have greatness thrust upon them but here – he waved a hand in the direction of the coffin – lay a man who was born with the gifts of greatness, goodness and graciousness in abundance. At this, an uncomfortable shuffling and coughing rippled through the congregation. RV heard a "Hummmph!" from his side of the aisle. Father O'Malley continued to speak of

Daniel Dwyer's life-long dedication to the cause of freedom and fraternity and how his burning love for the Motherland was borne out by the fact that he had chosen to be finally laid to rest among the green hills of Her bosom, to await the Angel's Final Trumpet. He spoke of Daniel's unswerving devotion to both families; the family of blood and the universal family of the one True Faith and of the unselfish love, generosity and kindness he always extended to both friend and enemy alike. RV distinctly heard Mrs Flanagan snort loudly and mumble something to Mrs Flynn, who suppressed a cackle.

"We have come, my dear brethren – " Father O'Malley threw a dark look in the direction of the two women and continued, " – to this hallowed place to pay our last respects to our beloved brother Daniel, who having lived a long, fruitful and holy life, having fought the good and noble fight, has departed this vale of tears here below to receive his just rewards in the life hereafter. Life!" his voice cracked with earnest solemnity, "is but the Shadow of Death! And Death is, my dear brethren, the Great Leveller – the Great Curer – the final Panacea of all our earthly ills. Let us not think, therefore, of our brother Daniel as being dead, but as being cured. Let us pray! Amen."

As the Mass came to an end, RV slipped outside as quietly as he had entered. Soon he was joined by the other members of the congregation, some who greeted him with a nod in his direction, as they gathered in small groups of two or three to smoke and chat and wait for the coffin to be taken from the church to the graveside. None of the villagers approached him to strike up a conversation, so RV was almost relieved to see Father O'Malley, a raincoat over his black and silver vestments, heading in his direction.

"Good morning, Sergeant," said the priest, a sardonic smile playing about his lips. "I'm delighted to see you among us in church this morning."

"Good morning to yourself, Father," answered RV. "I'm here officially, I'm afraid. Mr Dwyer, it would appear, rates as something of a dignitary and I've been instructed by my superiors to attend. On top of which, there will be volleys fired at the graveside. I'm here too to ensure that everything goes according to plan."

Father O'Malley and RV looked in the direction of the the three-man firing party, huddled together out of the wind by the church wall and deep in nostalgic meanderings.

"Ah yes! The – em – firing squad," Father O'Malley said heavily. "I suppose we have to allow it. I have to admit it *would* be a break with tradition if there wasn't a volley or two. I do wish it was blanks they were using in those rifles. I only hope that we don't have another funeral on account of them. Poor Mr Sweeney doesn't look strong enough to raise the shotgun he's carrying much above his shoulder."

"Don't worry, Father. I'm here to see the affair is carried out according to the rules. There will be no trouble, I assure you."

"Good. Good." The priest's look of preoccupied intensity returned. "It's rather strange, don't you think, Sergeant, that we've had no contingent at all from Ballyglen? I had expected a big turnout – but look about you – not a soul, other than the usual daily Mass-goers."

"That occurred to me too, Father, but you know, it is highly possible that there has been some misunderstanding about times of service and so forth. There have been some – er – difficulties, over the last few days, in communicating with Ballyglen. Nevertheless, I'm sure they will turn up any minute now."

"I hope you're right, Sergeant. But you know, it's usual for most funeral Masses to start prompt at ten o'clock. The PP in

Ballyglen knows that to be the case, so I'm surprised that he, at the very least, is not here. Not to mention the brass band and the choir! Did you see the pathetic turn-out in there!" He waved a hand towards the church. "I had expected – prepared for – the biggest funeral service ever conducted in Ballykeogh. I just don't understand it, Sergeant."

"It's puzzling, right enough. I had expected Sergeant Kelly with a guard of honour drawn from my colleagues below in Ballyglen," RV added and cast a glance towards the church gate. "They should be here by now – but I expect them to be here any minute."

"So, by the looks of it," Father O'Malley looked at the swelling ominous butterscotch sky, "will the rain."

"We can always be sure of that in Ballykeogh. The rain never fails us."

"Well, rain or no rain, we can't proceed until our expected visitors arrive. Anyway, the grave isn't fully dug yet. RN, your brother, is over there as we speak, putting the finishing touches to it."

At that moment, three latecomers came through the gate: Erasmus O'Regan, Jamie O'Connell and John L O'Shaughnessy. Jamie stopped for a moment to tether his red setter, Caesar, to one of the gate's spear-topped railings before sauntering up the gravel path towards the waiting groups of mourners.

"Good morning, Father. There's a drop in the eye of the wind this mornin'. It has the makings of a grand day for a funeral," Erasmus hailed the priest.

"Good morning to ye, gentlemen. Late – as usual." Father O'Malley cast a cold eye on the drawn, haggard faces of the men and realised that all three had the appearances of men who had not yet seen their beds and were somewhat the worse for wear.

"Would you believe it Father? The old alarm clock let

202

me down again this morning. But I see I got here in time for the main event," Jamie said, hunched deep inside a black Crombie overcoat two sizes too large for his slim frame.

"Well, you missed Mass! All three of you did!" the priest stressed then sighed. "But, yes, you're in time for the actual interment. Jamie, have you brought your instrument?"

"Indeed I have." Jamie held the canvas bag he carried at arms' length. His red-rimmed eyes took on a misty faraway look. "And I've got a piece in mind to play that will put goose-pimples on the gravestones, it's that powerful a tune. It's called 'Dark Lochnagar', as haunting a lament as you will hear in this life – or the next! Will I play you a bar or two?"

"Not now – not yet! Start to play it as they lower the coffin into the grave and that should be fine."

"Not too many mourners, I notice." Erasmus looked about him and tapped his pipe on a nearby headstone. "No bishops, businessmen or brass bands? *Not a drum was heard, not a funeral note as his corpse to the rampart we hurried.*' Charles Wolfe might have written that for the Yank himself. What do you say, Father?"

"Quite so Mr O'Regan, quite so. It is somewhat of a mystery, I have to admit that."

"By the way," RV cleared his throat and interjected. "I don't suppose any of you gentlemen have laid eyes on Mr O'Flaherty this morning?"

"Tombs? Not a sign so far, Sergeant. But I have to give the man full credit. I never expected him to arouse himself in time to make it down to Ballyglen to collect the old Yank there, that's for sure! But he obviously did – and more power to him," Jamie said, moving off to rejoin Erasmus who stood huddled by a large, angel-topped headstone, attempting to relight his pipe.

RV and Father O'Malley looked at each other and shrugged.

"Well," Father O'Malley said at last. "I'd better get along and see how the grave-digging is faring. I may have to call on you later, Sergeant, to help carry the coffin from the church. It would help give the ceremony a look of – well, importance! I'm sure you know what I mean, Sergeant."

"Eh? What? Oh, yes. Of course," RV mumbled. "You can depend on me."

"Right, I'll see you later then."

Plthocktic! RV winced and swore under his breath. He knew that sound and what it meant. Removing his cap, he could see that some cursed, winged defecator's aim was dead on target.

"What is it," he groaned and glared at a sullen sky, devoid of any flying creature, "about a uniform that attracts those filthy buggers?"

Chapter Fourteen

Reaching inside his cape, RV drew out a large chain pocket watch, given to him by his father on the day he joined the force, and scrutinised its aged face for a long while. The large minute hand slid up to cover its stubby fellow time-traveller to show twelve o'clock. Midday, and not a sign of the expected visiting mourners from Ballyglen.

"I just don't understand it." RV pocketed the watch and rocked back and forth on his heels. "What on earth has gone wrong? It's all very puzzling." The waiting was beginning to tire him. The small groups of people standing around were beginning to show signs that they too were losing their patience, as they intermingled and shifted, regrouped and shuffled. At eleven thirty-five, RN had appeared, his face flushed and sweat-stained, and whispered in Father O'Malley's ear. Father O'Malley nodded, looked at his watch, stared longingly in the direction of Ballyglen, and looked again at his watch before commencing to pace slowly back and forth between the church door and the main gate. The Yank Dwyer's three old soldier-comrades who made up the firing party had had their fill of waiting in the chilly drizzle and decided to let their feelings be known.

"Here! Father!" Ned Finnegan called out. "Are we going to bury old Danno at all today? Or are we going to stand around here waiting till resurrection day?" His two comrades nodded in vehement agreement.

"Patience, Ned, patience. All in good time." Father O'Malley checked his watch again, then turning to RV, added, "Well, I suppose there is not much point in delaying any longer. We may as well proceed with the burial. I can't understand why Mr Dwyer's nephew Jack isn't present. How on earth did he manage to miss his own uncle's funeral? And it doesn't seem like anyone else is going to arrive at this stage either, does it?" He threw a doleful glance at the graveyard gate. "So we may as well get on with it." His face registered bitter disappointment.

At that moment Guard Behan joined them at the church door.

"Ah, Guard Behan. You're back from your investigations," RV said. "Anything to report? Any trace of Mr O'Flaherty?"

"Not a sign of the man anywhere. I must have combed a good square mile of the bog and wetland in the immediate vicinity of the accident. I don't know where Tombs is, but I can tell you one thing, Sergeant, he's not down there in the marsh!" Guard Behan looked glumly at his mud-splattered boots and uniform pants.

"Extraordinary! Where on earth has the unfortunate fellow got to? Well, we'll have to tackle that problem later. Right now, you're just back in time to help carry the coffin to the graveside." RV removed his cap and entered the church porch.

Father O'Malley choose to ignore Guard Behan's audible groan.

"I'd better organise the other coffin-bearers. There's yourself, Guard . . . RN and Micho – and let's see – oh yes –

there's Mr McGarrigan. He'll want to lend a hand, I'm sure."

A few minutes later, a sigh of relief rippled through the waiting mourners as the tricolour-draped coffin, awkwardly shouldered by RN, Micho Farrell, Guard Behan and Big Tom McGarrigan emerged to begin its last short earthly journey from the church to the prepared grave by the church-yard wall, not fifty yards away.

The day had taken on a raw cutting edge. Single teardrops of driven rain plish-ploshed on the coffin-top and stung the faces of the four bearers. Slowly, the coffin and followers snaked between the gnarled gravestones and tufts of grass to arrive at last by the freshly-dug mound of black, bone and worm-rich earth. The men gingerly lowered the coffin alongside the yawning grave and stepped back to allow Father O'Malley to come forward to intone suitable prayers and splash copious amounts of Holy Water on the coffin-lid.

"Would anyone here like to say a few words?" Father O'Malley looked around him. A heavy uneasy silence descended on the gathering. From the corner of his eye, RV noticed Ned Finnegan manoeuvring his firing party into position at the opposite side of the grave. RV could hardly believe his eyes. Clutched in Ned's right hand was a huge rusted sword which he now brandished with pride as he prepared to give his squad their orders to fire. After a great deal of shuffling, Jacko Flannery and Willie Sweeney were in position, guns at the ready.

"Firing party! Aaah-ten-shun!" Ned pulled himself to attention, puffed out his chest and raised his sword. "Firing party! Ready! Take aim! Not at the church, Willie! Aim at the sky, you *cluisan*! Take aim . . . " The sword swished down. "Fire!"

Boom! Only Willie Sweeney's double-barrel fired,

leaving the old man staggering backwards under its recoil. Jacko Flannery swore, lowered his .22 rifle and began to fumble with its loading-breach.

"Your safety catch, Jacko! Release your bloody safety catch!" Ned hissed, once again raising his sword aloft to await his comrades to steady themselves and prepare to fire another volley.

"Right, men! Firing party! Load . . . Ready again? Take aim!" The two gun-barrels swayed in the air like metallic marsh-reeds. "Steady, men! Steady! Take aim! Fire!" Again the sword arced down.

Crack! Boom! This time both firing-pieces released their contents into the murky sky. Willie Sweeney staggered yet again, coming to rest in the arms of Erasmus O'Regan, who reached forward to grab him as he fell helplessly backward from the recoil.

"Eh – I think, Ned," Father O'Malley winced and whispered to the diminutive firing party leader, who was shepherding his men into position for yet another volley. "I think two volleys is ample, don't you?"

"It'll have to be," gasped a breathless Willie Sweeney, still wavering from the aftershock of his last volley. "I only brought two cartridges."

A scowling Ned Finnegan reluctantly lowered his sword and replaced it in the tattered scabbard attached to his overcoat belt before stepping back from the grave, his fine moment of leadership and glory past and gone.

Turning to Jamie O'Connell, Father O'Malley made a signal to him to begin his playing. "At the very least," he whispered to RV, "Mr Dwyer's last request will be honoured."

From his canvas bag Jamie drew his fiddle and bow, and proceeded to pluck the strings into tune. Happy that his ear and fiddle-strings were in accord, he settled himself on a nearby tomb and tucking the instrument under his chin, commenced to play his soulful lament for the returned dead hero. As the first long lonesome notes of "Dark Lochnagar" floated over the assembly, Father O'Malley nodded to RN who moved forward and slipped two ropes under each end of the coffin. He then signalled to the other coffin-bearers who stepped forward and, picking up a rope-end each, lifted the coffin and slowly began to lower it over, and then down into, the open grave. A single sniffle and a sob was distinctly heard as Father O'Malley leaned forward to sprinkle more Holy Water as the coffin came to rest at the bottom of the grave.

"We therefore commit our brother Daniel's body to the ground; earth to earth, ashes to ashes, dust to dust; in the sure and certain hope of Resurrection to eternal life. *In nomine Domini, et Filii, et Spir – "*

"Hold it! Hold it!" a voice called out from the church gate. "For God's sakes, hold everything!"

As one, all heads turned towards the shouter. RV squinted through the now heavy-falling rain and watched the figure approach. Even from this distance, he could recognise the enormous figure of Sergeant Kelly from Ballyglen. The gathering stood in frozen silence as the rotund Sergeant drew closer, his face beetroot-red from the exertion of running the hundred yards from his car to the graveside.

"Hold everything! Father O'Malley! Sergeant Mulrooney!" a waving Sergeant Kelly panted, recognising the two men.

"Sergeant Kelly! Please! Do you mind! In God's name, we're conducting a funeral here. Kindly show a little Christian consideration for the deceased!" Father O'Malley curtly admonished the breathless Sergeant.

"No, no! You don't understand! You can't bury that

man! Not yet. There's been a terrible mistake. That's not Daniel Dwyer you have there in that coffin. I don't know who it is you have down there, but it's not Daniel 'the Yank' Dwyer, I can tell you that much!"

"Not Daniel Dwyer? How can that be? For God's sake man, what are you saying?" Father O'Malley's jaw dropped open and a loud gasp rose from the gathered mourners.

"It's not Daniel Dwyer. I tell you! Daniel the Yank Dwyer is at this very moment below in a cell in Ballyglen, alive and kicking – and in the flesh!

"Dear God! And who then – is – down – there?" All eyes turned to peer into the grave.

"Whoever you have in that coffin down there is not the man you think it is. I can tell you that, for a fact! That is not Daniel Dwyer."

"Saints preserve us all!" Mrs Flanagan's voice cried above the excited babble.

As Father O'Malley stood slack-jawed and dumbstruck, RV moved to take command. "Quickly now, men! Let's get that coffin out of that grave!"

RN and the other coffin bearers stepped quickly to the graveside and grasped a rope-end each.

"Now – all together – heave!"

The coffin was a foot or so off the floor of the grave when a deep rumbling sound, followed by a strong ground tremor, halted the men at their work.

"Boom!"

The startled men released their grip on the ropes supporting the coffin. With a dull thud, the coffin dropped back into the grave. All heads turned once again, this time in the direction of the explosion. Yet another tremor shook the ground beneath their feet.

"Saints preserve us!" Mrs Flanagan crossed herself and dropped to her knees. "It's the Day of Reckoning, come upon us all!"

"What in heaven's name is that?" Father O'Malley pointed to a column of black smoke spiralling to the sky.

"Something's exploded!" Big Tom McGarrigan shouted excitedly.

"It's from the other side of the church!" somebody cried, as the expanding cloud mushroomed skyward.

"Oh, no. No!" The blood drained from RN's face as a dreadful possibility leaped into his mind. Dear God, he thought, don't let it be the still. Don't let it be that. Like a man demented, he dashed off at speed in the direction of the smoke and dust-cloud to learn the worst.

"Come on!" Ned Finnegan shouted and drew his sword. "Don't stand around here like tailor's dummies! Let's go see what's up!"

In a confused hubbub of excited near-hysterical voices, terrified crows, dislodged by the report from their church rookery, and Jamie's setter, barking wildly and fighting his leash, the crowd left the graveside and rushed en masse to the other side of the church to investigate this strange occurrence. Only Jamie remained, immersed body and soul in the sad beauty of "Dark Lochnagar" and continued to play on, oblivious to all, save his bitter-sweet music. For the time being at least, the funeral of the Yank Dwyer was forgotten.

First round the corner was RN, closely followed by RV, Guard Behan and Father O'Malley, with his soutane swishing about his legs. Behind them, weaving and dodging the knotted outcrops of matted grass and weeds, came the rest of the mourners and, bringing up the rear, the massive frame of Sergeant Kelly. At first sight, it looked as if the bank building, at the other side of the graveyard wall, was on fire, but as the group drew closer, the source and full extent of the disaster was revealed to them. A large area of the graveyard surface had collapsed into a huge, gaping chasm which had opened by the south-side graveyard wall and from it a column of thick black smoke and dust belched and snaked up to the overcast sky. The graveyard wall itself had been breached as if something, or someone, had hacked a V-shaped slice in it. Leading away from the breach to the rear northern corner of the bank a canal – more than five feet deep – had opened up, leaving the corner foundations of the building protruding like a rotting misshapen molar. The onlookers could do no more than stand and stare in shock and silence at this incredible sight.

"Good heavens above!" Father O'Malley said to nobody in particular. "Half the graveyard has collapsed."

"It's a bomb! As sure as God, it's them bloody Blueshirts! They're still around and they're still trying to get us!"

"Blueshirts? Never! It's the Republicans! It's the IRA!"

"Or Communists!"

"Don't be daft! It's no more than a slight shift in the earth's crust. It's a sort of mini-earthquake. Or," Erasmus paused, puffing hard on his pipe, "it could be the Day of Days – the Day Father O'Malley here has warned us about often enough – the Day when, as the Bard said *'the graves yawned and yielded up their dead.'* Julius Caesar." Erasmus removed his pipe and winked at Big Tom McGarrigan, who returned a blank uncomprehending stare.

Other opinions began to fill the air as each person there struggled to find an explanation for this seething, hissing pit.

"What's that God-awful stench?" Mrs Flynn screwed up her face. After a mass seizure of snorting and sniffing, it was unanimously declared that there was indeed a most horrible smell emanating from the hole.

"What do you expect from a hole in a graveyard,"

Erasmus said in dark measured tones. "The sweet scent of summer roses?"

Ker-rumble! Another section of the wall fell into the hole.

"Keep back now! Everybody back!" RV began to herd the more inquisitive back from the edge of the pit. "Move well back! This whole place could cave in at any second! We can't have anybody injured, so come on now! Everybody well back by the church wall."

"Looks to me like the remains of a couple of vaults or somesuch down there, Sergeant," Guard Behan offered, peering into the slowly settling dust and debris.

"Aye, lad. Could be. Could be. But we'll have to seal off the entire area immediately until we can afford to pronounce it safe. Then we can begin a proper investigation into the whole affair."

"Well, at least nobody was injured," Sergeant Kelly said, mopping his still-flushed cheeks and forehead with a gaudy polka-dot handkerchief.

"What do you figure caused this?" RV stroked his chin thoughtfully.

"Well, the sound and smoke would indicate an explosion of some sort. Graves or tombs don't explode of their own accord, that I do know. So we have to assume that there was something down there that caused the explosion. What exactly was that? Well – that's for us – for you – to discover."

The only person among those present who could have enlightened Sergeant Kelly as to a possible cause stood transfixed by the edge of the smoking chasm. RN, who had raced to the spot ahead of the rest, had his very worst fears confirmed. Now he stood as immobile as the headstones about him as he struggled to come to grips with the enormity and, more acutely, the consequences of the disaster. His befuddled brain tried to unravel the facts.

There had been a terrific explosion here. But what had caused it he could not, at this stage, determine. What RN could determine was that the vault – his vault, containing all his distilling equipment – had been entirely destroyed. His entire stock of newly distilled poteen – his best batch ever, bottled and ready for distribution, had also been destroyed. He saw too that the vault next door to his still – the one he had hoped to expand into – had also collapsed entirely.

His hopes and spirits swirled downward as the foul-smelling smoke drifted upward. His dreams and schemes of building a poteen empire lay crumbled and crushed in the bowels of this grumbling pit.

Chapter Fifteen

Black Jack Dwyer came awake with a start. For a moment, his existence was fluid, formless, lifeless. Try as he might, he could not command his eyes to focus on a single object about him. He was enveloped in absolute blackness. Slowly, the inky darkness around him gave way to a million fiery darts of searing pain which shot hither and thither inside his head, lighting up his brain like a Christmas tree. Some instinct, which automatically handled such functions, informed him that he was suffering a massive hangover following an equally monumental drinking binge. This was not a sensation unknown to Black Jack and in a way, it comforted him. Closing his eyes in a effort to ease the pain, he tried to relax and search the inner darkness for clues as to who, and where, he was. His immediate recollection was that of a dream – a prolonged and disturbing dream – in which he heard voices and saw shadowy figures gather around him and lift his powerless body into what he figured to be a small cramped and darkened room. The figures melted as he lost consciousness and he dreamed he floated on a cushion of air until the voices and shadows once again drew close around him. He had felt them lay their ice-cold hands on him once again and the closeness of these shadowy figures filled him with dread. He remembered struggling in vain to gain release from this nightmarish terror. Then, mercifully, the black fog descended once again and he sank back into the arms of welcome unconsciousness, where he had languished until now.

Slowly, ever so slowly, as the veil of unconsciousness lifted, Jack began to recall unrelated fragments of the previous day's activities. He remembered coming to Ballykeogh, he remembered drinking and being in a card-game, with whom he could not recall, then having more drink – a great amount of drink. He remembered, too, his leaving McGarrigan's Bar & Lounge in the early hours of last night. Or the night before? That he could not recall. He remembered getting on his bicycle and heading for home – then, no more. How did he get home? If indeed that was where he now was. He opened one eye and raised his head to inspect his immediate surroundings.

Thuck!

His forehead came in smart contact with something solid, a few inches above his head. His head fell back and his face contorted in agony as his brain exploded once again in a million slivers of white light. Gritting his teeth, he lay absolutely still as the pain subsided to a dull throbbing ache. Opening his eyes again, he raised his head a fraction and squinted into the darkness in the direction of where his feet should be. His feet! Where were his feet? His brain shot a signal to his toes, who waggled in response. His brain next signalled his hands, who answered that they were placed, folded, across his chest. So far, so good. He lay his head back and rested for a moment. Then, summoning up all the willpower he could muster, Jack commanded his mind and body to shake off the sleep-shackles which still held him fast. Suddenly, he became aware of a loud thumping sound. As his sense of

216

hearing grew more and more acute, he was shocked to realise that the deafening sound was that of his own heart and the ferocity and loudness of its beating sent a shock of electricity through his blood to his bones and marrow. Somewhere, high above his head, outside the ugly blackness that now pressed heavily on him, he could hear the sound of music being played, and beyond that, the sound of a dog yelping and the excited cawing of distant crows.

Where was he? And what in God's name had happened to him? Jack carefully moved one hand toward his lower torso. His probing fingers determined that he was without his suit jacket and pants and he was dressed in some sort of long shirt – flannel, by the feel of it, and damp too. Bringing both hands down by his sides, his fingers began to touch, then pressurise the hard substance on which he lay. Hard as a board. He quickly moved his hands to feel the area immediately above his head.

Solid! Solid board!

"Jeez Christ! I'm in some sort of wooden casing!" His voice sounded muffled, cracked and alien.

In that instant, the pain inside his head dissolved in an icy wash of stark terror. Something was very wrong here. Where, and what, in God's name was this place? He had to get out! Now!

Pressing both palms against the solid mass above his head, he pushed, and found the weight responding to his pressure. He pushed again – hard. The covering moved a few inches to allow a shower of white light splash his head and shoulders. He pushed even harder, his growing panic giving him the strength of many men.

With a creaking, grating sound the solid mass above his head shifted, slid sideways and fell away. In a blinding flash, his eyes clenched as the sky opened up above him and then fell in on top of him. Bringing his arm up to shield his face from the sheet of light and rain that showered upon him, Jack struggled stiffly to his feet. Now on his feet, he steadied himself, opened one eye, then the other, and looked at the high walls that surrounded him . . .

"Dear Jesus! Oh, God! This can't be real! It's a nightmare I'm in and can't wake up! Dear God, help me! Somebody save me!" Jack's voice rose to a keening wail as he gazed wildly about him. A cold sweat blistered on his face and his eyes bulged in sheer amazement, then in stark terror, as they took in the shroud in which he was dressed, the open coffin in which he stood and the crumbling earthen walls at either side of the grave. He looked up. There, above him, was a dark and bearded figure seated on a tomb, playing a fiddle in the rain. It was Jamie O'Connell. Or was it? His mind spun wildly and a sharp pain gripped his chest. He began to tremble violently.

"Oh, God help me! I'm dead! I'm dead and in hell! I'm dead and this is the Day of Resurrection. I'm to meet my Maker. Oh God save me! Sweet Jesus! Somebody save me!"

Wailing and crying, he frantically clawed and scrambled his way up out of the grave and on to the wet grass above. Jamie O'Connell, his concentration finally broken by Jack's frightened crying and moaning, opened his eyes to a sight he would never forget till his dying day and one that he would be called on to tell and re-tell in the Golden Gloves for many years to come. There, before his eyes, was Daniel the Yank Dwyer, still wrapped in his grave-shroud, moaning and clawing his way from the bosom of the grave as if answering the Archangel's Final Trumpet. Jamie spluttered, gagged, dropped his fiddle and bow and fell away in a dead faint at the awesome spectacle of the grave issuing forth its dead.

Black Jack did not wait to question, or identify, this

prostrate Angel Gabriel, who, in the guise of Jamie O'Connell, had summoned up the dead with his fiddle-sounding trumpeting. Gathering his shroud above his knees and calling loudly to the Gods for forgiveness, release and salvation, he turned and ran towards the graveyard gate.

"*Grrrrrrrrr . . .*"

Jack came to a halt and froze. There, lashed to the gate-railings, was the blood-red dog-demon of his deepest drunken nightmares. The animal's previous manifestations – though terrifying – had been mostly hazy and unreal. Now this monster – this infernal Hound at the Gates of Hell – its red eyes spitting fire, its teeth bared and frothing, growled and snapped menacingly and fought with all its might to escape its leash.

"I'm damned! My soul is lost! I'm in hell! I'm in hell!" Screaming and stumbling, Jack ran to get out of reach of the salivating animal and scrambled frantically over the graveyard wall to the street outside.

Sitting on a shabby, velvet-padded drawing-room chair, the last of a suite that her mother, Brigie, had brought with her to the house as part of her dowry, Miss Clara O'Dowd clutched a loaded double-barrel shotgun to her trembling breast. With fingers that twitched to every beat of her pounding heart, she gripped the stock of the double-barrel and peered at the drama unfolding across the street in the church and graveyard grounds. The explosion had come as no surprise to Miss Clara. Ever since reading of Germany's imminent invasion of Poland and the possibility of a full-scale war ensuing from the attack, she knew it would be just a matter of time before the barbarians that had killed her young English lover would arrive in Ballykeogh.

Miss Clara had not had a restful night. All night long, the village street fairly hummed with strange and unusual activities, giving her a sleepless night and confirming her worst fears. The Germans were coming! The authorities did not wish to alarm the general public yet, but they couldn't fool Miss Clara, who had carefully watched events unfolding. Sitting through the long night by her bedroom window, Miss Clara had witnessed with keen interest the furtive comings and goings outside in the street. Men, some of them strangers, moved up and down the street; vehicles moved in and out of the churchyard; lights came on and went off in Father O'Malley's house and in the church. Sergeant Mulrooney, and now, this morning, Guard Behan, had never ceased to-ing and fro-ing from the Garda Station since early yesterday evening.

"Oh, yes," she said to herself. "They know. They know the Germans are on the way. They think they can keep it a secret, but they can't fool Clara."

Her worst fears and suspicions were confirmed early that morning when she picked up a copy of the *Daily Mail*, dated September 4th, 1939, from the top of the pile of newspapers she hoarded in the kitchen.

"Britain's First Day Of War," the headlines cried out to her. *"Churchill Is New Navy Chief."*

"So, it's true! We're at war!" Miss Clara scanned the other headlines, nodding frantically as she read. Polish troops, she read, were launching a counter-attack to the German offensive, and the German passenger liner, the *Bremen*, had been captured by the British, after only one day of war. The Germans were finally on the way. The papers knew it, those in power knew it. She knew it and so too did Sergeant Mulrooney. Her mind raced and spun as she rushed about the house to ensure all doors and windows were shut and bolted. Miss Clara was going to be prepared, even if no one else in the village was. "Let them come!" she muttered over and over again to herself as she pushed a chest-of-drawers against her front door for added protection. "Let them come, and do their worst. They'll find Clara ready and waiting."

Secure in the belief that the house was now siege-proof, she went to the bedroom to retrieve her father's old shotgun and a box of cartridges from under her bed. If the worst came to the worst, she reasoned, the old gun would be her last line of defence. As she dusted and cleaned the rusty gun, she remembered the last time she was forced to use it. Many years ago, she was forced to fire both barrels over Jamie O'Connell's head in an effort to drive him and his fiddle away from beneath her window where he nightly played in serenade, hoping to win her heart and her favours. It proved to be Jamie's last attempt at courting Miss Clara, for she never again heard the sound of his lonesome fiddle outside her bedroom window. She had since often regretted that incident. This time, however, she would take the greatest of pleasure in using the gun should the need arise. As things stood at present, it looked as if that need would indeed arise.

"They killed my sweetheart," she said defiantly as she rammed two cartridges into each gun-barrel and snapped shut the breach. "But now, at last, I'll have my sweet revenge."

Taking up her lookout seat by the window, she continued to keep watch as the cold wet grey dawn grew to full morning. After some time sitting, the shotgun cradled in her arms, Miss Clara had nodded off to a restless uneasy sleep. She dreamed she was again sixteen years old and in Paris, and with her young English lover in her arms she waltzed and waltzed and held her lover tight until the gaily-lit Parisian night faded and dissolved. Then she was among the clouds – clouds that were heavy, dark and ominous – yet she waltzed on and on. Faster, ever faster, she spun with her lover, so fast she spun with joy and fear. Suddenly, the waltzing stopped and she found herself alone. She reached for her lover but he fell away through the swirling black clouds. From somewhere far beneath her, she could hear her lost lover call her name. She called out in answer, but she knew he could not hear, for though she cried out so loud she thought her heart would burst, no sound came from her lips. Then, as in all her dreams, her head was full with the drone of many bombers who filled the black sky and the scream of their falling bombs sent her spiralling downward, ever downward . . .

Jerking awake, Miss Clara reached down and grabbed the shotgun which had slipped from her hands and lay on the floor by her feet.

"Boom!"

What was that? An explosion? They were bombing Ballykeogh!

Across the street in the graveyard, she could see a torrent of smoke and dust gush from behind the graveyard wall. Her premonitions had become facts. The German Army was almost in Ballykeogh.

"So!" she said quietly. "This is it. They're bombing the town."

She could not now depend on anybody to come to her aid and she steeled herself for the coming onslaught. "I'll hold them off – or die in the attempt," she said, her eyes narrow with determination. Tightening her grip on the shotgun, she watched in amazement as a large group of people appeared from the other side of the church and collected by the bomb-stricken area. What on earth did they think they were doing? Was it possible they did not realise the grave danger they had exposed themselves to?

After the bombers, the tanks and land-troops would follow. They had to be warned.

"Keep away!" she shouted, her face pressed flat against the window-pane. "Keep away! That was just the first wave! This is war! An all-out Blitzkrieg! Don't you realise they'll be back to drop more bombs?" Then to herself, "Oh, dear! Those poor people are going to be blown to smithereens if they stand around waiting for the next bomb to fall. Why doesn't Sergeant Mulrooney do something? Why doesn't he get them away from that place?" She looked her half-crazed look and shook her head in confusion. For a man in authority, who knows the village is about to be attacked and possibly overrun, Sergeant Mulrooney, she thought, was taking the whole affair far too coolly altogether.

As she gazed out at the billowing smoke, a movement from the other side of the graveyard caught her eye. She could hardly believe what she was seeing. There, running down to the street from the direction of the church gate, was a tall figure dressed in what looked to be some kind of nightshirt. As the figure came closer, she got a better look at the person who was now obviously heading in her direction.

"Oh my God! It's the Germans!" It had to be a German soldier – only this one was not in uniform. A spy! That was it. He was a spy. From the look of him, he was more than likely an advance agent dropped from one of their planes and here he was running toward her, his parachute still wrapped around his body. The figure had reached the front gate of the post office and was still approaching – fast.

This was it! The moment Miss Clara had expected, but dreaded. She galvanised herself into action. Slipping the bolt off the window-fastener, she slid the window open just enough to push both gun-barrels through. Pointing the gun in the general direction of the approaching figure, she cocked both hammers, closed her eyes, gritted her teeth to stop her whole body from shaking, and squeezed both triggers. The double report resounded throughout the house and echoed down the village street. Miss Clara opened her eyes, swore loudly and pulled in the gun. She peered through the cordite smoke-haze. The running figure had come to a halt and stared wildly in her direction. She had missed. "Hell's bells! I'm not going to miss next time." Slamming the window shut, she retreated towards the bed, then fell on her knees to forage for the box of shotgun cartridges and reload.

The double report from the shotgun had stopped the running figure in his tracks. For a moment, he stared in open-mouthed horror at the sight of a smoking shotgun poking out of the post office window and aimed directly at his head. Then throwing his hands in the air, he turned and bolted, screaming for help and sanctuary, and disappeared around the corner. By the time Miss Clara got back to the window with her loaded shotgun, the street outside was empty leaving her to suspect the wily German had taken cover nearby. When he showed no sign of relaunching his attack, she began to wonder if the whole episode had been entirely due to her over-active imagination.

Chapter Sixteen

Thursday the fifteenth of October 1964 was a day that would be remembered and talked about in Ballykeogh for a long time to come. The last day the village had witnessed such excitement and activity was a day the previous year when it was announced that President John F Kennedy himself – then on his only visit to Ireland – was planning an official visit to the town. On learning that detailed research into his ancestral Irish lineage had unearthed a connection with Ballykeogh, it had been the President's burning desire, so the story went, to honour the out-of-the-way village with a visit. President Kennedy's great-great-grandfather, so it was claimed, had once stayed overnight in the village while looking for work as a potato-picker. On the strength of so "grand" and prestigious a visit, Big Tom McGarrigan had hastily converted a dingy bottle-room off the main bar to become the "John Fitzgerald Kennedy Lounge". Though the entire locality turned out to welcome the great man and his sainted wife, the Presidential party was duly diverted on a sight-seeing tour of Holy Wells when it was learned by advance officials that the Kennedy connection with Ballykeogh was little more than a speculative remark made by McGarrigan to a local Fianna Fail councillor, who in turn passed it on to a Party HQ-man in Dublin, who had the ear of de Valera himself.

Though the great man never came to Ballykeogh, McGarrigan allowed the lounge to remain so named and bedecked the room with a plethora of cheaply-framed photos of the President and the First Lady, replacing the old gallery of photos of Pope Pius the 12th, de Valera and a faded newspaper-clipping of the Kerry football team, dating back before the Civil War. The locals soon forgot their bitter disappointment at the mammoth non-event, but McGarrigan kept his cash-register ringing as wide-eyed Irish-American tourists "goshed" and "gee'ed" in awe at the proprietor's tales of the great day that John F and Jackie Kennedy sat in that very room, drank from those very glasses and indeed used that self-same toilet.

The last time the Golden Gloves had done so much trade was on the night Cassius Clay had pulverised Sonny Liston for the Heavyweight Boxing Championship of the World. On that night, as the packed pub gathered around the radio to await the commencement of the fight being broadcast "live" from the US, the proprietor, John L O'Shaughnessy had his finest moment. For almost an hour, he held the bar spellbound with an illustrated demonstration of how the Irish fighting tornado, the dark-eyed Son of Mars, Jack Dempsey, whipped Jess Willard into submission in three rounds to become World Champ in Toledo, Ohio, one hot July 4th night in 1919, in a fight so ferocious that men still gasp at the fury of it.

Today, it was Jamie O'Connell's turn to hold court in the Golden Gloves. Tightly grasping a tumbler of poteen in a still trembling hand, he told a tale he would be called upon to recount many a time in the years to come. Jamie had been in the Gloves since he had been discovered lying by the deserted grave in a dazed and confused

226

condition by Erasmus and John L. Now, with more than a few glasses of RN's poteen burning in his blood and surrounded by a large group of attentive listeners, Jamie re-lived his recent harrowing experience by the graveside of the Yank Dwyer.

"I swear to ye all, I've never seen – or hope I'll never see – anything like it again for as long as I live!" Jamie emptied his glass and accepted another from Erasmus. "We were all at the grave – Father O'Malley, the Sergeant, Erasmus, John L, RN, Ned and Tom Duignan there. I started to play my piece as they lowered the Yank into the grave. My fingers were frozen, but I was playing well, nevertheless! Anyway, the next thing I remember, I opened my eyes to find the place deserted! There wasn't a single soul left by the grave, except myself. Then I heard this noise at my feet – I looked down – and there – " Jamie took a deep draught from the tumbler, "God save me! There was the Yank himself, climbing up out of the grave we had just put him into! I – I don't remember much after that, till Erasmus and John L found me. Well, what would ye do if ye saw a corpse ye had just put down risin' up out of the coffin! I'll never forget that sight if I live to be a thousand!"

John L, delighted at the sudden windfall of customers, arrived with a tray of drinks and pushed a glass in Jamie's direction. "Here you are, Jamie. On the house. After what you've witnessed today, by God, you need it," he said and returned behind the bar to top up a long line of creamy black pints of porter.

"And it wasn't the Yank at all in the coffin! I knew it was too good to be true!" Erasmus puffed hard on his pipe and sat back on his chair, obviously savouring this deviation from the normal, the everyday and the humdrum.

"It was Black Jack!" said Jamie. "Wearing a habit and a face the colour of the top of a pint of porter. Crawling his way up out of the grave he was, crying and wailing like some demented banshee. But I took him to be the Yank – "

"What happened then?" Tom Duignan enquired, pulling his chair closer.

"Well, I kind of lost count for a bit after that. The next thing I recall was Erasmus and John L helping me to my feet. Then there was a shotgun blast from the street! I had just grabbed my fiddle and was heading for the gate to unleash Caesar when Black Jack came back over the wall like a scalded rat, still screaming and crying, and disappeared inside the church as if the very hounds of hell were on his tail! Erasmus and myself decided it was high time to get well away from the place – and here we are."

"Myself and Tombs were over in Tombs's house." It was the Piper Hanratty, having recently arrived in the pub and not wanting to miss the chance of playing a cameo role in the making of this legend. "The both of us had overslept and Tombs was in a bit of a state when he found out the time was after one o'clock in the afternoon and him supposed to be down in Ballyglen at eight to collect the Yank off the train. Tombs got into a panic and wouldn't even consider a hair of the dog. Anyway, just as we were coming out of the house, who should we see coming down the street, running like the hounds of hell, but this wild-looking boyo wrapped in what looked like a sheet and heading for the post office. The next thing we see is Miss Clara taking aim from the post office window and letting him have both barrels! She missed, thank God. Then your man turns on his heel and away he goes, back to the church at a pace that Ronnie Delaney would be proud of. Poor old Tombsy nearly passed out. I had to take him back into the house and put him back to bed, he was that shaken up. And that's where he is this very minute." The

Piper sat back to bask in the glow of the excited babble which spread through the bar.

"It was Mrs Flanagan who found Jack in the church." Old Ned Finnegan sat with the two other members of the volunteer firing party, a pint in one hand and his sword and scabbard in the other. "On his knees in front of the altar, the poor devil was. She says he was tearing his hair and ranting and raving about how he would give up the drink for ever or go into an enclosed Order if only the Good Lord would release him from his nightmare."

"Where is he now, Ned?"

"According to Mrs Flynn, he refused to budge an inch from the altar – not till Father O'Malley was called for and came to calm him down enough for him to go up to the house. I think he's there yet. Mrs Flynn told me she had to give Mrs Flanagan a couple of hot-toddies to sooth her nerves before she was carted off to her bed. The shock of going into the church and seeing the corpse kneeling at the altar was too much for her to take. It fair set her back, according to Mrs Flynn – who was fairly shook up herself!"

"Well, it'll give them both a good ten years of gossip. That's the least it'll do!" The Piper huffed.

"And after all that, the brave Danno the Yank is still alive and kicking," Erasmus declared to himself inside a halo of pipe-smoke.

"Aye! Would you believe it! Below in a cell in Ballyglen, according to Sergeant Kelly," Ned Finnegan offered. "After all the trouble we went to, organisin' the firin' squad to give the dirty quisling a royal send-off. I'd like to get five minutes alone with the bastard!" He spat in the direction of the spittoon, missed and fingered his sword which still hung at his side.

"What'll happen, I'm wondering, if the Yank comes

back to Ballykeogh when the Guards kick him out of Ballyglen?" enquired the Piper.

Ned Finnegan stiffened and bristled like a terrier preparing to attack. "What'll happen? I'll tell you what'll happen! If that turn-coated, blue-shirted, son-of-a-bitch Dwyer ever as much as shows his snout in this village, by Jeez, we'll see to it he'll get a proper funeral very shortly afterwards, won't we boys? And we'll put him down in a grave he won't crawl out of either. I guarantee you that!"

A rolling wave of laughter erupted around the bar, as empty glasses clinked on the marble-top bar.

"Fill 'em up again, John L," somebody called. "Drinks for the house and a glass of the Pure for the only man in Ballykeogh to witness the rising of 'Lazarus' Dwyer from the tomb!"

Black Jack Dwyer had been awarded a new nickname – a name he would have to wear for quite a while to come.

Seated in his usual chair by the window, Jamie O'Connell fought to banish the image repeating in his head – that of the grave giving up its dead. From inside his canvas bag he drew his fiddle and bow and and tucking the instrument under his chin began to play a lively version of "The Gold Ring".

Chapter Seventeen

"When you've finished trying to put that fire out," RV said to Guard Behan, who was on his knees by the station fireplace, "you can make us all a nice cup of tea."

Guard Behan snorted an indignant mumble and continued to puff life into a solitary dying spark sheltering amidst a canopy of soggy turf-sods.

"We could do with something a little stronger than tea, after all that carry on back there at the graveyard." Sergeant Kelly's gimlet eyes darted about the stark room as if looking for something. Still mopping his turkey-cock red jowls with his handkerchief, he planted his elephantine behind on the least stable of the station chairs. For a moment, it seemed the chair would totally disintegrate beneath the Sergeant's colossal frame. To RV's amazement and Guard Behan's disappointment, the agonised chair creaked and groaned, yet held firm.

The Sergeant from Ballyglen stuffed his handkerchief into his tunic pocket. "I'll say this for the place – this is a lively little town you run here, Mulrooney, and that's no lie. I've seen more action here in the last hour than I would below in Ballyglen in a month. Always like this, is it?"

"Thank heaven, no!" RV exclaimed. "It's never what you

might call dull here, but today has beat all. Most unusual and extremely puzzling indeed. I have to admit, I'm at a bit of a loss to explain it."

"Unusual? Unusual isn't the word! The boys back at the station in Ballyglen will never believe me when I tell them the carry-on here." Sergeant Kelly undid his tunic buttons, releasing layer after layer of the wobbly flesh encased in the folds of his oversized blue shirt. "I'm not too sure I believe it myself." As the last layer of fat found freedom, the Sergeant sighed a sigh of pure relief.

"Things were going fine until yourself came along to tell us that we were burying the wrong man! After that, everything seemed to go haywire!" Guard Behan said as he entered the room, having filled the kettle from a rain-barrel at the back of the station.

"So how come the Yank – that is, Daniel Dwyer – having been reported dead in the papers – is actually alive?" RV sat down at his desk, still wearing a confused, though quizzical, look. "You tell me that you have him safe and sound below in Ballyglen – in a cell! Are you positive the man you have is Dwyer?"

Sergeant Kelly drew his polka-dot handkerchief from his tunic pocket to once again mop his perspiring forehead. "Well, you will hardly believe this – " He was about to commence speaking when a light rap on the enquiry desk interrupted his explanations.

"Ahem!"

Three pairs of police eyes turned towards the polite cougher. Standing at the table-desk by the open door was Mr Cornelius McCraven, having quietly entered the room, unheard by either of the three men.

"Ahem!" McCraven coughed again. "I'm sorry to disturb your conference, gentlemen, but I wish to report a robbery."

"A robbery!" RV leapt to his feet. "Where?"

"It's the bank, actually, Sergeant. My bank. I went to my office at the bank less than half an hour ago to finish some business, only to find the place ransacked and the bank strongbox gone." McCraven's fingers nervously fingered his bow-tie and flicked imaginary dust from his sports-jacket.

His face registering utter disbelief, RV looked first at Sergeant Kelly, then at Guard Behan and then back at McCraven. "Now, let's see if I hear this correct, Mr McCraven. You're saying the bank – your bank – our bank – here in Ballykeogh – has just been robbed?"

"That's exactly right, Sergeant. The bank strongbox and its entire cash contents had been removed from my office where it's normally kept. Though I can't say exactly when it was taken. It may have occurred at any time since I left the office at around six o'clock last evening. What I can say is that when I went there not thirty minutes ago, what I found was a gaping hole in the floor in the corner of the room and the strongbox had disappeared – puffft – gone." McCraven clicked his fingers.

"A hole – in – the – floor – " RV repeated, scribbling furiously in a notebook on the desk in front of him. " – and the strongbox – missing. And can you say how much cash the strongbox contained?"

"How much?" McCraven lit a cigarette, inserted it in a silver and ivory holder, took a deep pull, exhaled the smoke through his nose and gazed at a point on the station ceiling. "Mmmm! Let's see now . . . two hundred and fifty – no – three hundred . . . in fact, three hundred and fifty pounds in cash – varied denominations – all used notes. The sum total of yesterday's takings. A particularly heavy day's business too, I might add. This is all most distressing, Sergeant. Most distressing!"

"Now, don't panic, Mr McCraven. We'll take over from here. Guard Behan here will accompany you back to the bank to carry out a full investigation at the scene of the alleged crime. If what you say is correct, then we will instigate a full and immediate search for the missing strongbox – and of course the speedy apprehension of the culprit or culprits responsible." RV beckoned to Guard Behan, who came to the table to receive his orders. "Guard, kindly accompany Mr McCraven down to the bank, examine the scene of the alleged crime carefully and take a full statement. Only don't touch a thing! Fingerprints, you know. I'll follow on as soon as I'm through with Sergeant Kelly here."

"Right, Sergeant!" Guard Behan headed for the door, delighted with this exciting, and for once, important mission. A real robbery! This was more like it. This wasn't the usual grind of issuing paltry dog or bicycle licences or summonses. This was a bona-fide crime – something that only happened in big cities – something he could get his teeth into. If he proved himself on this case, it could be the break he had been waiting for these long years. His spirits soared. No more boring work-shifts, tea-making or listening to the Sergeant's theories on KGB-organised poteen-making rings. If he got to grips with this one before Mulrooney got there to screw it up, it might mean promotion.

"Oh, by the way, Guard," Sergeant Kelly called out. "If you see RN – er – Mr Mulrooney, that is, on your way to the bank, can you give him this note?" He finished scribbling a hasty message and passed it to Guard Behan. "I meant to give it to him earlier, but in all that excitement it clean slipped my mind."

"I'll see he gets it, Sergeant, don't worry." Guard Behan followed McCraven out of the door, leaving the two sergeants to discuss this new and unexpected turn of events.

"Who's that little dandy?" Sergeant Kelly nodded after the two men.

"What dandy? Oh, that's Cornelius McCraven, our bank manager. He comes up here from Ballyglen twice a week. We only have a sub-branch here, you know."

"Mmmm, I thought I recognised him from someplace. He doesn't look too much put out about the fact that his bank has just been robbed, does he?"

"Yes, come to think of it, you're right. He does seem to be taking it all very calmly, doesn't he?" RV always considered McCraven's general attitude to be one of haughty arrogance, superiority and offhand diffidence.

"And to think, Mulrooney," Sergeant Kelly said with a dry grin, "that I figured this place as a real dump of a posting. How wrong could I be! It makes Ballyglen look like Sleepy Hollow. Explosions! The dead rising from their graves! Open gunfire on the streets and now, to cap it all, you've a bank robbery on your hands – and all in the course of a few hours! It's like bloody Tombstone! It's like a Hollywood film. It's bloody incredible!" He shook his beefy head and waited for RV to finish making the tea.

RV stirred four spoons of sugar into Sergeant Kelly's cup. "Now, about Daniel Dwyer? You were about to explain – "

"Ah, yes. That blackguard! Are you sure you haven't got a little drop of something stronger! No? Ah well. As you know, we had the same information as you did. Daniel Dwyer's remains were to be delivered to Ballyglen railway station on the 8.30 train from Galway and owing to the fact that he was a big wheel in the Troubles, we were to lay on a guard of honour to meet the train. Which we did! Six of the lads below turned out at the railway station at eight o'clock or so, and, by God, I was proud of them. They

235

looked good enough to be Guard of Honour to the Pope! Anyway!" He slurped the sickly-sweet tea, wiped his mouth with a greasy uniform cuff and continued, "There we were – standing smartly to attention at the station, waiting for the train – along with a contingent from the Cumann na mBan and a squadron of his old soldier-comrades. Dressed to the knockers, they were! There were that many medals clanking on lapels as would supply a fair-sized tin factory. There were a couple of priests and a gaggle of nuns to boot! On top of all that, the bloody Ballyglen Pipe and Drum Band were there too, squealing and shrieking and farting like stuck pigs. To cut a long story short, along comes the train, only a half-hour late and who do you think was the first man to step from the train?"

"Go on – go on!"

"Only the brave Daniel the Yank himself, that's bloody who!"

"Alive?" RV's eyes popped behind the reading glasses perched on his nose.

"As alive as you or I! Well, the place only exploded. First, we all just stood there – dumbfounded like – staring at him. Then the bastard takes off his hat, waves it at the crowd and says – cool as a breeze – 'Good morning to you one and all' says he, 'I'm delighted to see you all here to welcome me home. I hope,' says he with a smirk as wide as the Shannon, 'you're all not too disappointed that I didn't arrive in a box, as was expected.' There was a moment of stunned silence – you could hear a pin drop in the next parish – then all bloody hell broke loose! I had to get my boys to charge through and rescue the bastard before he was torn to smithereens by the mob. Which he would've been, if a couple of wiry old birds from the Cumann na mBan had him in their clutches for another five minutes. There was a couple of nuns who looked like they meant business too!"

"By Jove! Quite extraordinary."

"Well, as you can imagine, my men weren't exactly over the moon about having been taken for a ride by Dwyer's little prank, but they had to do their duty and protect him from any bodily harm. Which they did – though I do believe one of the ladies managed to place at least one good kick in a place that will help Mr Dwyer to remember his homecoming for quite a while to come. Not to mention hamper any chance of siring future issue! Anyway, we finally managed to extricate him from the mêlée and get him back to the stationhouse in one piece. That's where he is at the moment – until we decide what charges to press. There *has* to be some law against his masquerading as a corpse. The very least we can pin on him is causing public disorder."

RV could only shake his head and stare at Sergeant Kelly. "What on earth motivated him to do such a thing?" he said at last.

"Well, I interrogated a sore and rattled Dwyer when we got to the station and I asked him why he did it. 'I only did it,' says he, 'to see what kind of reception and turn-out I could expect to see at my own funeral. And as it obviously wouldn't be possible to fully appreciate the great occasion when that fateful day actually arrived, I thought I'd organise a sort of a live dress rehearsal. I never figured everybody was going to get so steamed up about it.' Can you believe the man? The scoundrel wanted to be there in person to witness his own funeral!"

"Extraordinary! Extraordinary!" Another wave of exhaustion swept over RV, who began to feel as if some unseen power had saved all the crazy, mixed-up, warped little chunks of unreality until this very day for the sole purpose of hurling them all at once at his unprepared person. He sipped his cold tea and forced his mind to come to grips with the day's events so far, events which seemed to plunge like an out-of-control roller-coaster from one occurrence to the next, each one as extraordinary, bizarre and mind-boggling as the last. Well, he thought, whatever else this day brought, he would have to see it through. "So what prompted you to come to Ballykeogh?" he enquired.

"Well, I tried phoning you but could not get through. Tell me, why is it nobody can ever phone in to Ballykeogh these days?"

RV rolled his eyes, wagged his head and clicked his tongue. "Can't phone out either. But that's quite another story altogether. Go on."

"As I said, I tried to call you and when I couldn't get through, I decided to let it wait. After all, we had Dwyer, alive and well, in the cell so all we had to do was wait for your undertaker – O'Flaherty? To arrive with his hearse to collect the body. We could then give him all the facts and send him back to Ballykeogh with the news. But O'Flaherty didn't arrive and then the mail-van driver arrived to deliver a garbled message from your Guard Behan to say that the coffin and body had arrived safely in Ballykeogh and that everything was ready for the funeral. Well! Naturally, at that news, the alarm bells began to ring. Your message said the Yank Dwyer had arrived safely. But, I asked myself, if we had Dwyer alive and well in our cell, whose body had in fact arrived in Ballykeogh? I realised I had only one course of action. I decided to come up here directly to see for myself what in heaven's name was going on! When I got here – and just in time, I might add – ye were about to shovel the turf on the wrong Dwyer. And ye don't even know how ye got the wrong man into the coffin?" Sergeant Kelly did not wait for an explanation and continued. "And, to top it all, I damn near got written off on the way up here."

"Written off? What do you mean, written off?"

"I had the foot on the floor, coming around a bend about five miles out the road, when I almost crashed headlong into a van broken down in the middle of the road. It looked like a wheel had come off and the bloody thing out in the middle of the road. I missed it by inches. Didn't get a chance to get the number."

"A van, did you say?" Something jangled in the far corners of RV's mind. "Would it be a Morris van? A black Morris van with two occupants?" His voice raised a semitone, while his mind groped to filter and focus on a dark unpleasant hunch. In all the commotion, RV had completely forgotten about his two helpers from the night before. What was it they had said? They were in Ballykeogh to do a wiring job. A wiring job in the bank, that was it! RV could not fight back the flowering seeds of suspicion and doubt. The bank robbery! The explosion in the graveyard! Good God, he thought, was it possible? Surely not – the two men were so helpful and they looked so – well – ordinary. But who else, if not them? They possessed the equipment to pull off the job – and the means to make a speedy getaway. It had to be those two.

"Come to think of it, it was a Morris van and there were two men. Why do you ask?"

RV sprang from his chair and snatched the phone receiver off the cradle with the suddenness of a rattlesnake striking out at its prey.

"Hello! Hello! Miss Clara! Miss Clara! Hello? Oh, Christ, what's the use!"

Slamming the receiver down on the desk, he rose from his chair and began to pace back and forth across the room in a highly agitated state.

"What on earth's got into you, man?" Sergeant Kelly enquired, struggling to his feet. "Calm yourself now. The van had a breakdown, that's all. I was as much at fault as they were. The road is barely wide enough for one car at that point, let alone two. It's nothing to get steamed up over. At any rate, you have more pressing problems to deal with, I would say."

"No! No! You don't understand!" An excited RV hurriedly reached for his cap and cape. "You don't understand! Let's get to your car. Quick! We've no time to lose!"

"Whaa . . . ? My car? What's going on, Mulrooney? Where are we headed?"

"Let's get cracking! I'll explain on the way! I think I know the men who relieved our bank of its strongbox and where to find them. A van, right?"

"Yes – as I said, a van – with two men. It was broken down. A wheel had come off."

"They're our men! They're our bank robbers! I'll stake my stripes on it! If we're in luck, they'll still be down on the road. C'mon! We've no time to lose! Let's get moving!"

Chapter Eighteen

Guard Behan found RN Mulrooney in exactly the same spot as he had seen him several hours previously, standing motionless by the lip of the pit which had mysteriously opened in the graveyard. He decided he had better deliver Sergeant Kelly's note before getting down to the serious business of assimilating the facts of this alleged bank robbery, reported by Mr McCraven. He halted by the bank side-door.

"You go on inside," he beckoned to McCraven, "I have a little business with Mr Mulrooney there." He walked to the now-breached wall separating the bank plot from the graveyard and called out to the immobile RN, "Mr Mulrooney!"

RN gave no indication he had either heard or seen Guard Behan and continued to gaze, in a trance-like state, into the deep depression at his feet.

"Hello there, Mr Mulrooney! A quick word, if you don't mind!" Guard Behan called out in a loud impatient voice.

RN slowly lifted his eyes and, with the look of a man whose mind is focused on something unseen, gave Guard Behan a cold vacant stare.

"I have a message for you."

RN did not respond.

"From Sergeant Kelly!"

Still no response.

"Here! Take it!" Guard Behan commanded. "I can't stand around here all day. I have important police work to be getting on with."

RN roused himself out of his trance to walk slowly around the pit and approach the wall. As he drew near, Guard Behan was startled to see his wan haggard appearance. Good Lord, he thought, he looks like he's been crying.

"Here!" He reached across the wall and pushed the note in RN's direction. "Sergeant Kelly from below in Ballyglen asked to make sure you got this message."

After Sergeant Kelly had given him the note, once he left the station he could not resist stealing a glance at it. It bore the simple message: 'RN, Please drop six bottles of your best, when next in Ballyglen. Signed Sgt. Kelly.'

RN took the piece of crumpled paper offered him, unfolded it and looked at it for a long time. Then, making a choked, sobbing sound, he rolled the paper into a ball and flung it with vicious force into the still-smouldering pit. Giving Guard Behan a last long forlorn look, he shuffled back to the spot by the pit to stare once again, glassy-eyed, into its twisted depths.

Guard Behan felt the hairs on his neck prickle and bristle. "What on earth is up with him?" He looked at RN stand by the jagged hole, as frozen as the headstones around him. "Has the whole village gone bananas, or what?" Shaking his head, he turned away from the wall to follow McCraven into the bank. "Well, at least," he said to himself, as he glanced back at the statuesque RN, "he's one less suspect to consider. If he had pulled the job on the bank, he wouldn't be standing around the graveyard, gaping into that bloody hole!"

RN Mulrooney's entire world, or so it seemed to him at this moment, lay crumbled and spent in the smouldering sodden pit that opened at his feet.

"Gone! Gone!" he moaned. "All bloody gone with the wind. All my hard work – all my long years of planning and labour. All gone up in one puff of smoke! What the devil caused it?" He shifted in his rain-soaked shoes and wiped away a stalactite of raindrops that had collected at the end of his nose, heaved a deep sigh, and continued to gaze into the pit which had swallowed his hopes and devoured his dreams. He had lost track of the passing of the hours, locked as he was in his deep dark thoughts. When the graveyard had finally emptied of babbling excited villagers several hours before, following the explosion, a gunshot and somebody screaming in the street, only RN remained. As he stood there, still motionless and trance-like, he slowly came to realise the full implications of the recent explosion. Buried deep in the stomach of this steaming pit lay the remains of his entire poteen-making empire. From the depths of the hole he could make out some of the distilling apparatus, protruding like some metallic skeleton, twisted and grotesque, from among the rubble. Now, standing alone over the hole, RN's fevered brain sought solutions to this catastrophe.

"I'm destroyed – finished – ruined is what I am! But how . . . how did this happen?" His mind reeled and raced, replaying over and over again his last minutes spent in the vault last night, just prior to being disturbed by the arrival of the Morris van, the two men and his meddling brother, RV. Then there was that whole episode with the coffin and Daniel Dwyer. All very strange, he remembered thinking at the time, but it had no bearing on the events which led to this present state of affairs. Or did it? Once again, his mind sifted carefully through events as he recalled them. Once again – apart from the interlude in the church – nothing seemed out of place or unnatural. So, what had gone wrong? What had caused an explosion – as an explosion it indeed was – down below in his poteen works? He had left the vault in a hurry – granted – but he had left the place as he had done on so many other nights, leaving everything ticking over as normal, with the silver liquid being extracted from the brewing mash, drop by precious drop.

"Unless . . . unless . . . " a possibility glimmered from the edge of his mind. "The lantern! Where did I leave the lantern?" Again, he retraced his steps for those last few moments before vacating the vault. "Jeez! Could that be it? Could that be the cause of the explosion?" RN remembered now that in his haste to leave the vault, he had placed the lighted oil-lamp on a shelf directly overhead a plastic bucket brim-full with the purest of poteen. "Was it possible?" He pondered. Any slight shifting of the lamp off the narrow shelf could easily tip it into the bucket underneath. He considered the possible results of such an occurrence. A lighted paraffin pressure-lamp falling into a bucket of pure alcohol in a small room surrounded by several gallons of similar flammable liquid . . . ?

"Yes! Yes! That's it! That must be it! The cursed Tilley-lamp! How could I have been so bloody stupid?"

The poteen would indeed ignite, or even explode, RN reasoned, and the other bottles would soon follow. Also present in the airless vault would be trapped various gasses – natural or otherwise. They too would ignite in a chain-reaction to the original explosion – as would the bottled gas used to fire the poteen-making apparatus. RN buried his face in his hands and groaned aloud, thinking of the consequences of such an occurrence. "Disaster! Utter bloody disaster! My whole life in ribbons down there in that godless grave!"

An evil-eyed crow had settled on a nearby gravestone and now sat eyeing RN accusingly.

"I may as well be down there in that grave with the whole shebang!" RN muttered at the crow, who thowocked her wet blue-black feathers in reply. "I mean – I ask you! How the hell was I to know? I always figured the vault to be as safe as the Pope's wine-cellar. Look at it now! Ruined! I had plans for this place – big plans. Now it's destroyed . . . and me with it! And to think of all the people from here to Ballyglen – and beyond – who depend on me to keep them supplied with the Pure Drop. It's a disaster, that's what it is! An absolute bloody disaster!" The crow blinked and nodded furiously. "Of course, it mightn't have been an accident at all!" he spat at the observing bird. "Of course, I could have it all wrong! I have enemies in this town, you know. Oh yes, deadly enemies. Men who despise the likes of me. Men who will stop at nothing because they hate to see anybody get something up and running successfully. Begrudgery – that's all it is! This country wallows in begrudgery. Like a noose about the throat of enterprise, it is. Take . . . " he pondered for a moment, "take Big Tom McGarrigan, for instance. Now there's a prime begrudger who would dearly love to see me fail and would go to some lengths, I'll bet, to see that I would! It wouldn't be beyond the man to try and force me out of business and then quietly step in and take over. I wouldn't put it past McGarrigan, or somebody like him, to be responsible for all this – this havoc! Look at it," he spread his hands over the hole, "I built it from zero – with these very hands – cared for it like I would my own home – now look at it – it's like a hill in Korea!"

The crow spread her glistening wings, mirroring RN's gesture, and cawed loudly. RN glared at the crow, as if expecting some comforting words in return. The crow glared back, flapped her wings, sending out a spray-shower of rain droplets in all directions, winked one hooded evil eye, settled herself once again on the moss-green gravestone and continued to suspiciously regard the disconsolate RN. "What's to become of me now?" RN said to the crow. "What am I to turn my hand to now that my hard-earned business is gone up in a puff of smoke? I can't waste my talents on ordinary work. Me – Ramon Navarro Mulrooney – a grocer? A postman? A taxi-man? Never! No way – no way!"

There was however, he fantasised, one job which could harness some of his special talents – politics. He would have to give it serious thought. Though he felt uncomfortable, this course of action might, he figured, offer one way out of this dreadful mess. His late mother, Cecilia, would turn in her grave at the idea of either of her sons pursuing such a career – "For the power-hungry and the plebeian," she would often say – but at this stage, RN reasoned, it could well be the only career left for a man of his calibre. "I've got contacts, after all. Friends in high places. I didn't spend all those years scouring the countryside supplying the gentry with the Pure Drop without making a few powerful friends. And some of them owe me a favour or two."

He would go to Ballyglen right away. From there he would launch his political campaign. Securing a seat on the county council should present no problem for him. After all, he thought, any fool with an IQ over fifty, a neck like a jockey's bollix and enough political pull could swing a council seat. Most of the serving councillors he had contact with were little more than primitive, inarticulate bogmen. From county councillor, it would only be a skip and a jump to the Dáil and government. Mister RN Mulrooney, TD! Or who knows . . . perhaps even Minister

Mulrooney! He savoured the sound of it. It had a luminous golden ring to it. RN scowl gave way to a slow, sly smile. He squared his shoulders, brushed a shower of raindrops from his coat lapels and straightened his tie.

The wetting drizzle had turned into a steady light rain. From the corner of his eye, RN spotted Guard Behan standing outside the graveyard wall and looking in his direction. He ignored the Guard, as he ignored the rain and the eerie fiddle-music wafting down the street from the Golden Gloves. He sighed and concentrated his gaze one final time at the remains of the vault that, up to a few short hours ago, had been his work-place, his office, his operational HQ, his refuge and indeed his home-from-home. He had plans to make. He had some thinking to do. He had a lot of hard thinking to do.

Chapter Nineteen

Sergeant RV Mulrooney was a man who liked things to be in order. As he walked, leaden-footed and utterly exhausted, down the hill to his cottage, he could not, by any stretch of the imagination, say that things at that moment were as cut and dried as he would have wished them to be. In all his days in the force, he had never had such a day. Nor in all his days as a guard, or a sergeant, had he willingly left his desk with so many things unresolved — so many loose ends, so many puzzling and frustrating aspects to the day's events. In little less than twenty-four hours, he had experienced more unusual if not downright bizarre occurrences than he might expect in an entire career in the force. Firstly there was the hearse accident, followed by the yet-to-be-explained mix-up of bodies, Tombs's mysterious overnight disappearance, the near-burial of Jack Dwyer, the as-yet unexplained explosion in the vault, Miss Clara's attempt on Jack's life and finally the robbery of the strongbox from the bank.

"Incredible!" RV said. "Quite incredible!"

There were so many things about the day's events he could not yet fully comprehend. For instance, how on earth did Black Jack come to be lying alongside the coffin destined for his uncle, Daniel? Only Jack himself could throw any light on that riddle and he was, so Father O'Malley assured RV, "still in deep shock and traumatised from his horrific experience", up at the priest's house. RV would have to wait until Jack had recovered sufficiently to attend the stationhouse for a lengthy interview.

Though thoroughly frustrated by the outcome of many of the day's events – his keenest efforts at flushing out the ring-leader of the poteen organisation had yielded nothing – he felt a glow of satisfaction at speedily and successfully identifying the culprits and apprehending them both.

"I must say!" he chuckled to himself, "Sergeant Kelly seemed quite impressed. Perhaps that'll change his belittling attitude towards Ballykeogh and towards myself. Today showed him there's more to running a town than having an official car at your disposal and having half-a-dozen young whipper-snapper gardai to serve you, hand and foot!"

The last few hours had been hectic. Even Sergeant Kelly marvelled at the roller-coaster speed and intensity of it all. After the initial and shocking realisation that his two nocturnal helpers from Derry and Waterford were not the innocent workmen they had at first led him to believe, RV took immediate action. Pushing a bewildered Sergeant Kelly towards his Ford Anglia police car, RV unfolded, as best he could, the events of the previous night.

" – and when you told me their van had broken down on the road to Ballyglen, I put two and two together," he concluded. "They are our men, I tell you! They are the villains, sure as eggs is eggs! Put your foot down, Sergeant, we're going to catch these two smart-alecs, even if we have to drive all the way across the country!"

With Sergeant Kelly at the wheel, the police car finally eased alongside the broken-down Morris van. The vehicle was exactly where Sergeant Kelly said it would be, its driver and passenger on their knees alongside a twisted, wheel-less back-axle. RV could hardly control or contain his feelings of both anger and elation. He got out of the car and slowly approached the men. For a moment he watched the looks of surprise, then panic, followed by despondent resignation, sweep over the faces of the two men like rain-clouds over Sliabh Cullen.

"Good evening, *gentlemen*." RV's voice was flint-hard. "Had a spot of an accident, I see. It's been a day of accidents, hasn't it? Well – perhaps I can repay your kindness of last night – by offering you both a ride – back to the station in Ballyglen where we can all have a nice little chat about recent events. I intend to take care of you two gentlemen – very good care indeed! In the meantime, I'd be obliged if you would slip your hands into these . . . " While RV handcuffed the two silent men, Sergeant Kelly conducted a search of the van's interior – to discover – as RV had predicted – a strongbox, as yet unopened. Returning to the village with their two captives and the bank strongbox, RV spotted a hunched familar figure emerging from Tombs's house and heading in the direction of the Golden Gloves. "Good grief!" he exclaimed. "It's Tombs! Where on earth has he emerged from?"

"O'Flaherty? Your missing undertaker?"

"The same! But, I'm glad to see, alive and well, thank heavens."

RV resolved to summon Tombs to the station as soon as possible to help unravel the mystery of the crashed hearse and perhaps throw some light on his own whereabouts these last twenty-four hours or so. For now, what was important was getting the two men responsible for the robbery behind bars.

When Guard Behan arrived back to the stationhouse,

his investigations at the bank complete, he found his superior seated at his desk in animated conversation with Sergeant Kelly.

"Ah, Guard! Back from your investigations?" a beaming Sergeant Kelly stood with his back to the fireplace.

"What delayed you? We expected you back an hour ago," RV said, peering at Guard Behan over the reading-glasses perched on his nose.

"I've just come from Miss Clara at the post office. I decided to interview her regarding the illegal discharging of her shotgun in a public place."

"And?"

"She's locked herself in her bedroom. Refused to answer any questions! Shouted at me through the window, she did – wild, mad talk! Ranted on about the Germans attacking – an advance party of Blitzkrieg bombers and parachutist spies infiltrating the village and the town being completely overrun – unless you and I, the keepers of the peace, did something about it. If we can't defend her, she said, she would have to defend herself. She's in a bad way up there. She needs medical help! And to make matters worse, she still has that gun – unlicensed – and probably loaded – in her possession! In my opinion she's finally flipped!"

"What are we to do with that woman? Well, Guard, we will have to deal with that little problem later. What did you find out from your investigations at the bank ?"

"Well, for starters I took a full statement from Mr McCraven. To me, the man seemed to be actually enjoying the whole afair. In fact, he seemd to me to be downright delighted that *his* bank had been robbed – very strange! He filled himself a sherry as we spoke – even offered me a glass . . . "

"You didn't accept, I trust!" RV glared at him.

"Of course not, Sergeant! Never on duty! Anyhow, then I carried out a detailed investigation of the office and general area immediately surrounding the bank."

"And what did you discover?" RV laid his pen on the desk, leaned back in his chair and folded his hands.

"I believe I know how the robbers got into the bank. I've come to the conclusion that the perpetrators of this devilishly cunning and well-executed crime entered the bank premises via an underground tunnel which originated in a graveyard vault – the one which exploded earlier today."

"What proof do you have of this?"

The proof, Guard Behan offered confidently, was borne out by the visible evidence. He had noted, and charted, the deep, collapsed trench running from the rear corner of the bank, through the graveyard wall and terminating in the large hole in the graveyard. This, he suggested, was the same hole which had appeared in the graveyard grounds following the explosion earlier that day. The sudden appearance of this large opening, Guard Behan also offered, had to be related in no small way to the disappearance of the strongbox from the bank.

"It would appear that the criminal, or criminals, responsible, tunnelled from an underground vault in the graveyard underneath the separating wall to the corner the bank, then broke through the foundations and the floorboards into the premises, removed the safe and made their getaway back down the tunnel."

"How do you explain the explosion?"

"Ah!" Guard Behan stated, delighted at the opportunity to advance his theories – especially with Sergeant Kelly present. "The explosion, which undoubtedly occurred in the vault, was entirely due to some fault or other in the tunnelling equipment or whatever advanced gadgetry the thieves used in getting in and out of the premises. Or they may have set a charge to detonate after vacating the vault – to cover their tracks and make good their escape. Or maybe – " a new possibility dawned on the eager Guard, "maybe . . . things went horribly wrong and they went up with the explosion! Maybe they never got out! Maybe they're still down there!"

RV and Sergeant Kelly looked at each other and after a moment's silence, began to chortle loudly. Guard Behan stared at RV in amazement. In all his days in Ballykeogh, he had never witnessed his Sergeant display any real emotion or show his feelings so openly; now he sat there rocking with laughter.

"Well done, Guard Behan! A very powerfully argued and astute deduction. You're right on all counts – with one exception. Go take a look in the cell." A smile still played about RV's mouth, giving his dour features an unfamiliar, almost benign, avuncular look.

Guard Behan walked to the doorway leading to the tiny cell and peered through. In the cell were two men – one lay with his face to the wall on the single bunk and the other stood with his back to the wall, hands thrust deep in his pockets and a cigarette dangling from his lips.

"Who? Wha? Who are they?"

"Those gentlemen, Guard, are our bank-robbers. Alive and kicking and not, as you suggested, at the bottom of the pit they most certainly dug, but where they belong – behind bars."

"But how? When?" Guard Behan asked.

"You can read my report later." RV tapped the document on the desk in front of him. "The strongbox is locked safe in the cupboard, until we can contact Mr McCraven. Right now, I have another mission for you. I want you to accompany Sergeant Kelly into Ballyglen as escort for these two scoundrels. You can overnight there and return in the morning. The suspects refuse to answer any questions or furnish us with any information until they speak with a solicitor and so we decided to transfer them both to Ballyglen where they can talk to the judge himself, if they wish. Then they will be officially charged with breaking and entering, the removal of the bank safe and its contents and of causing a explosion, endangering their own lives and the lives of others. I intend to see that these two gentlemen get what's coming to them and that they rue the day they decided to visit Ballykeogh."

"Yes, Sergeant!" Guard Behan snapped to attention, his eyes alight, delighted to be dispatched on any mission which would take him away from Ballykeogh; especially one that would earn him some reflected glory, and also the opportunity to see in person the now-legendary ex-corpse, Daniel the Yank Dwyer.

With Sergeant Kelly, Guard Behan and their two despondent charges departed for Ballyglen, RV, alone at last, returned his desk to jot down the day's salient events, before they became a jumble in his over-tired mind. For a long while, the room's only sounds were the tick of a clock, the crackle of logs on the fire and the scratching of a pen-nib on paper. After some time writing, RV paused, rubbed his eyes and pushed his note-pad from him. The clock struck 5.45. It had been a long, tiring and extremely confusing day. Slowly, he drew himself to his feet, stretched and yawned. It was time he signed off duty and went home.

As he drew close to his cottage, RV willed his mind to purge from it any troubling thoughts, nagging notions or irritating ideas regarding the day's events. Once RV entered his front door, he liked to leave his life as a garda sergeant, and the responsibilities and problems that attended such a post, on the mat outside his front door. There they would lie, until he once again emerged to pick them before taking up his duties. This, of course, was not always possible. Especially after a day such as today. It seemed to RV, as he walked up the leaf-strewn pathway to his door, that half-a-lifetime had elapsed since he set off on his bicycle at five forty-five the previous evening. Now he had to try to put all thoughts of coffins, bodies, explosions, gunshots and robberies out of his tired mind – until tomorrow, at any rate, when he would begin investigations in earnest, after a good night's rest.

"Still a few loose ends to be tied up," he said, as he bent to get his latch-key from underneath a stone by the doorway. "But tomorrow, as they say, is another day."

Entering the side-door, RV was disappointed to find the house deserted. In the warm kitchen he detected, laced with the familiar cooking smells, the aroma of perfume – subtle but definitely present. Strange, RV thought, Hannah never wears scent, except on very special occasions. A hand-written note on the kitchen-table caught his eye. He read that his dinner was in the oven, his usual admixture of milk and porter was in the blue jug on the dresser and that Hannah would be back from her needlework class not later than ten. RV scowled. He always felt slightly irritated that Hannah should have to go out each Thursday evening to instruct the other ladies of the village in the art of needlework, patchwork and carpet-making. He liked nothing better, after a long hard work-shift policing the village and environs, than to return home to a warm, tidy house, a good hot meal. He especially looked forward to those special peaceful – almost serene – hours by the fire talking with his wife, reading or listening to Beethoven. But, he grudgingly conceded, Thursday night was the only night of the week when Hannah got to go out and enjoy herself and he could not deny her that simple pleasure. As he prepared his simple meal, his mood improved. A sense of relief and peacefulness at being within the comforting womb of his own home swept over him. As he tugged off his boots before sitting down to his warmed-up meal, the images of events of the last twenty-four hours began to lose their sharpness as they faded, like a dying snow-shower, inside his weary mind. He ate his food slowly and with relish. Rising from the table, he padded to his bedroom and from underneath his bed, drew his collection of Beethoven 78 RPM recordings. He had no doubt as to which of the Master's works he most wanted to hear at that moment. The piece of music had been on his mind the night before and now, given the chaotic events of his day, it seemed to RV a most appropriate choice. Returning to the kitchen with a 12 inch shellac recording of Beethoven's "Pastoral" Symphony cradled lovingly in his hands, he placed the disc on the gramophone turntable and dropped the needle on the "After The Storm" passage from the great work. Soon his house and head were filled with the sound of the Genius's earthy bitter-sweet music. Lowering himself into his armchair by the warm range, he closed his eyes, sighed and lay back, letting the beautiful music swell, wash and lap over his consciousness in gentle luxurious waves. A tranquil landscape of sound, scent and colour floated down from the swirling mists behind his closed eyes to take possession of his mind and soul. Again, as always on hearing this particular piece of music, the scent of rain-sodden heather and hazel-bushes on the side of Sliabh Cullen give way to the heady perfume of sun-dappled new-mown hay, Alpine Daisies, Spring Roses and Mountain Flock and tinged with a hint of fresh snow. Somewhere, high in the air, a single lark piped an intoxicating melody, while nymph-like notes and sunbeams played hide-and-seek among the verdant woods and meadows of the Master's fertile imagination. On and on the golden waves of melody continued to lap over him, drawing him down at last into the welcoming arms of Morpheus and dreamless sleep.

Chapter Twenty

RV awoke to find Hannah sitting quietly opposite him.

She watched him open his eyes, yawn and blink rapidly at her. She put aside the unfinished rug she was working on and got to her feet. "You're awake, dear," she said gently, "Will I make you a nice cup of tea?"

"Yes, I could take a cup of proper tea." RV stretched and yawned again. "When did you get back? What time is it?"

"It's almost eleven. I got back just after ten. You were sleeping like a baby and I didn't want to wake you. I know you must have had a busy day at the station. Wasn't it terrible about poor Jack Dwyer! To think, he was almost buried – alive! Ugggh!" She grimaced and trembled.

"Busy, did you say? You don't know the half of it! Do you know that on top of all the shenanigans in the graveyard, we had a bank robbery to contend with?"

"The bank? When? Did Cornelius – Mr McCraven – did you talk to Mr McCraven?"

"McCraven himself reported the theft. But I solved the whole affair and the rogues responsible are in jail in Ballyglen."

"Oh my gosh! Is – is Mr McCraven in jail?" Hannah paled visibly.

"You don't listen, woman! I never said McCraven was in jail. Why should he be? He didn't rob his own bank now, did he! The guilty men are those two vagabonds who helped me with Dwyer's coffin last night."

"Thank heavens! For a minute I thought – "

"What a night it was! Not to mention the carry-on today. In all my days in the force, I've never witnessed anything quite like it – and never wish to again, I can tell you. I'm exhausted! Maybe it's time I started to take things a little easier." For the second time that day, the idea of retirement jumped from the back of his mind. This time he did not banish it and it now entered his consciousness like an unexpected, yet welcome, visitor.

"Well, when you've had your cup of tea," Hannah said as she rinsed the teapot, "you should slip off to your bed and get yourself a good night's rest."

"Aye! And while I'm sleeping in my bed, Tom Duignan will be busy at his still, manufacturing his next batch of poteen. He won't expect me tonight. If I go up there, I'm sure to nab him red-handed."

"Oh, for heaven's sakes, Rudy, have some sense! If I know anything, Tom Duignan, like the rest of them, will be either in McGarrigan's or the Gloves, and well-oiled they are by now, I should think! Tom Duignan will be lucky if he can walk home, let alone go to his still – if he has a still to go to. So save yourself another sleepless night of wet and cold and go to your bed. Look at you! You're all but done in! You've done enough for one day. And as you say yourself, there's always tomorrow."

Hannah handed him a mug of hot, sweet tea and returned to her chair opposite him.

"You're right, dear, as usual. I am dog tired. I doubt if I could make it to the top of the hill. I'll be off to my bed then." RV heaved himself from the comfort of his armchair and slowly shuffled, mug in hand, to the bedroom.

Hannah picked up the rug she had been working on to take up where she had left off, putting the finishing touches to the purple tassel of a green and red fez worn by a street-vendor in a Persian-market scene. "I'll be along in a moment or two," she called after him.

RV hovered on the edge of sleep, with the images of the day jostling and pushing for attention in his tired mind. He felt Hannah lift the bed-covers and slip quietly in beside him.

Soon she was settled and for a long while she listened to him breathe.

"Rudy? Dear?" she whispered at last. "Are you awake?"

"Whaa? What is it?" RV mumbled from the edge of sleep.

"I just wanted to ask you something," Hannah whispered from her pillow. "A big favour, really. I wonder – I wonder if you could see your way clear to lending me fifty pounds."

"Lend you *fifty* pounds? What on earth for?"

"Oh – er – materials for my rugs and so forth. Will you?"

"In the morning, dear. I'll discuss it with you in the morning. Good night now."

With a long sigh, RV Mulrooney reached across the bed to gently stroke his wife's hair before giving himself utterly to the waiting outstretched arms of deep untroubled sleep.